Destiny

C. E. Giannico

NEWMAN SPRINGS PUBLISHING
320 Broad Street
Red Bank, NJ 07701

First originally published by Newman Springs Publishing 2024

ISBN 978-1-68498-506-7 (Paperback)
ISBN 978-1-68498-507-4 (Digital)

Printed in the United States of America

This is dedicated to every woman who ever wondered, "What if?"

AUTHOR'S NOTE

Since I can remember, I would write down my thoughts on paper, and it would bring clarity to my reality. As I got older, I realized I was not doing it as much as I did when I was young. I guess growing up and having a family didn't allow me the free time to do so.

For the most part, my life has been filled with happiness, but there have been some trials and tribulations. Sometimes I find myself wondering what my life would be like if I had let my innermost desires guide me in my adolescence, even my early twenties. I fantasize about what could have been—the lovers, the friendships, the adventures.

In the pages ahead, Alisa finds herself in a similar predicament. A successful business woman, devoted daughter, and trusted friend, Alisa can't seem to find love. She realizes a steamy encounter from the past may be the reason she hasn't found true satisfaction in any of her romantic relationships. In an effort to find the missing pieces to lead her to her destiny and find true love, Alisa recounts instances from her past where she found herself at a major crossroads.

Simultaneously, we hear from Brent, the commissioner of the East Hampton Police Department, assigned to solve the case of actress Kim Killian's missing diamond necklace that mysteriously disappeared at Alisa's restaurant opening.

Destiny may find a way to answer both questions.

I'd like to thank the following people who have supported me in this process:

My family who had to do without my attention while I fulfilled my dream of publishing a book.

Louise Butera-Smith, Valerie Gildard, Katerina Plew, Teresa Rosalia, Maria Kurtoglu, Melissa Santell, Bethany Egbert, my friends and family who have read and gave me their honest feedback. Marissa Delaurenti-Panicci who assisted me in typing all of my handwritten notes.

I would also like to thank Christine Meir who I met through a book signing of *The Mister* by EL James. She guided me through the publishing process and gave me information I was not aware of that brought me to getting this book published.

Thank you to my content editor, Jenna Troyli, for her feedback and support.

And finally, a thank you to Effie Kammenou, who has also helped me through the process of making my premiere publishing a success.

PROLOGUE

How our story began…

The peak of high school was saved for junior and senior years. You are beginning to feel adult, invincible even. A time to take risks. Friends come first, especially my best friend Sharon. Boyfriends, well, I don't have too much experience in that department. I never dated anyone really. I had no interest in anyone in particular, but that all changed about two weeks ago.

It was at the end of math class, and I gathered my books and headed down the hallway to the stairs. It was a day just like any other. Ms. Stevens droned on about geometry, and I itched for the bell to ring. It was about to be the most exciting time of the day. Freed from math, I collected my things and headed to the stairwell. I reached for the banister, and I felt a jolt that brought my body to life. I could feel the hair stand up on the back of my neck, my palms began to clam up, and my nipples started to tingle. Somehow, even after days of this phenomenon happening, it always surprised me. In the next few seconds, I was going to see *him*. Aching with anticipation, I began to make my way up the stairs. I slowly gazed up, and there he was. I couldn't help but wonder if he was stopped in front of the window waiting to see me. But I was glad he did so I could see the sun kiss his face, pouring its rays across his jaw that was so sharp I wanted to run my finger across it to see if it could draw blood. At that moment, I wished I was the sun. His T-shirt looked painted on, highlighting every muscle. My fingers, again, would happily oblige to test the landscape. Before I knew it, I was halfway up the stairs, like some sort of animal magnetism was subconsciously pulling me closer.

The last few days felt like foreplay. We'd lock eyes on the stairwell as he made his way down and I made mine up. We'd never speak a word, but the feeling was electric. His eyes, light gray, would magically transition to a smoldering shade by the time we'd brush shoulders.

It was like the entire world ceased to exist when we were in each other's presence. Everything moved in slow motion, my heart beating so loudly that it would drown out the chatter of my classmates. The seconds felt like hours but it was never long enough. I nearly black out before landing at my desk for Mr. Brown's class only to be shocked back into reality with the ringing bell. For the rest of the day, I couldn't shake that aching feeling. I needed to know what his mouth tasted like. What it felt like to wrap my arms around him. Who was this mysterious guy? I wasn't going to let another day pass without finding out.

The very next day I made a promise to myself that I'd make a move. What kind of move? I wasn't sure. What I did know is that I needed to be in the south wing of the school, in that stairwell immediately after math class. I could feel myself becoming a hunter, tracking my prey. I knew his route and was ready to make the ultimate catch.

The bell rang and I leapt from my seat, headed onto the trusty route I knew would take me to him. I needed to know if this was all in my head, a fantasy I kept replaying that he wanted me *too*.

Body tense, mind in a flurry, I made it to the banister, I glanced to the top steps and there he was, right on time. I exhaled slowly, trying to plan my attack, my lower lip trapped between my teeth. His brown curly hair bouncing along his neckline, yet another tight shirt hugging his chest begging for my hands to keep it company. My body pulsating, it was time.

Those eyes, I found myself caught in his trance again. As I reached the last step, I found myself in front of him, and I couldn't help but drink in every ounce of his beauty. My hands began reaching toward him but they stopped just inches away as if he was too hot to touch.

Now was my chance, his eyes gleaming, I watched his Adam's apple bob as he gulped, noticing my hands eager to meet his body. All doubt of my affection being one-sided was erased in that moment and the tension was thicker than ever.

Anxiety hit, and the words just flew out.

"Do you have a girlfriend?"

I nervously chewed my bottom lip, awaiting a response. What was I doing? I had never done this before. I never thought I would be so forthcoming with a boy. But there was something different, something calling me to him.

He looked at me from head to toe, staring into my eyes, his tongue moistened his bottom lip. "No," he whispered.

I put my hand on his chest, the other hand feathered on his cheek, and crushed my lips to his. Pure electricity, my body molded to his as we melted into each other. We broke apart briefly to look into each other's eyes. He leaned down and gently kissed me again. It wasn't long that the kiss started to deepen. He placed his hand around my waist, spinning me around and put my back against the wall. The spark became an inferno. He raised his hand to my breast as mine felt for the hardness hitting my abdomen.

The bell rang to start the next period. We were both panting trying to gather our thoughts. His hand ran along my cheek. The gesture of pure affection. He swallowed as the look in his eyes changed. He lifted my chin with his index finger, and we locked eyes.

"I'll remember you. Don't forget me," he said with a sweet kiss on my lips and another on the tip of my nose.

I replayed what had just happened as I shook my head and smiled. As he walked away, I found myself stuck in concrete, unable to leave this now sacred spot. He slowly turned around at the last stair and reached his hand to his heart and tapped it twice with a little grin. Was this the end or just the beginning? Either way, I had my answer, he yearned for me too, and that was enough for now. The kiss burned into every fiber of my being. It was exactly as I expected. A volcano explosion of feelings I never had before. The wait for tomorrow, to capture his lips again, was going to be treacherous. Yes, I am seventeen, but wow, just wow. I never thought I was capable of feeling like we were the only ones in the stairwell. More than anything, I have surprised myself with my courage and appetite for adventure. I could still taste my trophy hunt on my lips.

Now it was time to sneak in late to class to tell Sharon every detail. She'd been hearing about this mystery guy for the last two weeks; she'd be shocked I actually pulled the trigger. I was still shocked. "Do you have a girlfriend?" That's so unlike me.

I turned the corner to head down hall. There was a commotion in the hallway. It's not normal to see this type of entertainment in my high school. I mean other than the Friday school spirit brigade, where the cheerleaders and football players parade the halls as if they were the monarchy of the school.

Sharon was outside the classroom trying to see what all the ruckus was about. Sharon doesn't usually indulge in this type of excitement, but something was different about this episode of a day in the life of a Long Island high school.

"What's going on?" I asked, still slightly out of breath from my encounter.

"Not sure," Sharon mumbled as she briefly turned to me, pre-occupied by the scene unfolding. Her head quickly snapped back in my direction.

"Why are you glowing?" she asked with a raised eyebrow. She turned her back to the commotion and turned her attention to investigating me.

"It can wait. I'll tell you later! This is too juicy to miss."

Was it that noticeable? I couldn't help myself from blushing at even the thought of sharing the details. But my entanglement could be on the back burner for another few minutes. Whenever something happened in the halls—whether it's a lovers' tiff, a fight, or even a visit from the cops—it's your obligation to stop and watch it all play out.

Unfortunately, this time our friends were the stars of the show. Two brothers, Joey and Richie Futzelli, were in handcuffs. To make matters worse, Joey's girlfriend Teresa was screaming and trying to jump on top of the arresting officers. The principal pulled her back and tried to calm her down, but she was hysterical, proclaiming

Joey's innocence. The crowd around continued to build; the air was filled with gasps and whispers. I thought my kiss would be the most exciting thing to happen today, but I was wrong. I felt like I was an extra in an episode of *NCIS*.

The whispers grew louder as everyone tried to fill in the blanks.

"Looks like they took bags out of Joey's jacket."

"I saw that."

"Do you think it was drugs?"

"Possibly."

We continued to watch. Richie was trying to struggle out of the security guard's arms. He yelled out.

"You, pigs, will never get anything out of us!"

Men in FBI jackets entered the hallway. They grabbed Joey, Richie, and another guy we couldn't see and escorted them to an FBI van just outside the exit door.

"Get back in class, ladies," Mr. Brown said, smiling.

Mr. Brown was one of those rare chill teachers. The type you could hang out with in between classes and talk without feeling like you were going to get in trouble for sharing your feelings or what *actually* happened over the weekend. He taught business management, and I loved the way he made us think about owning our own business. I always felt empowered after one of his lesson plans.

The crowd started to disperse, and Mr. Brown waved us to our seats, shutting the door behind him.

"Sharon, could you share with the class what you saw outside the classroom?" Mr. Brown asked with his feet propped on his desk and hands laced behind his head.

Sharon gave a detailed briefing of what she saw. The class discussed it for about five more minutes. Mr. Brown redirected the conversation right into the lesson for the day.

"Alisa, I need to talk to you for a moment," Mr. Brown said to me as the class was being dismissed. As the class emptied, Sharon and I went to speak with Mr. Brown. I knew that look on Mr. Brown's face. He was trying to set me up with someone. Sharon read my mind and whispered in my ear, "Who do you think it is this time?"

I giggled, and before I could say another word, Mr. Brown began his latest match making spiel.

"So, Alisa, I hear you don't have a date to the prom yet." Mr. Brown was in his late sixties, but he loved getting involved with my and Sharon's love lives. There was no doubt that we were his favorite students. I mean one time Sharon and I really wanted ice cream. He allowed us to leave class to go to the local shopping center to get it. Of course, there was a hitch, we had to pick him up a double scoop of chocolate peanut butter in a waffle cone.

"No, not yet, but..." My head dropped down and glanced at Sharon. Sharon looked at me with confusion in her eyes.

"But what, Alisa?"

"That might change after today." I lifted my head with a huge smile on my face letting her know we had to talk.

"Well, if that doesn't work out, I hear Austin wants to ask you," Mr. Brown said with his arms folded across his chest.

Austin was a boy in our class who was not bad looking, but he had a weird bounce to his walk. It was as if he was trying to trick everyone into believing he was taller than he actually was. He liked Sharon for years, but as of the last couple of months, he gave up hope. Once that dream was over, he redirected his affection toward me. Whenever I was in eyeshot, he would make his way over, hug me, and give me a wink with a smile as I walked away. His flirtation skills needed work; a little less "notice me" would go a long way.

"Good to know, Mr. Brown. See you tomorrow!" Sharon and I left class, and we barely made it out of the door before I could feel her eyes like lasers on me waiting for the details.

"So...," Sharon said with a shove on my arm.

"What?" I teased.

"What happened today?" I looked at her and began to relive that moment in my head. The feeling that was so intense I never experienced before. I felt the mutual attraction—no, that's not the right word. It was desire.

"Okay, spill it. Who is this guy? What's his name?"

Oh my god, I never got his name. His tongue was in my mouth, and I didn't even ask for his name!

My eyes widened, and before I knew it, I started relaying every detail. The stairwell, the question, the kiss, the *bulge.*

"You can't be serious!"

Sharon's hands were holding each side of her face like she's trying to keep her head from exploding. Her eyes were searching my face like I was a long lost acquaintance and she was trying to remember my name. Her best friend Alisa, who she has known for her entire life, would never do something like this. And I didn't, *usually.* I mean, if my mother knew I became a *puttana*, she would make me say ten Hail Marys and go to confession.

I never got his name. I don't know his name. One of the most remarkable moments in my life, one that will always hold a place in my heart, and all I have is the visual, no name attached to my mystery man.

"He said, 'Don't forget me, I will remember you.' Sharon, I have no idea what he meant. Do you think he really has a girlfriend? Am I being stupid, Sharon, naïve even?" I put my hand in the air and shook my head as if I was crazy.

"Alisa, I don't think you're stupid. I just don't understand why you wouldn't get his name. I mean, really, the kiss must have been amazing for you to lose your mind," she said, making me feel less of an idiot.

"I know. I might not know his name, but I know how his lips feel, how his arms feel when holding me tight, and how I feel when I'm near him. I will just see him tomorrow and talk to him."

"Alisa, you did something spontaneous. You never do that. I'm actually proud of you. You literally grabbed something you wanted and went for it." She smiled with me.

The next morning, all I was thinking about was the reaction I would have when I saw him post-kiss. What would I say to him? What would he say to me? Unlike any other day, I was feeling nervous, and excitement hit me. The bell rang for the period to end, and I rushed up the stairwell, almost tripping over my own feet. I was overwhelmed with the feeling of anticipation—to once again experience the intensity of being in each other's arms.

But my smile quickly disappeared once I realized my mystery man was nowhere to be found. I waited another ten minutes after the bell rang, hoping he would show. Maybe he got stuck talking to a teacher after class? Maybe he had to go to the bathroom and there was a line? Who am I kidding? They never have a line. My heart sank. Where could he be?

Heartbroken and confused, my mind kept replaying that moment. Did I read too far into it? Did he actually have a girlfriend and now he had to change routes to his class? I needed answers, but that was pretty hard to do when you didn't have a name.

I began to ask around, describing him to friends to see if I could get a lead. One person remembered a guy with his build hanging out with Joey and Richie. The same Joey and Richie who were in jail and accused of selling drugs at school with possible mob affiliation. I was in shock. Could my mystery man be behind bars with them? There was a third person who I couldn't make out down the hall also in handcuffs. Left with more questions than before, the happiness I had been filled with for the last twenty-four hours slowly started to leave my body in exchange for heartache.

Would I ever see him again? I wasn't sure. But what I did know was that if it was meant to be, our paths would cross again.

The guy with the mysterious gray eyes with just one kiss somehow set the standard of how I should feel when a man kisses me, leaving me helpless and entranced simultaneously.

Destiny, perhaps, would bring us together again one day.

CHAPTER 1

Alisa

Ten years later

"Congratulations, my Alisa," my father said as I cut the ribbon. The opening of Sicilia's, my second restaurant, was today. It was a great compliment to my first restaurant on the North Shore in the little town of Port Jefferson. The restaurant was hard work, but I was proud of what I achieved. Designed to transport hungry customers to the Venetian coast, water features embellishing the cobblestone walls, trestles climbing from floor to ceiling laced with wisteria and jasmine, and table centerpieces of peonies, my favorite—my own little Italian paradise in New York.

All the stars aligned to make my first location a success. It was in an ideal part of town, just close enough to the ferry so tourists, and locals alike, could take advantage of the easy access. It was even becoming a hot spot for celebrities! Once it had become a staple in the community, my regulars encouraged me to expand; and luckily, investors were easy to come by and had a major pull.

The second restaurant was on the South Shore of Long Island, the infamous East Hampton. It is known for its notoriety of the rich and famous. It's the weekend getaway for the Manhattan hustle and bustle. One of the socialites wanted to back me in an investment in East Hampton. Kim Killian, the Oscar-nominated actor and humanitarian. She felt a restaurant that served the finest food and gave the most comfortable atmosphere needed to be right in the middle of East Hampton. So we rented the building on the corner of Main Street and Newtown Lane. The restaurant was more beautiful than I could have ever imagined.

The place was swarmed with socialites, celebrities, and the who's who in the Hamptons. Page Six is outside the front door, with cameras flashing. Kim Killian, the actress, investor, and now friend, was working the room. She was taking photographs, pouring champagne, talking to the local paper—she did what any celebrity would do to make this evening successful. My dad, being the proud father, was checking the kitchen, making sure it ran smoothly, and assisting the bartender. Michael, an old customer of Sicilia's in Port Jeff, now East Hampton's restaurant manager, was greeting our customers. He took pride in making sure their glasses were filled and food was to their liking. I was rather calm considering the hype that came along with opening. With Kim's backing and the press, I was elated.

I was talking to Kim's boyfriend, Jaime Worman, supermodel extraordinaire, about his new project with Macy's, the New York City department store. It was very exciting to hear about his upcoming shoots and the models he would be working with. I would be jealous, but Kim didn't even bat an eye. If my boyfriend were around flawless women all day in barely any clothes, I would be one jealous lunatic.

Suddenly everything went dark. I held onto Jaime for dear life. Breathing heavy with fear, we heard a scream. The lights flickered and came back on. Everyone was looking around to find out where the scream came from. Kim was holding her neck, tears streaming down her face.

"Where is it?" Kim's face turned white. "Who took it?" Her hands frantically searched her neck for the diamond necklace that adorned it just moments ago.

Jamie ran to her side and consoled her, and I followed right behind while Michael called the cops.

"Kim, did the robber say anything to you? Did he hurt you? Is there anything I can do?"

"I just need to sit down. Alisa, that necklace was worth a lot of money."

Jamie chimed in, "Sweetheart, all that matters is that you didn't get hurt. The necklace is not worth more than you, the love of my life."

Kim kissed Jamie for the words he spoke from his heart. If she didn't love the man before, she does now. Kim began drying her tears and transitioning to slower and deeper breaths.

"Alisa, can you please get me a glass of Merlot. I am going to need it."

"Yes, you want a shot of tequila on the side?"

"Make that two," Jaime blurted out.

Kim and Jaime were settled and preparing themselves to talk to the police.

Michael and I began making our rounds trying to calm the startled guests who were now checking their purses and pockets to make sure nothing was missing or out of place. Complimentary wine began flowing in hopes of reviving the vibe before the cops showed up. Speaking of backup, maybe the surveillance system caught something

Before I could pull the footage, the police arrived, along with a crew of detectives who didn't waste any time gathering the evidence and statements. I panned the restaurant to find Kim sitting with a distractingly attractive detective. Didn't take long for Jamie to swoop in, to place one hand on Kim's thigh while the other wrapped around her back to hug her close. Jealousy never slept. I found a smile start to creep over my lips as I watched it unfold, but just then, I felt a hand on my waist.

"Hey, are you okay, baby girl?" It was Michael.

"Yeah, how about you?"

"Fine, leave it to you to have the wildest restaurant opening of the century." He giggled his way through the sentence.

"Well, normally you would tell me I needed to spice up my life, but I think as of tonight, I'm good for a while." I giggled right with him.

"Well, baby girl, you never know this night might be the start of a whole new beginning," he said as one eyebrow lifts.

"You know, spice of life," he said.

"Well, I have enough spice. I do own two restaurants. Spice, I have plenty of that," I said with a wise-ass tone. He kissed the top of my head as he told me he's going to assist the detectives with anything they needed.

Some guests began to make their way home after being questioned, hoping this freak incident didn't deter them from returning, I made sure to slip each of them a free dinner and gift card. There was still so much left to be done.

I started to look around for my father and saw him in the kitchen assisting the pastry chef with the tiramisu. He was the cutest thing. After my mother died, he was glued to me. I was his pride and joy and proud to be known as the typical "daddy's girl." The love he had for mother is the type of love I wish to find. I hope one day he'll find someone the way he loved my mother.

CHAPTER 2

Brent

I walked into Sicilia's, the newest restaurant of East Hampton. I had to put extra patrol out for its grand opening. Rumors were around that there would be plenty of celebrities and press around. It's that time of year when Manhattan comes out to the east end for the weekends, and social media feeds are littered with photos of celebrity sightings and captured sunsets. For the A-listers, it's the place to get their tension released and their bodies bronzed.

I'm the person who ensures everyone's weekend goes according to plan. So tonight, when I got the call about a grand theft at Sicilia's, I wanted to make sure I had an eye on the investigation. Being in the business as long as I have, something as small as missing one witness's testimony could jeopardize the case.

Kim Killian, the actress from *My Heart's Desire* was talking to my top detective in this investigation. Being that Kim was an A-lister, this meant that the incident would be publicized beyond the local papers and hit national television stations. This also meant that the local gossip press, *Dean's Paper*, would be all over this case. Dean was ruthless. He'd bribe unsavory characters for tips, dig into people's pasts for skeletons in their closet for a juicier headline. He wasn't above spinning a story or twisting a quote to fit his agenda. It was *the* paper in the Hamptons. No need to turn on your TV, Dean knew the juice and he was ready and willing to spill it.

I looked around the restaurant for clues that my men may have missed, looking where the entrances and exits were, pleased to see surveillance cameras in the right areas. Looking around, this place felt familiar somehow, but I couldn't place my finger on it.

I continued to look around. The feeling started to overwhelm me like my body had some strange gravitational pull to this place. I only had this feeling once before. It was a long time ago, but it was the same sensation that made my heart beat faster and left my body tingling. My head turned on its own as if someone was doing it for me. I couldn't believe my eyes. I took a double take because simply it couldn't be, not after all this time. It was her—the girl that left me breathless that day—Alisa. The one person that ruined me for any other woman. I have dated many girls, but there was no one that made me feel the way she did, the day I got lost in her kiss. Yes, it might have been just a kiss, but the way it made me feel, I never wanted to settle for less. There were days that I wondered what would have been there when I was released from my duty, hoping to start our lives together.

I was only twenty-two when the agency put me undercover in her high school. The two guys we finally charged were a small part of a big ring. Joey and Richie Futzelli were the nephews of Mario Adamo, head of the Marino crime family. They were dealing drugs and recruiting kids to peddle them. Drugs weren't the only thing they were doing; they also did small robberies like taking Amazon packages left on doorsteps, stealing from the mom-and-pop stores. After much convincing, the investigators were able to get the bastards to talk. Mario went to trial and two of his lieutenants. Mario never survived prison. The other families put the hit on him. After two weeks in the state jail, they buried him at St. John's cemetery at the Adamo mausoleum.

Oh, how I wanted to go back and find Alisa. I wanted to explore more of what we started ten years ago. I remember the day when she walked up those stairs of the high school. She came to me, with a look between fear and want. Our eyes met; the feeling of an electrical current went through me. She brought herself just inches away from my lips before pausing. It took everything in me not to grab her close and devour her mouth, I wanted to feel those pouty lips on mine. The innocence to ask if I had a girlfriend and the longing look she gave when she waited for my answer. It was much more complicated than that, but I couldn't bring myself to tell her the truth. Not then.

I remember being amazed by her beauty. That day I looked up and down for any imperfection, and there was not one I could not find. I knew I should have said yes—I didn't want to start something I knew couldn't last more than that one moment we shared. But I couldn't help myself.

I looked into her hazel eyes, gold speckles shining through. She moistened her lips awaiting my answer with bated breath. I was helpless in her gaze. Before I knew it the word "no" slipped from my mouth.

She lunged in and kissed me. I felt her soft lips. Her hands were in my hair, tugging me closer to her. The sensation was getting stronger. I lost full control of my mind and body. The sweet taste of her lips, the soft moan coming from her mouth enticed me to make the kiss deeper. The deeper the kiss, the more I wanted to take. I turned her so her back was against the wall. I got a feel of her breast as my hands roamed her body. I knew she felt how much I needed more. I never wanted this moment to end. My jeans were growing tighter as I felt every god damn curve of her body. I wanted to take her and make her mine right there. As soon as I was going to grab her shirt and pull it out of her jeans so I could feel her skin, the bell rang to change classes, and I was forced to snap back into reality. I had a very serious, and dangerous job to do. The arrest of the Futzelli brothers was happening today.

As we broke apart from the distraction, we stared at each other. Neither of us wanted that moment to end. Those hazel eyes turned a light green after our encounter. Deep down I knew this would never be able to happen again. I needed to tell her to remember that moment because I knew then I would never forget her.

She was seventeen, and I was twenty-two, a five-year difference. At that time in our lives, it was not a good idea. I was undercover, and most likely after the case, I would be put under protective services. The repercussions of the mob finding out I was the cause of their takedown would be fierce. I never blew my cover. Imagine hanging with the nephews of the infamous NYC crime families for four months and pretend you can't wait to heist a smoke shop for expensive cigars or sell cocaine without even touching a bag of it. If the Federal Bureau of Investigations (FBI) did not put me in protective services, I would be at the bottom of the Hudson River with cement shoes.

At the end of that investigation, the agency did indeed put me in protective services for two years until the trial was over. I was in Sedona, Arizona. Beautiful little town with the red rock mountain landscape and the famous Bell Mountain. While Sedona was the prime place to clear my mind, I was consumed with thoughts of Alisa. I only received one phone call during that exile, and it was to inform me that Joey and Richie were missing. As far as I was concerned, my job was done, I wanted to be through with that high school and everyone in it. Well, almost everyone. I was sure karma would handle Joey and Richie, but maybe destiny had something else in store for me.

I haven't thought about the past for years, but I had to get my head in the present. I was the commissioner of the East Hampton police department. I needed to get a hold of myself. I straightened up and continued with the investigation at hand. My detectives were finishing up the questioning of the guests, while the forensics squad was taking the pictures of the crime scene. Channel 12 wanted a commissioner statement for the ten o'clock news report. I couldn't help but wander toward her. I watched the way she presented herself so confident and controlled. She looked amazing, her curves just the way I remembered, and her eyes still captivated me. The way she moved made me want to grab her and finish what we started the better of ten years ago.

She didn't even notice my presence. This was ridiculous. Why would she remember me? For all I know, it was just a dare. That day her friends dared her to kiss me. She probably won a spa day, but realistically that was not how I remembered it.

I told her not to forget me.

Deep down, I know she didn't.

I found Detective Doherty; we needed to do a briefing of what he found out. I needed the details to be prepared for the reporters and the press. He rattled off the main details—victim, what was stolen, the value of the necklace—but the information I really wanted to hear was about the owner of the restaurant. When he finally came up to the part I wanted to hear, a slight smile grew across my face when I heard "Alisa Rossi." Doherty continued with his bullet points—Alisa Rossi owns two restaurants, the first being in Port Jefferson. The East Hampton restaurant manager, Michael Davis, is accounted for and willing to cooperate. Kim Killian, the victim of the burglary, may have been the only target in the incident, which means this could have been a premeditated attack.

As Doherty was finishing up his report, the sensation from earlier returned. I wanted to turn around. I just could not make that happen. I did not want her to see me tonight. There was so much to be said, and I was not ready to tell her what happened to me after that day. Additionally, this was not the right time to explore the past.

It was great timing when Gayle from Channel 12 News wanted me to do the interview. My eyes moved to get a glimpse of her to hold me over until the next time our paths crossed.

CHAPTER 3

Alisa

Everyone was frazzled. I can't believe it. Why tonight! Who would ruin tonight for me? Everything was going so smoothly. Detective Doherty was doing his best to comfort me during our conversation. He knew I was anxious and wanted this chaos to end. I provided him with all sorts of information to help him find the criminal that put this night in shambles. The information included the invite list, the layout of the restaurant, the names of the construction crew and general contractor I used for the improvements, the access to the camera footage from the security cameras, and the employees' names and phone numbers that worked tonight.

I glanced at where Kim and Jamie were sitting. Kim calmed down from all the commotion, as Jamie was rubbing her back and lacing her forehead with small pecks, refusing to leave her side for even a moment. I hoped one day I would meet the man I was destined to be with to provide me the love that Jaime had for Kim. I shook my head out of my dream when my dad called me.

"How are you holding up? I wanted to make sure you were good before I left, *bella*." Always making sure I was not overwhelmed.

"Dad, I'm fine. You can go. Just be careful." I gave him a kiss and a big hug before he ventured back home. He was here all day. He must be tired.

"*Bella*, always looking out for Papa," he said as he kissed each side of my face and held my face in his hands.

"I'm so proud of you, honey. Don't let this ruin the whole night. The police are going to find the thief. Kim is so rich she can buy another necklace. Look on the bright side—it's like free advertising." He smiled, trying to make me laugh.

"Dad, really?" I rolled my eyes. "Is that the best you can do?"

"*Bella*, you have worked so hard on this, and I don't want you to feel upset. You know your mother would be so proud." Just hearing those words from my father made my eyes well up with tears. My mother passed a while ago from cancer. She was my rock, always pushing me to be my best, and she would give me advice that I would never forget.

My father was right. My mother would be proud of me. She always told me, "Nothing is impossible if you have the will to succeed." A hand touched my shoulder. On impulse, I jerked my head toward a familiar voice. He's right. My mother would be proud of me.

The familiar voice belonged to Sharon, apologizing for being late while standing next to her flavor of the month boyfriend, Louie. I could see her face go from guilt to confusion as she began to realize she was in the middle of a police investigation.

"What's going on here?"

I rambled through the events of the evening, how I went from flying high to possibly hosting the greatest jewelry heist the Hamptons has ever seen. Not to mention how this ordeal will most likely grace the cover of tomorrow's issue of *Dean's Paper*. Unable to find the words, Sharon opted for a hug to console me after my night of chaos. As I laid my head on her shoulder, I overheard Kim's celebrity posse complimenting my restaurant. Kim was sure to thank them with her Oscar-winning smile, and I could feel one creep across my face as well.

Suddenly the energy in the air shifted. A familiar feeling I couldn't shake. A chill ran down my spine, I haven't felt this way in years. After all of today's excitement, what could this mean?

"Alisa...Alisa?" Sharon said as she was waving her hand in front of my face.

I was in my own little world, beginning to reminisce about that gray-eyed guy who used to give me chills. All of a sudden I was transported back to those stairs, his arms around me, my body pressed to his…

"Earth to Alisa! Jesus, what planet are you on?"

Sharon's hands were on my shoulder, shaking me back and forth, trying to pull me from the grips of my fantasy.

I could feel myself slowly drift back to reality. She was right. I turned into a total space cadet, paralyzed by what was and now aching with what could have been.

Desperate to change the subject, I flipped the attention back to Sharon.

"What took you so long to get here?" Sharon's expression went from concerned to annoyed.

"There was an accident on the Long Island Expressway at Exit 68 for Smithpoint Beach. A food truck and a Pepsi truck collided. Well, anyway, a two-hour delay."

It's 12:00 a.m. The detectives and guests have left, and Michael closed the restaurant. We went back to the house I rented for the weekend. It was off Hands Creek, a beautiful beach house. Michael, Sharon, and Louie came back to the house with me. We stayed up for a while longer and talked about the evening. After two bottles of wine, some cheese and crackers, we decided it was time to get some sleep.

I was getting ready for a well-deserved good night's sleep. Grabbing my toiletry bag, I ventured toward the suite's bathroom. It was one of those en suites you'd swoon over while flipping through a spread of a millionaire's home in *Architectural Digest*. The walk-in shower was bigger than my bedroom back in Stony Brook. Slated tile and floor-to-ceiling windows that allowed the moonlight to pour in. The beam from the lighthouse would dance across the walls as it made its rounds. I was thrilled to see the rainforest shower heads. I couldn't wait to feel the water cascade my body.

The water was warm and pulsating on my skin. I thought about that feeling I got tonight, wondering what caused that reflection of my experience I had from high school. After ten years, I still did not know his name. The man with gray eyes, dark hair, that square jaw-line, and muscular chest seen through his tight T-shirt. I relived that passionate kiss and that encounter many times over the years. I have yet to find that same connection with anyone else. Maybe that was why I am still a virgin at the age of twenty-seven. I dated, sure, but I never truly connected with anyone I felt was worthy enough to have intimate sex. It was embarrassing to say I was waiting for someone to make me feel like that again, but I don't want to settle for less. It was the way he touched me so seductively. He made me feel as if I was the most beautiful girl in the world. When the bell rang for class to begin, the look he gave me was as if he never wanted it to end. He told me not to forget him, and I never did.

Hot water was running down on my breast. I continued to remember how bold I was that day. I needed to feel his lips against mine. As I relived that encounter, I found myself moving my hands toward my breast and reenacting the way he touched me. I moved my hand down lower, fantasizing what could have happened that day if that bell did not ring. Remembering his mouth being so warm as he sucked on my tongue. I wanted so much more that day, and I know he did too. I imagined him playing with my clit, and my hands found their way there, sliding in and out, faster and faster. I became on edge when suddenly my whole body thrusted back, my back being pressed against the wall. My body released. I stood there as the water continued to drip down over my breasts and couldn't believe what I had just done.

My mind came back to reality. The emptiness too. The feeling of loss reentered my mind. I have to find a way to move from the past. I finished my shower and laid on the bed closing my eyes to an eventful day.

The next morning Michael made breakfast fit for royalty. The smell of waffles, eggs, and bacon filled the air. He cut up strawberries and made fresh whipped cream. The table was set in the kitchen, the windows open to see the beach and the pool in the backyard. The sun was glimmering off the water, and the seagulls flew across the inlet. Sharon and Louie made their way down, searching for their coffee.

"Alisa, this is a really beautiful house. How did you find it?" Sharon asked, looking around in amazement.

"One of Kim's personal assistants got it for me." It's good to know people, but to know someone who is famous—that's a blessing. I can't believe she was able to get it in the middle of summer.

"It must have cost a fortune. Look at that view. It has a private beach." This was Kim's gift to me for the weekend.

Sharon was a photographer for an up and coming socialite magazine. It will give *Dean's Paper* of the Hampton a run for its money. Sharon's camera was out and set for a day of picture taking. The coastline was amazing out here. She also had a clear view of the shores of Amagansett and the Montauk lighthouse. Any photographer's dream.

In the background, the television was on. I heard the news. "Kim Killian's 2.5-million-dollar necklace stolen" came through loudly. Leaving the kitchen to enter the den, I took my breakfast and sat down on the couch. My eyes grew wide, I couldn't believe what I was seeing. It wasn't that I saw my restaurant on TV or even a picture of Kim. I moved closer to the set to make sure I wasn't imagining it. I could feel my hand subconsciously reaching for the screen in hopes of touching him, as if caressing his face would confirm his identity. After ten years and many nights of wondering where he went, it was *him*. Coming out of my trance, I focused on the newscast.

"More from Commissioner Collins," said the anchor lady as she introduced him.

"Last night around 8:10 p.m., at Sicilia's grand opening, Kim Killian, the actress from *My Heart's Desire*, was robbed. We are still questioning and investigating the robbery. If anyone has any information about last night's incident, please contact East Hampton Crime Stopper, and folks, the food at Sicilia's is delicious. Please don't have this incident prevent you from eating there." He shook his head and stood to the left of the podium. Detective Doherty took over the microphone to answer questions from the swarm of reporters.

I stared at the television, understanding why I felt something last night. He must have been there. Why didn't I see him? His eyes have not changed. I became hypnotized by his smile. It felt as if he was staring right back at me through the screen—those lips. I felt seventeen again, my face started to heat up with excitement.

In the background, I heard Sharon. "Earth to Alisa. What is going on with you lately?" She shook her hands in front of my face just like in high school.

"It's *him*." I pointed to the television.

"Huh?"

"It's him, gray eyes." Read my mind Sharon.

"No." She already knew who I meant. This is the best part of having a best friend since childhood. Sometimes you just don't need to explain yourself.

"Yes!" I said, shocked.

"Louie, I'll meet you outside. I have to talk to Alisa." I knew she thought I was losing it. She was going to give me the speech, the "you need to move on from him" speech.

"Okay, hun, don't be too long; I want to show you a great spot I found out here a couple of years ago," Louie said with a hint of disappointment.

"Yes, dear," she said sarcastically. As Louie left the room in a huff, Sharon spun around with urgency.

"Okay, spill." She put her hand on my shoulder, showing me the support I needed to explain my sudden tongue-tied moment.

"Okay, remember in high school the day those two guys were arrested for drugs in school?" I looked for a reaction.

"Yeah."

"And I was, as you put it, 'glowing'?"

"Yes, I remember. You haven't glowed like that since. Hence one of the reasons why you have commitment issues…and other issues."

"Well, it's him. The police commissioner, Collins—Brent Collins."

"What? Are you sure, Alisa?" She spun around to look at the TV to glance at the commissioner. "You're telling me your Mr. Destiny, the man you have been waiting for to pop your cherry, is the commissioner of the East Hampton Police Department? You have to be shitting me."

"Yes. That's exactly what I am telling you."

"What are you going to do? I mean are you sure it is him? It's been ten years. Did you notice a ring on his finger?"

"I don't know what I am going to do, and yes, I looked—no ring." I realized I needed a plan.

"Why wouldn't he want to talk to the owner of the restaurant that his men are doing the investigation on? Was he there last night? Alisa, what would you have done last night if you saw him?" Frantic energy was filling the room. Sharon hopped up and began pacing as she attempted to wrap her mind around the situation.

"True. Probably run, or worse, grab him and—" Hmm.

"Alisa, I can't see you doing that." She looked over her shoulder with that sarcastic look again saying that I would never do that.

"Sharon, that day when I kissed him, it wasn't me at all either. He has this—"

Sharon cut me off before I could finish. "It doesn't matter. You need to find him."

"Really, you think so?" I looked at her as if she was the crazy one now. Sometimes this girl…

"Yes. Also, are you really drooling right now?"

I giggled as I wiped my mouth. "No, I'm not," I said, giggling even more.

"Alisa, you need to clear your mind with him, to see if what you are feeling is real. You have to at least tell him it was you that day in the stairwell at high school."

She knows me well enough to know I need to do this. If anything, to get closure of this insane hope I have for him.

"And how would I go about doing that?"

At this point I was relying on Sharon to map out my reunion. Give me my next clue, Sherlock.

"It will all come together. I mean, as the owner of the restaurant, you may need an update on the case. Right?" Sharon looked outside as she heard Louie calling her name.

"I have to go. Talk later," she said as she headed out of the den. I went to the couch to sit down.

Brent Collins, East Hampton police commissioner, he is real. I must admit I gave up hope in finding him. Some days I even convinced myself that I imagined the entire interaction. I didn't have any other witnesses, it's as if I implanted myself in a romantic movie as the lead.

Shaking my head in disbelief, I can't believe he is real. How am I going to make my move? Should I just walk in the police department and see how the investigation was going? I mean, Sharon had a point: it is my restaurant. It's normal for the owner of the restaurant to want to know how the investigation was going. It would work. That's it!

I started to get myself ready, going through many scenarios in my head how the conversation should go, anticipating any outcome of our interaction. The one I hope does not happen was the one where I was mistaken and I have the wrong person. The worst case would be he forgot about me. After digging through my luggage I packed for the long weekend, I pulled together an outfit I thought would perfectly encapsulate the more mature version of the girl he met ten years ago on those stairs. A valero jacket layered over a cowl neck blouse, jeans, and a heel. As I was fixing my hair, I caught a glimpse of myself in the mirror. My wardrobe said sophisticated yet sexy; my face said nervous but excited.

It's two o'clock. I called Michael to let him know that I would be late to the restaurant for the evening's service. "Okay, I am going to do this," I said out loud to pump myself up. I took one last look in the hallway mirror to compose myself and headed to the police station to meet Mr. Brent Collins.

My Mr. Destiny.

CHAPTER 4

Brent

I haven't stopped thinking about her since I left the restaurant last night. I remembered the tinge of jealousy I felt when I saw Doherty talk to Alisa, then again when he spoke to me about their conversation. It was how he snickered when he said certain things. He was impressed with her sense of resolve and in her willingness to assist in the investigation. She even gave him her cell number if he wanted to view the security tapes or needed to enter the restaurant in off hours. He said he planned on using it. I sensed he was attracted to her. I couldn't tell him to back off. Okay, maybe I could in a professional way. I was already feeling a sense of possession, and she doesn't even know I exist.

I knew I felt it within five minutes of her being near me. I couldn't help to think she may have felt it too. *Brent, you're losing it*, my conscience spoke loudly in my head. It's been ten long years. She probably has a boyfriend. I didn't see a ring, but she does own a restaurant and cooks, so maybe she doesn't wear it. Alisa and her manager seemed close last night. Yeah, they were probably dating.

I was interrupted in my thoughts as Detective Doherty came into my office with the updates on what we were now calling the Kim Killian case.

"What do we have so far, Doherty?"

"Well, it looks like an inside job."

"Why do you think that?"

18

"Everyone was accounted for." James explained, "The cameras were dark when the lights went out, so we couldn't see anything on tape. I'm going to call Alisa to see if I could view them in her office." I saw the smile forming on his face. I knew he was interested in her.

"Hmm…keep looking. Oh yeah, Doherty."

"Yeah, boss."

I leaned forward on my desk to show him this was nothing to joke about. "You're in charge, the point person in this case. It's high profile. We need to find the thief."

"Yes, boss. I understand. Thanks for trusting me with this. I won't disappoint." Doherty was a no-nonsense type of person. His loyalty to the department was not lost in my eyes.

Normally, with a high profile case like this, I am the lead. This case was different in many ways. I do trust Doherty to do all that's necessary to close the case efficiently, but I wanted to be involved in the background, so I could dig a little deeper. I can't let this take longer than it needs to, knowing this was part of her. I needed to make extra strides to solve this. I have to protect what was hers. I have to protect what will be *mine*. I know I was getting ahead of myself. This was not about hope; it was about need.

I looked out of the window of my office; it faced the shoreline of the Atlantic Ocean. The Montauk Lighthouse was in sight. I was thinking of the best way to make her know it was me that day. It's been a long time since that day and many changes in my life. I am not sure how; she may have changed too. This was something I needed to do. I will never be able to move on until I talk to her. So many thoughts of what the next few days could hold flooded my mind.

How am I going to react when I approach her? Will she remember? Gathering my thoughts, I created a plan of action. It's 1:00 p.m. She should be at Sicilia's. Usually restaurant owners were at their establishment for the lunch crowd. I cleared off my desk for the afternoon and headed out the door. Passing my assistant Jen, I let her know I would be out on patrol for the rest of the day. Exiting the station, excitement started to ignite the fire that's building in my heart. This was it. I found my lost treasure.

I walked into the restaurant. A skinny male with a confused look on his face approached me.

"Sorry, sir, but we don't open until 4:00 p.m."

"I'm Commissioner Collins. Is the owner in? I need to speak to them about the incident last night."

"Alisa is running late. She should be here in fifteen minutes. I'll get Michael. He is the manager. He could help." This was not part of the plan I came up with in my head.

"No, no, I can wait for Alisa," I said, being patient.

"Could I get you anything? A coffee or sparkling water perhaps?"

"Yes, coffee, black please."

The skinny kid ran toward the double doors and must have told the manager, as I saw Michael walking through the doors texting someone. He went to get my coffee.

My nerves got the better of me. I wanted to leave and come back when I had this all figured out. I haven't felt like this since I asked Melissa Locastro to the junior prom. My buddy Tom will never let it go that I ruined his Nike sneakers with vomit. The good part was that she said yes. She also said yes to the question I asked her in the back of the limousine that night where we both lost our virginity. Talk about awkward. I'm surprised she didn't get pregnant. Trying to put on the condom, well, let's just say a comedian would have had a field day explaining that one with his audience. I heard a man's voice. It brought me back to reality.

"Hi, Commissioner Collins, I'm Michael, the manager. Alisa will be here shortly. Is there anything I can help you with? I'm assuming this has to do with last night?" His hip leaned against the counter.

"No, Michael, I'd rather wait and talk to Alisa." As I finished that thought, that feeling of electricity through my body came back, and I knew...she was here.

"She just walked in. I texted her. She knows you're here. Just give her a couple of minutes." Michael left to catch up with her. I was still trying to figure out if they were together. I sensed a connection but couldn't make out the intensity of it. He hugged her tightly and headed toward the double doors.

I looked toward her way with a calmer feeling than I expected. I knew this was the right time to confront the one person that has held my heart for way too long. I made it this far. But what do I say to her? I can't do what she did ten years ago, or could I? I checked my watch, trying not to look too eager and took a sip of my coffee, waiting for her to approach me. She was still looking down at her phone texting. The occupied look on her face had me uneasy as if something else was wrong. The feeling of protecting her overflowed me again. I stood up to approach her when she darted through the double doors. She didn't even glance over my way.

CHAPTER 5

Alisa

Michael said that someone needed to talk to me about last night. It's probably that detective Doherty. He made me feel like I knew who the thief was. Although I believe he did flirt with me. It was a slick move when he asked me for my cell number by saying it was to make an appointment to see the surveillance cameras. It was when I walked through the front door that I knew it wasn't the detective. I felt it again, the feeling of electricity running through my body. I quickly looked up from my phone to see not Detective Doherty but Brent checking his watch just casually standing in the middle of my restaurant with a cup of coffee. Panicking, I made a beeline for the kitchen.

"Shit, shit, shit! Okay, control yourself. He probably forgot about you!" I said to myself. Breathe. Suddenly Michael was by my side.

"What?"

"Hey, Alisa, remember Commissioner Collins is in the bar. He wants to go over last night's events," he reminded me, giving me a kiss on my cheek.

My heart was racing. "Oh, yeah," I responded, twisting my hands together.

"What's wrong, baby girl? You look like you have seen a ghost." His forehead was scrunched up.

"I'm good, Michael. Just feeling overwhelmed about everything." Not really a lie.

"Ali, I got your back, baby girl." He pulled me to his chest to give me a hug, the ones I love, the great big bear hug.

"I know you do." I finally gained my composure and reassured myself that Brent probably won't even recognize me.

Buying myself some time, I poured a fresh cup of coffee for him. It was a good idea until I realized Michael had already got him one. Flustered and desperately trying to slow my heart rate, I stuck my hand out to shake his, "Commissioner Collins, I'm—"

The tension of the room changed from me being nervous to being mortified. I felt my body lunge forward, then float to the ground. I tripped over some invisible object and in slow motion I watched in horror as the scalding hot coffee sailed through the air and drenched Brent's polo.

"Oh, I am so sorry. So very sorry. How embarrassing." I took the towel from the counter and started to wipe my hands.

"It's okay. I mean, it was an accident, right?" He winked.

He began to take off his shirt. Our eyes met, and my heart stopped. My eyes darted to the ground and silence took over.

All of a sudden, I felt Michael swoop up behind me.

"I am so sorry, Commissioner. Alisa is feeling pretty overwhelmed with everything going on." Michael had no idea how right he was. I was overwhelmed—overwhelmed to finally be standing in front of Mr. Destiny after all of these years of fantasizing about that day, of what could have been and now what could be. I apologized again, my eyes still avoiding contact. I don't think my heart could handle it, I might lose it.

"It's okay, Alisa." I felt his eyes on me. Him saying my name was the same sensation I get when chocolate melts down my throat, silky, smooth, and delicious. Embarrassed by my clumsiness, I kept my gaze on the floor. Brent began talking, but consumed with my thoughts, I couldn't hear one word.

"Mrs. Rossi," Brent said a little louder.

Just the cue to snap me out of my trance. "No, it's Ms. Rossi, but please call me Alisa."

A smile hit his face. "Alisa, would it be okay if I come back later?"

"Yes, Commissioner, I'll treat you to dinner. Come back tonight as my guest. It's the least I can do," I said as I continued to clean the floor from the spilled coffee.

"Sure, what time?" Brent's tone was different. I couldn't tell how he was feeling.

"How about 8:00 p.m.? That way I can sit and answer your questions."

"That sounds good. Excuse me, I need to put on a clean shirt. Was that a cappuccino you were drinking?" A smile hit those luscious lips trying to make light of the embarrassing situation.

"Yes, Commissioner. With a double shot of espresso," I said with a smile. "Again, Commissioner, I'm sorry!"

He headed toward the door, but just before he left, he turned back. Our eyes met just like they did back in high school. I noticed Michael smirking.

"What?" I said with annoyance.

"I think someone wants a piece of this comish," he said, singing it as if it was a playground song.

"Shut up!" Okay, he's got me. Michael continued to look at me with a smirk on his face as if to say, "You know I'm right."

"Get back to work, you," I said with a knowing smile.

"What are you going to cook for him? I suggest that you start off with the oysters. It's an aphrodisiac," he said, lifting one eyebrow.

"Shut up. It's not like that." I took the rag I was using to clean the recently spilled coffee and slapped his ass with it.

All right, I made it through the first meet cute, as they say in the movies. Brent Collins was the commissioner of not just the East Hampton Police Department but now the commissioner of my heart. The feelings I had at that moment were of intense longing. I can't be clumsy tonight. I continued to clean the floor and tumbled back on my ass and started to laugh.

"What the hell did I trip over?" I said to myself. The look on his face as I saw the coffee go midair—priceless, probably the same look I had on my face when he took off his shirt. I'm glad he kept up with his workout routine over the years. His body was even more defined than I remembered. I could feel my loins tighten at the thought of grabbing his shirt and planting my lips on his, running my hands along his abdomen, and unbuckling his pants did cross my mind. I'm ready to finish what we started all those years ago.

CHAPTER 6

Brent

I sat in my car buttoning up the spare polo I keep in my cruiser and retraced what just happened. I was confident that she truly remembered me. She was just as she was ten years ago. Those hazel eyes that were caramel brown with light green around the edge and golden specs peering through. Those luscious lips that I tasted ten years ago and craved, the curves of her body that drove me crazy. She was wearing jeans that accentuated her figure and fit beautifully around that ass. She wore a low-cut blouse teasing me by showing off the swell of her breast. I needed to make a good impression tonight. I mean if she does remember me, she may have some hatred toward me. I mean I left. She would think I never cared enough to say good-bye. I never forgot, wanted to write her or send her flowers to explain, but what good would that have done? If things were different back then, who knows.

Get it together, Brent, I said to myself. *You have a grand theft robbery to solve!* I just couldn't help it. That look she gave me before I left, I just knew she felt it too. That's why I deliberately took off my shirt in front of her. To ensure her attraction to me. Her eyes looking me up and down, seeing her lick her bottom lip. I thought Michael even took a glimpse of her doing that. I knew if she licked that lip again, I wouldn't be able to restrain myself.

I walked through the doors of the precinct down the hallway to my office. Doherty was at his desk looking through files, piecing everything together. As I approached his desk, my assistant, Jen, ran with a sense of urgency down the hallway.

"Commissioner, someone came in to speak with you today."

"Did they speak with anyone else, who was it? Do I need to reach out to them? Give me more details, Jen." I was aggravated that she found it important enough to chase me down the hallway but yet she leaves out the important information.

"Sorry, sir, she said she wanted to talk to you about her restaurant's case and she would come back," Jen stated as she tried to catch her breath.

Holy shit, she was here looking for me. I wonder if she knew who I was. Wait, she was here when Michael called her. My mind went adrift. Doherty got me out of my trance.

"I have a suspicion about her. I don't know why, but something," he said, nodding his head up and down.

"Well, spill, what do you have on her?" My mind was now in full focus. Could she have turned criminal?

"Really, nothing, but there is something there. I can't put my finger on it."

"Well, when you figure it out, let me know. I'm actually questioning her tonight for due diligence. I'll let you know if I feel the same way. Doherty, in the future, you need facts to support your intuition. Was it her body language or something she said? Understand?"

I was now agitated about his speculation of Alisa's involvement in the case. I reviewed the notes Doherty had on the case thus far. I couldn't find any evidence that backed his suspicion. I looked up at the clock and realized I needed to go home and get ready for my dinner at Sicilia's. The excitement of seeing her again caused me to pay more attention to what I usually do when I go on a date. I shook my head. This was not a date. I am going to question Alisa about the grand theft. A smirk appeared in the mirror as I put the finishing touches to my appearance.

27

It's 7:50 p.m. when I headed over to the hostess at Sicilia's. "Hi, I'm Brent Collins. Alisa is expecting me."

"Okay, Mr. Collins," said the hostess. She looked in the reservation book as I looked into the crowd. I hope I was dressed properly. I was wearing a button-down shirt and dress pants. No one was staring, so I guess I was fine. I saw her manager Michael, the guy with the retro look. I had to admit he was one of those types of people that had you guessing which team he was pitching for. Slowly looking toward his way, I found my answer. He played for my team. In the middle of the restaurant, I saw him kiss the blond. My eyes followed his hand as he released it from underneath her shirt. That's daring. I have a feeling we will be good friends.

"Mr. Collins…Mr. Collins." The hostess was looking at me impatiently. I smirked and followed her to the table.

"Alisa will be with you soon," she informed me as she looked me up and down. I couldn't help but give her the look that said, "You're not my type."

"Would you like something to drink?" She tried to seduce me with her voice and winked as if that would make a difference.

"Just a club soda for now." I showed my smile as she turned away. Flirtatious bunch that worked here.

"I'll have the waitress bring it over. Alisa already put in your dinner order." She walked away making sure that her ass swayed so I would be forced to look in her direction.

"Thank you," I said, trying to hold in my laughter.

Michael came up to greet me. "Mr. Commissioner, I see you changed your shirt," he said with a giggle.

"Yes," I said with a smile.

"Alisa will be here in fifteen minutes to sit with you." He was smiling at me as if he knew something I didn't.

"Thank you." I sensed a flutter in my stomach. I never had that experience before. I was suddenly nervous to see her again. Michael was looking at me with a purpose I hadn't figured out yet.

"Please let me know if you need anything." Michael put his hand out to end our conversation with a handshake. He had a strong grip. That was his way to make me understand that he cared for her.

The waitress arrived at the table with a basket of bread and olive oil with some sort of spices in it, as well as my club soda. My mind drifted to the encounter from this afternoon. I will make it known to her that I know who she is tonight. I have waited too long. As I started to plan in my head what I was going to say to her, I heard Alisa greeting some of her guests. When I turned my head to see her, my whole body became stiff. Yes, every part. She was wearing a cranberry red halter dress that clung to every curve of her body. It sat about four inches above her knee, exposing most of her legs. The legs that one day will wrap around my waist. I'll have her up against the wall making passionate love to her until she screams my name. *Get your mind out of the gutter, Brent!*

"That dress is a Versace," I heard a woman say to her. She nodded in agreement. She excused herself when she saw me. There was a hesitation in her stride as she walked over toward me. I stood up showing the respect she deserved.

"Please, Commissioner, sit."

"Ms. Rossi—I mean Alisa, it looks like last night's incident has not affected business." I kept searching her face to make eye contact to see if there was any familiarity.

"Yes, thank God. Your speech on the news seem to help. I hope you don't mind that I picked the menu for dinner tonight." She couldn't look into my eyes. I think she knows—the keyword being *think*. I hoped that by the end of the night I'd have the answer to my question.

"No, I don't mind at all." I hope she put herself on the menu for dessert.

Within seconds, oysters in a half shell came out. Alisa handed me an oyster. I looked at them not knowing how to eat them. Do I use a fork? She sensed my confusion.

"Put the oyster shell on the tip of your lips and let it slide to the back of your throat." I watched her go first and promptly followed her lead.

"Well? It's good, right?" she asked.

I look at her and said, "Delicious," wondering if she knew what oysters were. Every man knows oysters are an aphrodisiac, as I smirked after the word.

"So, Commissioner, what questions do you have for me?" she asked, still avoiding eye contact.

"Well, Detective Doherty oversees the case. I wanted to ask if you have any idea of who would want to ruin your grand opening." I looked at her and noticed that she finally looked up and was trying not to stare.

"No, I don't know who would want to do that to me," she replied, shrugging her shoulders.

"No boyfriends or ex-lovers?" I got the question out. That will give me the green light to my thoughts and wants for this woman.

"No boyfriend now, or ex-boyfriends. To be honest, Commissioner, I never had a relationship long enough to have a man care that much." She looked into my eyes for any reaction.

"Okay. I find that impossible for a woman like you," I responded as our eyes locked.

"Why would you say that, Commissioner?" she asked, intrigued by my comment.

"Well, Alisa, I find you to be a successful, personable, and attractive person. The added feature of being a good cook is just a bonus," I told her, smiling at her. It's time to go for it, asking her the question that could change the course of the evening and even our lives.

"Alisa, have we met before?" My body became tense anticipating her response, and my eyes made their way toward the swell of her breasts. The breasts that I felt before. The breasts that I want to put my mouth on and suck the nipples until they pebble.

Her eyes left mine. "You do look familiar. Where did you go to high school?" she asked with her gaze remaining on her empty plate. At this point, I knew that she remembered me. My heart started pounding, and before I could respond, the main course came out—filet mignon with mushroom risotto and grilled asparagus. It looked delicious. I'm hungry, but not for food.

"I went to Ward Melville High School in Setauket." I didn't lie. I really went there. Ironically the high school I was undercover for was only two miles from mine.

Her eyes met mine. "Oh, that can't be it. I went to the high school in the next town over. Comsewogue. Did you go there or have friends you visited there?" She was disappointed in the answer I gave her. I was there. The time that I had to go undercover, there was a girl that blew my mind with just one kiss. There it was, that look that I was waiting for—silence.

"So, Alisa, did Detective Doherty look through your surveillance video?" I purposely ignored her question and waited to see if she would bring it up again, putting the ball in her court.

"Yes, he did. Now that I answered your question, can you please answer mine? Did you go to Comsewogue at any time or visit friends you may have had there?"

"Oh, just for—"

Michael bent down and interrupted our conversation. "Alisa, there is a major issue in the kitchen that needs immediate attention."

"Excuse me, Commissioner," she said as she rose from her chair with urgency.

I can't believe I ruined the moment. I should have answered her question right away. Instead, I tried the arrogant prick approach. I swore under my breath. This wasn't supposed to be so difficult.

Some time passed when Michael came back. "Commissioner, Alisa apologized, but the chef had an injury, and Alisa's needed to manage the kitchen," he informed me with a smug smile on his face. I think he knows something, or perhaps he was jealous because he saw the attraction between Alisa and me.

"She asked if she could meet you at your office tomorrow if you needed to continue your questioning." The look on his face told me to take the deal.

I contemplated my answer. If I said yes, I will get to see her again and hopefully make up for the mess I made out for myself. If I say no, she may think I'm not interested in giving her the answer to her question that could bring us back to the place where we could begin our journey together. This was a no-brainer, of course.

"Yes, please let her know I will be available at 10:00 a.m. Please give her my card. If she has any issues, she shouldn't hesitate to call me." Michael nodded and took my card.

"Please, Commissioner, finish your dinner. Is there anything else I can get you? Perhaps a glass of wine or something stronger?" he said, waiting for my response.

"Michael, I would love a Jack Daniels, if you don't mind. It's been a long week." Damn, this night was nothing how I expected to go.

"Coming up," he said with a smug smile.

I sat and finished my meal. I couldn't believe the way I reacted. I don't blame her if she blew me off. Scratch that—I hope she blows me off in the physical way. I shook my head. The image of that made me hard. She looked amazing tonight. Her curves, one word—*beautiful*—but I had to screw it up.

Michael came back with my Jack Daniels and sat at the table. My curiosity has piqued. Two things could happen right now. First, he could feel the attraction between Alisa and me and tell me to back off his girl, which, to tell you the truth, I was not sure I could. Or he could tell me that Alisa liked me, and if I hurt her or use her, I would have him to deal with. I hope it's the latter.

"Was there something you need to ask me, Michael?" I asked him as I tilted my head to the side waiting for an answer. He looked back with a sarcastic smile.

"What are your real intentions here, Mr. Collins? I see the way you look at Alisa. So I'll bring the question back to you. Is there something you need to ask me?"

Touché, nice move, Michael, bringing the ball in my court to take a swing. It's a testosterone showdown. Okay, I'm game.

"Well, Michael, Alisa is very attractive. I do believe I've seen her before." I stopped at that. I waited for his response to see where he would take me.

"Really, Mr. Collins, let me help you out. Alisa likes her men to be straight shooters in and outside the bedroom, if you catch my drift. I could see it on your face. No, I'm not your competition, but I do have the power to cockblock you. Alisa is the only family I have.

She is the purest person you will ever meet. If you hurt her or her heart—consider yourself hurt yourself, Commissioner. Got it?" His hands were on top of the table with his fingers entwined waiting for my response.

"Understood. I'm glad she has someone like you to protect her." The man just passed the baton to me. He was giving me his brotherly approval. If I screwed up, he was my consequence.

"Now, Mr. Collins, let me let you in on something. You two have something. Not sure what, but I see it. Alisa smiles whenever you are around. The coffee thing this morning, not like her at all. You got her twisted. Why am I telling you this? I need her to be happy. She pours herself in her work. She needs to be romanced, not wham-bam. You look like the guy who will do that for her." Big brother has spoken.

"Michael, I can assure you my intentions are pure." I really mean that. Okay, I do want her, but it's not just that.

"Mr. Collins, this conversation is between us. Remember, I'm the one who can cockblock you. Not a word to Alisa." His eyes were telling me that he wanted a verbal confirmation.

"Yes, between us. This goes both ways, correct?"

"Brent, I think we will get along just fine." He got up and patted my back and extended his hand for a handshake.

I finished my dinner, downed the rest of Jack, and headed out.

After I closed the door to my car, I sat and thought about tonight. The food was delicious, but what I really enjoyed was Alisa in her element. So controlled and confident. She cared about her staff and her friends. Michael made me understand that. This was not what I expected her to be like. It was better. All those years I imagined what it would be like if I saw her again. I could feel a smile begin to form on my face at the thought of seeing her tomorrow. The anticipation of taking the next step in this game of cat and mouse has my heart beating faster than ever before.

CHAPTER 7

Alisa

I rolled over to look at my alarm clock: nine o'clock. I was over-come with nerves; in exactly one hour, I was going to see Brent again. The saga continued; what happened last night? Why was Brent so arrogant? Why wouldn't he admit he remembered me? All these years I hoped our reunion would be a reenactment of that passionate embrace we shared. He'd see me and immediately want to throw me up against a wall and kiss me until I couldn't breathe. I would rather suffocate in his kisses than take a moment to pull ourselves apart. Wow, that would have been something. Instead, it seemed like he was playing hard to get, full of himself even. Someone I could never see myself with. Footsteps interrupted my thoughts. I looked over my shoulder to see Sharon coming down the hallway.

"Earth to Alisa," she said with her hand on her hip.

I blurted out, "He said I looked familiar," as if Sharon had just been listening to my thoughts. I sat staring at her with a confused look, waiting for her to somehow clear things up for me.

"Who?"

"Brent."

"Oh, of course, how could I forget? Brent! The guy who has been haunting your dreams and putting unrealistic expectations on your love life."

"Wait, you wore your cranberry dress, didn't you? The one some guy actually said makes you look like a piece of filet mignon that he wanted to get their teeth into. Maybe he was just flirting with you, trying to get in your panties."

I looked at her with fear in my eyes. Maybe he was only looking for a one-night stand.

"Sharon, stop being a bitch. It has to be destiny, right?"

"Alisa, stop playing games with him. Why didn't you just ask him straight out?"

She has a point, I missed a prime opportunity.

"Ugh, I know I should have."

I could tell Sharon was nearly fed up with the conversation. She took a deep breath and exhaled, letting her shoulders sink before giving me a final pep talk.

"Go over to his office and do what you did ten years ago. Take what you want!" That's what I needed to hear. Go get what I want, sounds like a plan.

"I mean, really, Alisa, what's the worst thing that can happen?"

Again, good point, but—

"Well, I can embarrass myself."

"Isn't it worth another kiss?"

She's right. There's so much riding on this, but at the very least I could feel those lips again.

"You go get him, girlfriend."

Sharon had her fist clenched, giving me a stern look like she was sending me off to war. Now wanting to get the heat off of me before I was struck again with a lightning bolt of insecurity, I changed the subject.

"Hey, where's Louie?"

"He had to go back early. Your father came to get him."

"Really? Why?" I didn't know Louie and my dad had bonded. I knew my dad saw Sharon as his daughter too. I guess he was just making sure he was worthy for Sharon's virtue. My father was a protective one when it came to the women in his life.

"Just for a ride." She shrugged her shoulders. She didn't get it either.

Looking at the clock, I realized I needed to get myself ready. I carefully chose my outfit. It's snug around the right areas but more casual attire than my Versace last night. I can't look that sexy all the time, or can I?

I hopped in my BMW, a treat I bought myself after my first restaurant turned a profit, and began my quick journey to the station. I declined Sharon's invitation for her to ride shotgun for moral support. I needed to do this on my own. My nerves were building, I needed to somehow channel 17-year-old me, the lioness who hunted down her prey. Once I hit the parking lot, I took one last look in the mirror for a makeup check. "Showtime, baby."

Not quite in the right mindset but wanting to make sure I was prompt for our meeting I swung open the precinct doors.

Bang! Detective Doherty had his head down on his way out and we collided, knocking me to the ground. This makes my third tumble to the floor in just over twenty-four hours.

Suddenly, I felt an arm around my waist helping me up. I know that touch. Shockwaves were now vibrating through my body.

I turned my head and saw those gray eyes.

Meanwhile, a startled Detective Doherty stood nearby with his eyes wide.

"Ms. Rossi, I'm so sorry. I was looking down at my file."

I should be thanking him. He put me exactly where I wanted to be, in Brent's arms.

His arm was still around me. It's a sensation of an electrical current running through me. In that moment, I decided, *I'm going to do what Sharon told me to do*. That's right—be the woman I was that day, that should jog his memory.

"Alisa, are you okay? Doherty has been working overtime hours to try to put this case behind us." He stared into my eyes, so deeply it felt as if he could read my thoughts. I pulled away from the intensity of the stare.

"Yes. I'm fine." He released me and guided me to his office. I should have just kissed him. I shook my head. *Coward. Don't mess up the next opportunity*. We walked down the hallway to his office. He allowed me to precede him as we walked through the doorway.

"Please take a seat."

He closed the door and headed toward his desk. I needed to kiss him before he got to his chair—the anticipation was killing me. I popped up from my seat and somehow that damn invisible object got me again. As if we were in slow motion, I began falling. Brent lunged to catch me, but it was too late. I hit the floor and all 6'5" of Brent had fallen right on top of me. The tension in the room must be so thick I trip over it. After the initial shock of the fall wore off we looked at each other, simultaneously realizing how every interaction of ours ends in chaos. I started to laugh and watched him give me a once over to make sure I was okay, then he shook his head and let out a laugh.

His hand brushed against mine, and that current went through my body once more. We stared into each other's eyes, and I knew this was my chance to go for it, and I did. It was the same way I did ten years ago. This time I did not care if he had a girlfriend or not. It was magical. I pressed my lips to his. The memory was crystal clear, and we mimicked what happened ten years ago in the stairwell. He deepened the kiss—fireworks exploded inside me. My libido was waking up from being in hiatus. Our hands were entwined above my head. He rolled over so he was on top of me. That move, just a fantasy of mine, came true. He began to kiss my neck. My breathing changed to panting. My hands roamed, feeling his muscular arms. He began to unbutton my shirt. I reciprocated, feeling his bare chest. He began caressing my nipple with his thumb and looked into my eyes before kissing me again. His kiss devoured me. At this point, I felt right. I have been waiting so long to feel this way again.

He stopped, gently pulling his face away, holding my chin between his pointer finger and thumb, he locked his eyes on mine and I began swimming in those cool gray pools.

"You didn't forget me."

"You told me not to."

We continued celebrating our reunion with our lips glued to one another. The connection was still there and just as hot ten years later. He rubbed his erection against my thigh. I slid my hand up from his knee up to his throbbing penis. He groaned, parting his lips just enough to slip out a few words. "Alisa, not here."

Once our breathing became regulated, he got up and held out a hand to help me up. We began buttoning up our shirts when the intercom went on.

"Commissioner Collins, Special Agent Vogel from the FBI is on the phone for you." He looked at me as he was apologizing for the interruption. I looked at his Adonis body and bit my bottom lip.

"Okay, Jen, give me two minutes."

"Sure, boss."

He turned to me. "What are you doing tonight?"

"I'll be at the restaurant."

"Okay, I will come by around nine. We need to talk." His voice sounded like he was concerned about something.

He's married. Got to be. *You're getting ahead of yourself, Alisa.*

"I agree. We need to talk. Nine will be fine."

That moment was everything that I'd been waiting for. It felt like a rerun of ten years ago, a little more intimate, but if the bell hadn't rung that day, we would have found ourselves under that stairwell. I loved how he took control, pinned me down and took me.

"Alisa, I wish I didn't, but," he said and gave me a kiss on my forehead, "I have to take this." He walked toward his desk and picked up the phone.

I left his office, slowly closing the door behind me. Did that really just happen? I could still taste him on my lips, my hands were trembling, and my head was now swirling with questions.

As I made my way out of the station I walked past the front desk and got a snarl from a woman behind it. *Sweetheart, nothing will wipe off the smile on my face.* I kept bringing my hand to my lips and tracing them with my finger, his kiss imprinted. I could just melt into a puddle right here. I was right, it was him, and he remembered me, remembered *us*. Just that alone made my heart skip a beat.

But why didn't he come back for me all those years ago? He was right; we do need to talk. I wasn't going to let another day go by without knowing. Before I knew it, I subconsciously made my way to Sag Harbor Marina. It was a beautiful little lookout point where I could be alone with my thoughts. I sat in this exact spot when I made the decision to expand my restaurant, to bring Michael on, to accept

Kim's offer of backing my new venture. Hopefully this spot could help me with this crossroad.

Am I getting ahead of myself? What did he have to talk to me about? Maybe he was in a relationship, and this was a fluke. A moment of passion never to be had again.

Just then a song came on the radio, *Now that I found you, I won't lose you again.*

The universe was speaking to me. I was not going to let Mr. Destiny slip away again. But before we moved forward, I needed to know what happened that day after we parted on the stairs. Why didn't he come back for me?

I'd get my answer, and hopefully more, in just a few hours. Now it was time to go back to the house. I needed to change and head to the restaurant for the dinner shift. I know Michael will be curious to hear how my meeting with Brent went. Michael and I had grown closer over the last few months. He was such a great listener and would never give unsolicited advice. If he had something to say, he'd ask first. Any time I brought up one of my dilemmas with men, he'd lend an ear.

He'd make the most entertaining facial expressions while listening along, and turn on Big Brother Mode if he didn't like the way I was being treated. He was the brother I always wanted. I think I even saw him giving Brent the "hurt her, and I hurt you" talk. The thought of Michael defending my honor would be heartwarming but it worries me. I think Brent would have the upper hand in that battle.

Tonight, I would get the questions answered. I am not sure how I feel right now. This could be the most wonderful night of my life or could end in heartbreak. It won't be long until I discover what fate has in store for me.

CHAPTER 8

Brent

"Special Agent Vogel," I said while smoothing down my hair and adjusting my shirt. My erection refused to subside as I continued to straighten up my office after our steamy exchange. It finally happened. We were reunited, and the chemistry was stronger than ever.

"Commissioner, are you there?"

Vogel's voice snapped me back into reality.

"Yes, sir." I shook away the fantasy and went back to work mode.

"We might have a lead for you on the Killian grand theft robbery case." If the feds were involved, there was more to this case than just a missing necklace.

"Yes, sir. I am listening."

"Well, it seems our undercover heard about a big cash exchange occurring in East Hampton." This could be a small layer in a huge investigation. I could tell by his voice that he couldn't share too much information. But if this could wrap up the case and make Alisa's life easier, I needed to find a way to get involved.

"Tell me, Special Agent, I need to talk to him." I knew that would not happen; it could ruin the whole investigation.

"Collins, really, I know you're ex-fed. Tomorrow, in our office. Let's shoot for 11:00 a.m."

I nodded and confirmed, "Sounds good, eleven hundred hours."

I hung up the phone wondering how deep this really went. I saw a glimmer shining on the floor—it's Alisa's earring. It must have come off while we were reenacting our past. I slid it into my pocket, keeping it as a small memento.

I sat at my desk going over the recent hour of events. My pants immediately grew tighter when I saved her from falling when Doherty knocked into her. I didn't want to let her go. I felt myself getting hard just thinking about it.

I can't believe she tripped again in my office, as if some invisible object kept taunting her whenever she was in my presence. I was thankful for any opportunity to get my hands on that body. On the floor, she leaned in and kissed me like she did ten years ago. This time there wasn't a bell that made us stop before we were able to touch each other. The softness of her skin, the way she rubbed up against me—I had to stop because I needed more, and I couldn't risk getting caught frisking a potential suspect in my office. She's like a drug to an addict. I could never have enough. "Listen to me. Who am I? I don't talk like this," the words slipped from my mouth as I was in a dream state. She does something to me no other woman has ever tapped into. I needed to explore this animal magnetism we have. First, we'll need to talk about that fateful day that brought us together a decade ago. She might ask me questions I may not be able to answer. I just hope she will understand. I looked up and saw Jen at my desk. How long had she been standing there for?

"I was going to get a drink after work today. Did you want to come? I know it's been stressful around here. I can ask the other guys if you want." Did she just bat her lashes at me? No, Jen was not like that.

"Sorry, Jen, I am heading to Sicilia's to continue my questioning with Ms. Rossi." The look of disappoint on her face made me feel guilty.

"Okay, just make sure you get your rest." Her eyes were welling up. She turned around and left my office. That was an odd encounter. I may be overthinking the situation.

As promised, I arrived at Sicilia's restaurant promptly at nine o'clock. I always had that feeling when she was in the same room as me, and she's not there. Michael came over to me. "Hello, Collins, come with me." Michael took me through the dining area, through the kitchen, down a set of stairs.

"Alisa is in there. She is expecting you. Give her five minutes." He shook his head with a smile. I walked into the room. It is decorated with a Tuscan flair just like the restaurant. Mahogany woods, cream walls, it looked like she kept the very expensive wine down here. I looked around the room and saw a door ajar. The water was running, and I saw a light coming from the corner of the room. I didn't think twice and invited myself in. I saw her shadow; she was in the shower.

My eyes were glued to her silhouette. The curves of her body were calling for me. At that point, my body moved on its own. I instantly took my shirt off, then my pants, and next thing I knew, I was entering the shower. *Who am I right now?* This woman possessed me to do these types of things.

Shocked by the intrusion, she turned around covering herself. Her eyes met mine, and her arms fell away. It seems I do the same to her.

"Wait. How did you get in here?" Her breathing started to deepen.

I said nothing. I prowled toward her. Her mouth opened, my arms wrapped around her waist, and my tongue slid right into her mouth. The kiss was deepened in seconds. She put her arms around my neck guiding me to her. My hand slid over the curve of her ass. I grabbed it causing her to moan. She was holding back. The water was streaming over us, and I pushed her against the marbled wall. My fingers slid down her body, approaching their target. I have been dreaming about tasting her. Alisa's hands made their way to the base on my cock, stroking it. Her nails scratched the bottom of my sack giving me the friction that made me groan. I couldn't take it. I enjoyed the journey I was taking with open-mouthed kisses down her body. My heart was pumping; her legs were already apart when I began to feast on dessert. Her hands were in my hair. She was in euphoria, arching her back, when I felt her release. I grabbed my cock and began stroking it. "Brent, oh, don't stop," she begged. I inserted two fingers and picked up the pace. "Brent, Brent," she chanted as she gasped for air.

A taste of her honey was coating the inside of my mouth—delicious—but I didn't stop. I needed more. I continued to stroke my cock and looked up to see her looking down on me. She got to her knees, grabbed my cock, and kissed it. My fingers continued to explore, and I started my expedition for the sweet honey again. She seemed to be in search of her honey, too. My cock hit the back of her throat. "Ahh. Alisa," I whispered as she took it deep. At this point, it was an adrenaline rush, both of us picking up the pace. She grabbed my hair and exploded. The vibration from her orgasm put me over the edge. I exploded in her mouth watching her swallow. We were there for a couple of minutes. She sucked me clean. She crawled over my body and gave me a kiss. The taste of each other was a taste I would never forget.

Spent but not wanting to leave our close quarters, we remained under the steady flow of warm water and and she took a cloth and soaped it up.

"Turn around. Let me look at that ass," she commanded.

"Yes, madame."

She giggled.

As she washed my back, I felt for her entrance. She smacked my hand away.

"Commissioner Collins, keep your hands to yourself. This civilian needs to thank the servicemen in East Hampton properly." She messaged my shoulders and turned me around. Taking the cloth down my neck, down my chest, and she caressed my cock. I lifted her chin, pulled it up toward me, and kissed her.

"All clean, Commissioner," she whispered on my lips.

I grabbed a towel and slowly dried off her body from top to bottom, pulling it up over her head to dry her hair. She gazed up at me, eyes wide and features softened. Maybe she thought it was only physical for me. She shyly got dressed, and we headed back into her office area.

"Alisa," I said and stared deep into her green-gold eyes, taking me back to our first encounter.

"I'm sorry, Brent. I never—"

I placed my finger over her lips.

"I've been waiting for you to find me, Alisa. I needed to—"

She put her finger over my lips. I kissed it.

"Brent, I don't regret what we did, but I would understand if you wanted to leave." She was ashamed. It's the cutest expression on her face. I could tell this was not her normal way she handled her men. Just the thought that she may have done these things with other men made me furious. I already claimed her as mine, and she didn't even know it yet, but she will soon.

I grabbed her by the waist, pulling her into me, and kissed her tenderly on the back of her ear. "I'm not leaving, Alisa. This is only the beginning." I kissed the top of her head.

She looked up at me for a minute and hugged me around my waist, her head in my chest.

"You really remembered me. You never forgot," she whispered.

I lifted her head up and gave her a gentle kiss on her lips.

"Every day of my life, I dreamed of this moment," I said, quickly following it up with another kiss.

"Every day I wondered where you were. If you were thinking of me." She looked at me, waiting for an explanation. We looked into each other's eyes waiting for the next sentence to be spoken. The battle of wills were in control. You saw that both of us didn't want to ruin the moment we were both entwined in. She pulled me down and gently kissed me.

CHAPTER 9

Alisa

"Every day of his life." Did I just hear him say that? I stared at him and gave him a gentle kiss back.

"Brent, tell me what happened."

He took a deep breath, grabbed my hand, and headed over to the leather couch. I had wine and cheese at the table. I poured two glasses. I could tell he was nervous, he was rubbing the top of my hand with his thumb. It felt like a flip had switched in him. Yesterday, he was so arrogant, today, he proved he's the man I was looking for. The one who was passionate in everything he does. I decided to start the conversation, give him the opportunity to chime in.

"One day back in high school I kissed this amazing boy. I did something I never thought I had the guts to do. Every day for a week I saw you in that same spot. I would look at you and—"

"Sparks," Brent said before I could.

"Yes. I knew you felt them too." I needed to understand it. "You told me that you will remember me and asked me not to forget you." I stared into his gray eyes.

"Alisa, I'm just happy I have the opportunity to explain it all to you," he said, soul-searching as he looked deep into my eyes.

"I was part of an investigation of a drug ring. I was twenty-two. You were seventeen. I should not have kissed you that day, but as you said, there were sparks, and you, you were captivating. I wanted to feel your lips on mine." He placed his hand on my knee.

Our eyes locked as the energy between us started to spark. I couldn't help but just kiss him, I couldn't fight the craving of wanting his skin on mine. I straddled him and began to take off his shirt. His kiss had become my addiction, and I couldn't get enough. I wanted to be lost in it, give myself to him in every way.

"Alisa," we heard Michael say at the door. "I'm leaving. Are you locking up?" He looked in and was surprised by our position on the couch.

"Yes, Michael, have a good night," I said with my hand over my face, frustrated and slightly embarrassed to be caught wrapped around the Commissioner. Thank god it was Michael and not just any employee.

"See you tomorrow. Have a good night." By the tone in his voice, he knew what I was doing. He wasn't so innocent. I mean I could tell he used my shower yesterday—the blond hair on my desk gave it away. Oh yeah, and the skip in his step this morning. A dead giveaway he got some last night. Mr. Casanova with a metro flair.

I continued my predatory move on Brent—kissing his neck, kneading his biceps, and worshipping his body. I took off my shirt. *What am I doing?* I thought to myself. This man has casted a spell over me. I was possessed with sexual want. He looked up at me biting his lip. Oh, how that drove me crazy. He grabbed my breasts, suckled my nipples, and grabbed my waist. Within seconds, I'm flipped onto my back, and we were both completely naked. We were all over each other. His hands were exploring my curves. His touch was igniting my libido. I caressed his chest. My hands worked their way down. I felt every contour of his muscles. This man worked out regularly that was for sure. I suddenly felt the tip of his cock hit my vagina.

"Brent," I said, breathlessly trying to slow down the actions.

"Yes, my princess," he answered as he put two fingers in me.

"I'm still a…"

He needed to know I was still a virgin. I was not sure how he will take it; he might not want me.

"Are you telling me you're a virgin?"

"Yes," I whispered with my head down.

"Alisa, were you waiting for me?" At first that sounded con-ceded, but looking at him, I can see that he was hopeful.

"All this time you knew we would find each other," he said knowingly, and I continued to melt into him. That's what it was. It wasn't that I hadn't found anyone worthy, it was because he was the *only* one worthy.

"It's destiny," I whispered.

He grabbed me and kissed me as if it was his last. Passion in its fullest form. He broke the kiss, panting.

"Not here, not like this. You deserve more. Tomorrow?" he said as he started to pull away from me. My body was already getting comfortable with him and felt his absence.

"Tomorrow?" I said with a hint of disappointment.

"Yes, Alisa, tomorrow." He gathered me in his arms and kissed me in the one spot I now call my explosion spot right below my ear. Every time he kisses the spot, I instantly get wet with desire.

"Tomorrow you will be mine," he said, the lust written all over his face. "You deserve to be treated like the princess that you are."

I know it sounds corny, but coming from him, the hairs on my arm stood up. I felt special. I bit my bottom lip. I have suddenly turned shy.

After we got dressed, he walked me to my car—a true gentle-man. The silence of the night was getting me nervous. I had this uneasy feeling. He held my hand. As we got to my car, he turned to me.

"Tonight was special to me, Alisa." He blew out a breath.

"I never realized how much I really needed you to complete my life." My heart was fluttering as he said those words. Don't get me wrong. That's exactly what I wanted to hear. The ironic part of those words was that I felt the same way.

"I feel the same way. I can't explain it, Brent, but—"

"Like a feeling that you never felt before?" He asked as he raised an eyebrow to see if he finished my sentence.

"Yes, you make me feel things—do things I have never done before. It scares the shit out of me and thrills me at the same time." I knew that might not make sense to him, but it did to me.

"Alisa, you want this? Us?" he asked as he lifted my chin so he could see the answer in my eyes. Those gray eyes so light I see the moon in them.

"Yes, more than I imagined I would." His soft lips touched mine as he enveloped me in a heartwarming embrace.

"Brent, I just want to know something. These meetings were never about the case, were they? You just wanted to explore this, right? You and me?"

"Yes, and it was exactly what I expected—until tomorrow when we grant each other the first day of our newfound relationship." He bobbed his head and gave me one last kiss before he opened my door and closed it for me. I looked in my rearview mirror and watched him get in his car. He waited for me to leave before he pulled out of the parking lot. I still felt his lips on me. And felt his hands around me. I left the parking lot and headed to the house in the happiest moods I have had in a while.

When I arrived home, I sat in the driveway with the images of the night playing like a movie in my mind. It was amazing, better than I ever could have imagined. And he said it was just the beginning.

It will be more than a decade-old kiss. We were going to grow something together, something more than physical. Although, the physical parts have been the most thrilling moments of my life. Tonight was the first time the feeling of my libido was taking over my body. Who knew I could be so passionate? I guess I needed to meet the right person. Crazy to think that all of this came from a necklace. All of the events that needed to align to make way for my reunion with Mr. Destiny.

CHAPTER 10

Alisa

I walked into the house at 11:30 p.m. I threw my pocketbook down looking to tell Sharon about the most amazing night I had. In desperate need of a glass of red to celebrate the moment and calm my nerves, I snagged a bottle of Merlot from the kitchen and two glasses. Just then, I overheard Sharon on the phone sitting by the pool.

"Okay, I'll bring her there as soon as she gets to the house. Louie, stay there with him." I tensed up, whatever it was, it couldn't be good.

"Everything okay?"

Startled, Sharon jumped out of her seat, which set off a chain of events ending with the bottle of of wine and the glasses in the pool. Watching the glassware float, Sharon broke the news.

"Your father…he's at Stony Brook Hospital. He was attacked."

My head nearly exploded. I was riding such a high from the last few hours and this hit me like a ton of bricks. I stared at her in disbelief as my eyes began to well up with tears. My father is all I have.

"What happened? How? Who?" I was so frazzled I couldn't speak clearly. Not my dad.

"Come on, Alisa, I'll take you to see him. I'll tell you everything I know on the way." She grabbed her pocketbook and headed toward the door. My feet felt like they were in cement blocks. I was stunned and couldn't find the strength to move. Without a word, she grabbed me by the wrist and pulled me to the car, gently situating me in the

49

passenger's seat before we ventured on the back roads through Sag Harbor. He's a strong man; he'd pull through this. Attacked? Why him? Why would anyone want to hurt a sweet old man?

At least Louie was with him, someone there to talk to the doctors, he wasn't alone. Louie was a good guy, I remember the day Sharon met him during our weekend getaway aboard a party cruise, which is essentially a cruise to nowhere. It went from South Street Seaport, New York City, to North Carolina and back. No stops in between and just pure partying for forty-eight hours nonstop.

Louie was there celebrating his friend Patsy's bachelor party. Sharon and I were the only women in a corridor of fourteen men. This was one for the record books. The first thing we heard getting off the elevator was, "God has answered my prayers—two Italian women!" Louie's friend Drew shouted.

All the guys were cheering. Sharon and I went with the flow; it was the best time. They all treated us with respect. Although Sharon and I had different intentions. Sharon shacked up with Louie almost immediately, while I kept my options open. I made out with Ralph the first night while we were in the casino. The second night Johnny; he was built, abs of steel. That night we were dry humping and fooling around for hours. Little did I know that Johnny was Ralph's first cousin. Oh, and that Johnny had a jealous girlfriend who was counting down the minutes for the boat to dock. Oops! Sometimes New York feels like the smallest world. The guys were from Ozone Park and Howard Beach, Queens, home of Aqueduct Racetrack and fifteen minutes from JFK airport. This made it easy for Louie and Sharon to spend nearly every day together since. This was the longest relationship that she's had, and it might be the last. As she put it, "her time to settle down has come."

"Alisa, are you okay? You've just been staring at your hands since we left. Did you hear anything I said?"

She was concerned but trying to keep her cool to keep me calm.

"No, can you say it again, please?" I said under my breath, still trying to rationalize the situation.

"Louie and your dad went to Queens. Louie needed to clean up a couple of things at work. They stopped at Aqueduct Raceway, placed some bets on a couple of races. Your dad hit for fifty thousand dollars on the ninth race," her voice went up trying to lighten the situation.

"Wow, finally the old man hits," I said.

"Yeah. He wanted to take Louie out to lunch, so they went to Louie's cousin's restaurant on Cross Bay Boulevard." She looked over to make sure I was still paying attention.

"Sharon, was he attacked in Queens?" I asked, looking for her to hurry with the story.

"No, just listen," she replied, sounding annoyed.

"Well, get to the point." I rolled my eyes in frustration.

"After lunch they headed back. Louie's car broke down on the Belt Parkway. His brother and friend and," she used air quotes for the mention of a friend, "picked them up and drove them to your dad's house so they could get his car. They kept talking about how your dad won the money on Let It Shine. The horse was 12–1."

Again, she glanced over to make sure I was conscious. My eyes must have been piercing in her direction because I heard her gulp.

"Sharon, what happened? Get to where my father gets attacked," I asked, starting to lose my patience.

"His brother's friend went crazy and swung a bat that was in the back seat. They swung at Louie's crotch, hit his brother in the ribs, and hit your father over the head, taking all of his winnings as well as Louie's brother's car. Your father is currently in the ICU with head trauma." She kept glancing over to gauge my reaction. I could feel my heart pounding in my ears. I was overwhelmed with feelings of both rage and fear. Stony Brook is ninety minutes from East Hampton, the drive was beginning to feel like an eternity. My anxiety was through the roof. All the happiness was sucked from my soul and replaced with fear of losing my father.

"I'm sorry, Alisa," she said as she patted my lap showing support.

It's 1:15 a.m. when we arrived at Stony Brook University Hospital. Dr. Pappas, head of neuro, came up to me and introduced himself.

"Ms. Rossi, your father fractured his skull during the attack. The swelling is bad. We needed to induce him in a coma. We are going to keep him in the ICU until we can pull him out of the coma."

"What! Coma?" Tears were streaming down my face. Sharon was hugging me tight. We saw Louie running down the hallway toward us with his shoulders heavy and head hung.

"I'm so sorry, Alisa. The cops just left. They think they found my brother's car in Hempstead." He thought that was going to make me feel better.

"What kind of friends does your brother have?" Louie's face dropped. I know it sounded accusatory, but we were talking about my dad's life here. I mean, the emotions were speaking, not me.

"It was my brother's dealer." Sharon and I both looked at him. He put his head down in embarrassment.

"I had no idea he was on drugs. My brother apparently owed him two thousand dollars." He looked heartbroken to be part of the equation.

"Where is your brother?" Sharon asked angrily.

"The cops brought him down to the station to look at mug-shots." His hands were clenched on either side of him. It wasn't Louie's fault, but he felt responsible. I went to my father's room. The beeps of the heart monitor made me start to cry again. I went to his bedside and placed my hands on his.

"Dad, can you hear me? I need you."

Grief-stricken, I made a promise not to leave his side. I needed to make sure I was there when he woke up. Sharon and Louie headed back to my house in Stony Brook not far from the hospital. I realized with all the drama, I never had a chance to let Sharon know what happened earlier that night. My long-awaited interaction with Brent, which seemed so minute compared to my father's health. I have been on a single passenger emotional roller coaster for the last couple of days and it was starting to catch up with me. I was so exhausted that I kissed my father's hand and fell asleep.

The next morning, Sharon was back at the hospital with a cappuccino and egg sandwich for me.

"How is he?" Sharon asked.

I took a big swig of coffee and began fixing my hair after a night of sleeping on a hospital bed.

"The same. The doctor is coming in at eleven o'clock to talk to me. I have to call Michael and let him know that I probably won't be around for a couple of days," I said, feeling guilty. The new restaurant hasn't even been open a week and I've been asking a lot of Michael.

"Okay. Louie and I will go to East Hampton and get your things from the rental. You only had it until tonight, right?"

"Yes, thank you, Sharon." She was my rock, always thinking of my well-being, making sure I have everything I need.

"Oh, by the way, what happened with Brent yesterday?" I perked up, straightened my posture and looked to the sky like a schoolgirl in love.

"Sharon, it was everything I could have imagined and more."

I gave her a rundown of the events that transpired at the police station, to the floor of Brent's office, to the steamy moment in my office. Her eyes were as wide as a river when I told her about the visitor I had in the shower and the unexpected pleasure I endured.

"Does he know you're still a virgin?" she asked, sitting in the chair with her elbows on her knees, waiting for my answer.

"Yes. I told him. We were fooling around on the couch, and the moment was getting intense. I stopped him and told him."

"Whoa, girl! This isn't like you at all. What did he say?" she asked with the biggest grin on her face.

"Nothing really, other than he wanted to wait to make it special for me. If it's even a fraction of the passion we've shared so far, it'll be worth the wait, Sharon." I clapped my hands together with a smile on my face.

"I'd say so. Maybe he was the one you were waiting for. Did he tell why he never showed up at school again?"

"Vaguely. I mean I kinda interrupted him by biting his lip and caressing his chest. I just can't keep my hands off of him."

"Alisa, when are you going to see him again? I mean, don't you want to know what happened?"

"We were planning on seeing each other tonight." My head was spinning. I have to call him and cancel. I didn't want to, but I had no choice.

"Whoa, just take your time, Alisa. I don't want you to get hurt." Sharon was giving her sisterly advice. She kissed my cheek and headed into the hallway.

I couldn't help but think about all that has been going on. My life was normally uneventful, but within the past couple of days, it has been a whirlwind. My second restaurant opening; Kim's necklace; finding Brent, the passionate reconnection; and now my father is in critical condition after being attacked by a total stranger. I don't like it when I don't have control.

I met with the doctor about my father's current condition. Good news, the swelling went down in his head, and he believed that he should come out of the coma within the next seventy-two hours. He warned me that once he was out of the coma, he could have massive headaches due to the trauma and suggested that he should be homebound once released from the hospital for two weeks. I nodded in agreeance and made a mental note to plan for his recovery. The doctor said his goodbyes, and the nurse came in to check his vitals. I decided to call Michael to let him know the new event of this week.

"Hello, Michael," I greeted, trying to sound cheery.

"Hey, Ali, how was your night?" I could tell he had a smirk on his face over the phone. He knew I was in the middle of some passionate positions when he entered my office last night.

"Good…until I had to rush to the hospital."

"Oh my, Alisa, did you give Brent a heart attack?" I heard him laugh on the other end.

I laughed. "No!"

"Are you hurt? Is everything okay? What happened?"

His tone changed quickly to the concerned older brother. I told Michael about my father and let him know I will be in my home in Stony Brook until he came through. He completely understood and told me not to worry about the restaurant; he would be able to handle it. He was always looking out for me. From the day we met, I knew he'd always be an important part of my life.

One night at my restaurant in Port Jeff, he made a point to introduce himself and compliment the food and the atmosphere. He was a wine consultant in New York City at the time and quickly became one of my regular diners. He came up with some great ideas, and after a few encounters, I offered him the position of restaurant manager. He brought in so many clients, people from all over NYC. Everyone knew Michael. He had a major following, even on social media.

That was how I met Kim Killian. She was making an appearance at Foxwoods Casino in Connecticut. She took the ferry from Port Jefferson to Bridgeport and decided to come into the restaurant for dinner. Michael being the ultimate socialite, befriended her and introduced me. It wasn't long before Kim began frequenting the restaurant with some of her fellow showstopper friends from Manhattan. One night, Michael snagged a picture of Kim and her gang having dinner and posted it to socials—the restaurant became an overnight success.

After the conversation with Michael, I knew I had to make one another phone call to cancel tonight's date with Brent. I didn't want to, but I couldn't imagine being anywhere else other than by my dad's side. Losing my virginity while my dad is in a coma? I don't think so. Looking at my phone, I realized I didn't have his number. I called information to get the number to the East Hampton Police Department hoping he was at the office.

"Hello, may I please speak with Commissioner Collins?"

"Who may I say is calling?" asked the receptionist with an attitude.

What a bitch.

"Alisa Rossi, owner of Sicilia's restaurant."

"Well, Ms. Rossi, Brent, I mean Commissioner Collins is busy at the moment. Would you like to speak with Detective Doherty?" I wanted to tell her it's personal, but I was not sure if Brent would appreciate that. I mean, there was an ongoing investigation involving my restaurant.

"No, no, thank you. Does he have a voicemail, or may I have his cell number?"

After a lecture for five minutes on how she cannot give out the police commissioner's personal cell phone number, she put me through his voicemail. He was in a meeting and could not be disturbed. I thought quickly what to say and not to sound too disappointed that I would not be able to see him tonight.

"Hi, Brent, it's Alisa. I wanted to thank you again for last night. I am so happy that we reconnected. I know we had plans for tonight, but I need to cancel. My dad is in Stony Brook Hospital. I need to be with him, I hope you understand. My number is 631-555-1213, call me back whenever you can."

As much as I wanted to see him, I needed to stay with my dad. I waited this long to see Brent, what's another few days?

CHAPTER 11

Brent

My 11:00 a.m. appointment was here—Special Agent Stewart Vogel of the Federal Bureau of Investigations. He came in to talk about the Killian jewelry theft.

"Special Agent Vogel." I held my hand toward the chair for him to sit down.

"Commissioner Collins." He nodded his head in a greeting and continued to get to the point of his visit.

"My people have been working on an ongoing case, and the recent occurrence in your neighborhood came up in a conversation that was recorded by our team." As he sat in the chair in front of me, he looked around my office. Typical FBI protocol to always be aware of your surroundings.

"Commissioner, are you familiar with the Marino crime family?"

My ears perked up, this ought to be interesting.

"Yes, Special Agent. I am very aware of their dealings, as you may already know," I said with pride.

"I thought you would," he said, tapping his finger on my desk waiting for my reaction.

"To our knowledge, you were involved in the big takedown of Mario Adamo?"

"Yes, that is correct."

I never realized what a major role that case would play in my life. It springboarded my career while simultaneously ripping me from the possibility of true love.

"Well, the family has gotten stronger. More drugs, gambling, trafficking, and now they are part of the underworld," he said with concern.

"Excuse me, Vogel, but why is the robbery of Kim Killian's necklace of such interest?" Curiosity struck.

"Well, Collins, we believe that this theft was part of the larger scheme that could catapult the Marino family to the upper crust of the underground."

He was staring right through me, his eyebrows furrowed, thinking of the chaos to come.

"You see, Commissioner, Killian's necklace had a microchip in it—a microchip filled with information to bring the entire organization down."

"Does Killian know?" I asked.

"We are still investigating that, as well as where the other copies of the microchip are located."

"What do you need our department to do?" I leaned back in my chair.

"We had two of our undercovers at Sicilia's that night. Well, I should say one because the other was delayed in traffic and arrived after the theft. However, I am not at liberty to expose their names." His eyes were searching my face to gauge my reaction.

"Collins, do you have any other leads?"

It felt like I was back in the FBI again. Over the last few years, things have been pretty quiet at the precinct with simple open-and-shut cases. It's been a while since I've felt this kind of rush.

"Well, I was going to ask you about the conversation you overheard," I asked knowing he couldn't share much, but my interest was piqued.

"We got wind that the theft was on the books and that the mission was accomplished." He wasn't going to provide me with any further details. I might've felt like an agent again, but I certainly didn't have the clearance of one.

"Detective Doherty is in charge of the investigation. So far we know the suspect is male and that they have an infinity tattoo on their wrist," I told him. This was a fresh discovery. Doherty was able to trace some of the surveillance from the back door of Sicilia's.

"That's the loyalty tattoo. In the Marino family, an infinity is a sign that they are a loyal soldier," he explained, giving me a clue for our investigation.

"I'll get a briefing from Doherty and send it to your office."

"Brent, this case is almost ready to close. I mean this is bigger than the one you were working on. Understood?"

"Yes, Director Vogel."

Vogel stood up and gave me a knowing look of secrecy, nodded his goodbye, and exited my office. Within seconds, Detective Doherty was knocking at my door.

"Brent—I mean, Commissioner."

You could tell Doherty was itching to tell me the latest details on the case.

"Yes, James, come on in." Detective James Doherty, my protégé, I know he has what it takes to take over my position one day. He was loyal, hardworking, and would do whatever was necessary to get to the bottom of a case.

"Do you have any updates?" I asked.

"Yes, we are going over the invite list and employee list, and Alisa had her manager call her guests to get their plus ones' names. There were a couple of people of interest, but the one that caught my eye was Louie Vaccaro. He was on the plus one list, but we did not see him enter the event." He looked like there was something special about the name. I don't remember his name from the past.

"Louie Vaccaro? Why is he a person of interest?" I asked.

"We believe he may be connected to the Marino crime family," Doherty stated.

Damn, Doherty *is* good. He's connecting the dots even without the help of the FBI. The only problem was that I wasn't at liberty to share the information Vogel provided me with to confirm his hunch. This was going to be tricky, but I had to play this right for the sake of the investigation. Who knows how deep this goes?

"Why would you believe that? What evidence do you have?" I inquired.

"Well, he was recently seen with Carmine Rossi, a known affiliate of the family. We also have reason to believe that Carmine may even be a captain," he explained.

I tried not to look alarmed recognizing the last name. Alisa's last name is Rossi. I mean, Rossi was a pretty common Italian last name. It could be a coincidence. I needed more information to be sure.

"Please explain."

"Mario and Carmine went to school together in Aragona, Sicily. They both came to the United States in the '60s. Carmine's brother, Alfonso, had already set up shop in Queens. Alfonso made sure that Vincenzo, Carmine's sister's husband, was part of that business, but Mario pushed him out. He didn't want Vinny to be part of any of it. Mario became the head of the family. They call him 'Godfather.' Vincenzo moved to Long Island and had a family with Rosalie Massaro who's family had connections in Sicily. Well, anyway, five years ago when Mario was put in the slammer, the heads of the Marino family realigned their organization, and over the past two years, Carmine had been giving the honor of being second in charge. That's not the end of my find. Get this. Carmine is Alisa's father."

James was nodding his head proud of his discovery. I was in shock about the news. Alisa's dad was Carmine Rossi.

"Oh shit."

My hand raised to my temple, and my mind went to the worst possible outcome. Was Alisa part of this? Has she known all along? Or even worse, was she in on it? Looks like this reunion just got more complicated. Suddenly, there was a knock at my office door that ripped me away from being lost in thought. Shortly following the knock, my assistant, Jen, let herself in.

"Commissioner, the mayor is on the phone. He says it's important."

"Great timing. Tell him I'll be with him in a minute." Jen left my office with a smile. She looked different today. I noticed her shirt was not up to par with the dress code. It's lower than allowed she was actually showing cleavage. I ignored the fact and decided to address it at a different time.

"Excuse me, Commissioner," Doherty politely waited for me to snap back to reality.

"Okay. Who else knows about this?"

"Just me and you, boss. Why?"

"Okay, well, let's just keep it that way for now, and keep investigating alternative theories. We will reconvene tomorrow," I said with a nod to dismiss him.

"James, remember, do not tell anyone. We need to confirm your findings are correct before we discuss your efforts with others. Understood?"

"Yes, Commissioner."

Detective Doherty left my office proud of his efforts. Honestly, I was proud of him too. While I now know that this case is much bigger than just a stolen necklace, I have to give Alisa the benefit of the doubt. I can't keep letting my mind go to darker places, that would only put a strain on what we are trying to build on after so long of being apart. Until then, it was time to listen to the mayor drone on about budgets.

"Hello, Mayor. How can I help you today?"

The mayor was going over some of the summer events to make sure we had enough support from my department, especially after all of the buzz from the recent theft. Summer in the Hamptons was like a playground for the rich and famous. They let loose of the stress of the city, the locals make big money from the crowds, and tourists try to get into the memory making bashes and exclusive clubs.

"Yes, Mayor, we brought some extra patrol in from the county police, and the Southampton Police have our back as well."

"Great, Brent, after the Sicilia's robbery, I am glad that everyone is on high alert for the summer season."

"I understand the urgency of safety, sir. I give you my word we have total control over the security of these events and the streets of East Hampton," I reassured as I rolled my eyes.

He was always on high alert, especially being that it was an election year. Once I hung up the phone, I started to go through the pile of paperwork on my desk. The last couple of days I have been ignoring it, a few documents needed to be signed, others needed to be filed away. Busy work really, but I had other things I had my mind on—better things. Most importantly, the hazel-eyed girl who has turned my world upside down once again.

I looked up from my desk to see Jen. She had an intercom to contact me, but it must be broken. She was always coming into my office to give me my messages.

"An Alisa called you. She wanted me to give her your cell number. You believe the girl? I told her that it was against policy and to leave you a voicemail. She seemed annoyed. I couldn't interrupt you."

She waited for my response, searching my face to see if there was something more to my relationship with Alisa than strictly business. But I wasn't going to budge.

"Yes, Jen?"

"I read about her in *Dean's Paper* last month, he covered her restaurant. She seems to be a woman that means business. I have to give it to her—she's pretty and successful." She was relentless. She really thinks she could get something out of me that easy. I refused to give her the satisfaction.

"Jen. I have no idea what you're thinking."

"I know you know what I'm thinking. You could tell me to mind my own business, Brent."

"It's not like that, Jen."

I've been keeping this relationship close to my chest, especially with all this new information and possible mob involvement. I'm not having this conversation with anyone, especially not my assistant.

"Okay, so what's it like?"

My eyebrows raised. I was totally taken aback by her audacity. I really don't have that type of relationship with her to divulge my personal life to her. I knew she could see the expression on my face because she followed her question up with a sarcastic laugh.

"None of your business."

"I'll get it out of you one day," she said smugly followed by a wink.

"Oh, Jen, don't make this water cooler talk."

I raised my eyebrow letting her know that I don't appreciate the accusation, and if the rumor did start, I will know she was the one to start it.

"You got it, boss."

I quickly retrieved her voicemail. The sound of her voice saddened me. She was torn—the raspy tremor told me she longed to continue what we started last night but she needed to be with her father. She wanted both. I grinned, putting her cell number in my phone. While I had enough paperwork to keep my chained to my desk all night, I was disappointed I no longer had the option to sneak away to see her.

The last couple of days have been some of the most action-packed days of my life. The feeling of an electrical current running through my body the moment I saw her at the night of the theft was only the beginning. The clumsy run-ins that followed that led us to the connection we had on the floor of my office when her soft lips touched mine, transporting me back to my twenty-two-year-old self on that stairwell. Last night in the shower, letting my intrusive thoughts steer the ship.

Alisa was different from anyone I have dated; the animal magnetism I had for her was untamed. If Michael didn't interrupt us while she was straddling me on the couch, things would've escalated. It was for the best. We were getting too heated, considering her virtue was still intact. I couldn't believe she was a virgin at twenty-seven years old. She had been waiting for me. Well, not exactly, but she didn't deny it when I suggested it. I missed the taste of her. Being with her was no longer a want but a need. All I could think about was how to make her first time memorable. Now that she's back at home, I didn't know when I was going to see her next.

Wait, could her father's hospitalization have anything to do with the case? A possible retaliation? Oh, this keeps getting more and more interesting. I can't let her know about the information Doherty dug up. Could he be wrong? I shook my head knowing that this was wishful thinking on my part. His leads on the mob involvement were confirmed by Vogel's visit.

"Innocent until proven guilty," I mumbled, trying to keep hope alive.

I can squeeze in a quick text before my next meeting, maybe follow it up with a call after. This woman was turning my simple life into one with complexity and excitement, and I thought working for the FBI would be my biggest thrill.

"Your appointment is here," Jen said through the intercom.

"Send her in."

CHAPTER 12

Alisa

Sharon made the drive back from East Hampton to the hospital to check in on me. I was so lucky to have her. She had been with me through thick and thin. She was by my side around the clock after I lost my mother. Now she's holding my hand again while my father was fighting his way out of a coma.

She put her hand on my shoulder and could see how exhausted I was. "Alisa, go home, get cleaned up. I'll stay with your dad until you get back."

I knew if I didn't take her up on her offer she'd make a scene, so I changed the subject to buy a little time.

"Where's Louie?"

"He went to go talk to his uncle to help him with his brother."

"Poor Louie."

"Alisa, Louie feels horrible. He had no idea that his brother was on drugs. Let alone indebted to anyone."

I wanted to ease his guilt, and her guilt by association.

"How would he have known? I don't blame him at all—really."

"Alisa, I really like Louie. I may even love him," she said, getting verklempt, looking down at her twisted fingers.

"I never even heard you come close to saying that word, Sharon," I said, shocked by her confession.

"Well, I have never met anyone quite like Louie. He's so caring. We like the same things. He would do anything for me. Not to mention we have incredible chemistry in the bedroom."

She couldn't keep herself from blushing just mentioning it.

"Let's just say we can go all night long."

Looks like I wasn't the only one with exciting bedroom escapades.

"I'm so happy for you, Sharon, opening your heart up. You deserve someone like Louie to love you," I said, grabbing her in a hug.

"Speaking of love, did you call Brent?"

I shrugged my shoulders and mumbled, "I left him a message."

"Alisa, what's that about?" She saw the disappointment on my face.

"I'm tired, Sharon." I was trying to get her off the subject again. "In fact, I am going to take you up on that offer. I'll be back in like an hour or so." I looked to her for approval to leave.

"Take your time. I'm going to do my reports," she said, taking out her laptop and placing it on the rolling table.

"Sharon, I thank God every day that you are in my life."

She knew I meant it.

"Ditto," she said with a wink and blew me a kiss on my way out the door.

Twenty-five minutes later, I was walking through my front door. I felt like I hadn't been home in weeks. In the kitchen, I found that Sharon had left me a sandwich and a bottle of Merlot. What an angel.

I checked my phone to see if I had any correspondence from Brent. Nothing. Maybe he was busy...or no longer interested. I shook my head. Now's not the time to spiral into that mess. Instead, I found a voicemail from Kim.

"So that was a great grand opening. Thank God I had insurance on that necklace. Call me."

While Kim had become such a good friend and business partner, I was still dreading a conversation centered around a mishap at my restaurant. Thankfully, she was upset but relieved, and didn't place any of the blame on me. She mainly called to tell me that regardless of the investigation, she planned on hosting her movie premiere dinner at the restaurant in a couple of months.

I couldn't help but think of how Michael opened the door for this type of opportunity. I have surrounded myself with such incredible people. Kim went on to say that she appreciated my work ethic, and she trusted me to make sure that night goes without a hitch. Another sigh of relief.

After the conversation, my phone buzzed. It's a text from Brent: "Sorry to hear about your dad. Let me know if you need anything. Brent."

I was a little annoyed. No "miss you" or "can't wait to see you again."

Alisa, don't overthink it. You're not in high school anymore. "I do need something. I need you, Brent!" I called out in the middle of the kitchen with my fist clenched and raised to the sky. A smile broke. I decided I was getting delirious and headed into the shower. Feeling like a whole new person when I got out, I decided to venture to Port Jefferson to visit my restaurant. I couldn't be prouder. This restaurant ran perfectly. My staff had been with me for five years now. Sophia took Michael's role as manager, and she was doing a great job.

"Hi, Sophia."

"Hi, Alisa, I didn't expect you," she exclaimed, wondering about the surprise visit.

"I figured I would swing by since I was in the area. Unfortunately, my dad is in the hospital."

Sophia gasped, she and my dad had created a bond. He has a gift when it comes to connecting with people and making them all feel special. For some reason, Sophia and my dad had a joint love for imported olive oil. It was silly, but they'd spend hours taste-testing, and they'd grown close.

"Is everything okay?"

"Not really, but it should be," I replied with a half-smile.

"Aw, Alisa, let me know how I can help. Oh, Mr. Mangels came in and booked his annual golf outing dinner here."

If the president of the country club wasn't spooked by the theft, that was a huge relief.

"That's great to hear! Any other updates?"

"And we have been very busy with the free advertising of last weekend's event. We've had a very high volume of customers."

I couldn't help but let a little smile creep across my lips. My dad was right; this mess brought some good.

"Last night we brought in eight thousand dollars, a record-breaking Wednesday!"

A sense of relief washed over me, it felt like one part of my life was falling back into place after all of the commotion this case has caused.

"That's great news, Sophia. I can't even imagine the madhouse this place was over the last couple of days. Thank you so much for holding down the fort."

"Oh, by the way, Detective Doherty called here for you. He sounded really cute," Sophia said with a smirk.

Every time a man calls me, she assumes it's my boyfriend. She actually isn't too far off this time. After denying any sexual or emotional involvement with the detective, she interrogated me on Doherty's appearance. Maybe she was on the hunt for her Mr. Right too?

"Okay, okay, Alisa, I'm just looking out for you. You deserve a hottie to escort you around town."

I smiled, waved her off, and walked into the kitchen. My senses were immediately taken over by an overwhelming aroma of fresh tomato sauce. Basil, garlic, onion—each component was playing its own part in the delicious symphony wafting through the air.

"Joe, it smells delicious," I said as my mouth began to water.

Joe was like my uncle, I grew up watching him cook side by side with my dad in our kitchen, sneaking me spoonfuls of whatever he was making. He was an old-school Sicilian.

"Thank you, *bella*."

I grabbed a piece of bread so I could dunk it. Before I could finish chewing I blurted out, "Perfecto! The sauce is to die for." Which turned his face a shade of pink from embarrassment.

Ready to rip off another chunk of bread for another taste, I heard a crowd come through the door for the dinner rush. I was so happy to hear the restaurant buzzing, it was one less thing I had to worry about in this time of uncertainty.

Speaking of worry, as I was headed back to the hospital, I couldn't help thinking about how Brent went radio silent on me after his short text. What is going through his head? I was lost in thought until I stumbled into my dad's hospital room. I was stunned to find Sharon standing over my father who was now awake and looking around the room.

"Vin, Vin, it's Sharon. Can you hear me?"

"Thank god you're here, he just woke up! I have to get the nurse."

I rushed to his bedside, both elated and shocked that he was conscious. The nurse anticipated him to be in a coma for weeks.

"Dad, are you okay?"

He nodded.

Sharon looked at me. "I have to get the nurse. He literally just woke up."

"Dad, can you talk?" I was excited to see him respond.

"Yeah," he said in a whisper. "Where am I?"

"Stony Brook Hospital. You were attacked. Do you remember anything?" His eyes grew wide. The machines started beeping like crazy from his accelerated heartbeat.

"Dad, calm down. Everything is going to be okay," I said, trying to be calm and rubbing his hand.

The nurse came in. "Hello, Mr. Rossi. I'm Nurse Kelly. You are in the ICU. You suffered a head trauma which seems to be getting better."

Slowly the beeps from the monitor became steady as my father began to settle. After she took his vitals, she invited me to the hallway to talk.

"Dr. Pappas will be in soon to do more tests, Mr. Rossi."

"Hungry," my father mouthed.

"No eating until you are seen by Dr. Pappas," Nurse Kelly reassured us. My dad gave her puppy dog eyes, which made us laugh.

"Nurse Kelly, is he okay?"

She grabbed my hands, I wasn't sure what was coming next.

"Yes, Ms. Rossi. It's a miracle that he survived that kind of hit."

"What do you mean?"

"Your father has a skull of steel. A normal person would not have made it out of the coma that quick."

I've heard that before. My grandmother used to call him a stubborn, hard headed Sicilian regularly. At least it did him some good this time.

Sharon gave me a hug on her way out to share the news with Louie, who was currently competing in his bowling league on Howard Beach at the Ozone Bowling Alley. Sharon loved to watch him play, apparently, he'd play like a typical New Yorker—so animated, using his using his hands to emphasize his excitement or dismay.

I settled back down by my father's bedside. We mostly sat in silence watching television holding hands. A few hours passed before my father told me to leave and get some rest. Although my heart told me to stay, I didn't argue. I decided to go to the Port Jefferson Marina to watch the sunset and unwind. It's so calming, watching the pinkish-purple hues of the sky meet the waves swaying the boats tied to the dock. Sitting at my favorite bench by the old shipyard building, I opened Brent's text again. I debated whether I should call him—I didn't want to seem desperate, but I wanted to hear his voice. I took a deep breath and hit the call button.

"Hi, princess."

Did he just call me princess? I tried to stifle my excitement.

"Hi, I hope I didn't call at a bad time," I said, biting my bottom lip.

"I am sorry about tonight. How's your dad?" he inquired, concern in his voice.

"He woke up from the coma about an hour ago."

"Coma?"

He would've known how intense the situation was if we would've called! Compartmentalizing my frustration, I told him the series of events that landed my father in the hospital. His detective nature kicked in, and I nearly felt like I was being interrogated. Damn, this guy is good at his job. After he got all of the details, he quickly shifted gears.

"So have you been thinking of me?"

"Maybe," I said playfully.

"Maybe, huh?" He paused for a moment. "Did you think of me putting my mouth on that pretty little pussy?"

I was taken aback, I covered the speaker to hide my gasp. My body ablaze, I bit my lip a little harder. I needed to find out how far this would go.

"M-hmm."

"I thought of your lips surrounding my cock," his voice deepened and I could hear him breathing heavily like his lips were pressed against the phone.

My hand subconsciously made its way to my zipper.

"Oh, Brent," I moaned his name, he had the power to make me wet just with his words.

"Are you alone, Alisa."

"Yes," I said while looking around the marina to make sure. I would be mortified if a family came out from around the corner. I didn't want anything to interrupt.

"Do you have any idea what I wanted to do to you tonight?"

I'll bite.

"Mr. Collins, please enlighten me with your fantasy." I couldn't believe we were doing this. Phone sex? I felt like I was in college again. My only experience had been with a fling—Jimmy Rizzo. Our schedules were packed but twice a week we'd make time for a phone sex session. That relationship lasted exactly six weeks—talk was cheap I guess.

"First, I would have taken you out for a quiet dinner. Intimate, just the two of us, where we could sit side-by-side in a hidden corner without eyes on us so I could have one hand gripping your upper thigh. My fingers tracing the inside, working my way up to the apex of your thighs. I'd outline your panties with my fingers until I could feel them slowly start to get wet. I wouldn't slip my fingers in just yet. I'd keep teasing you to let the anticipation build. After we fed each other dessert, I'd take you back to my place to surprise you with candles lit, sultry music on the speakers, and rose petals surrounding the bed.

I'd grab your hand and spin you around you, laying your head on my chest as we'd sway to *Versace on the Floor* by Bruno Mars. Can you hear it? You'd look up and mesmerize me with those hazel eyes, I'd lift your chin to steal a kiss. I'd start working my way down from your lips tenderly down your neck."

"Brent," I gasped, interrupting him, feeling every word coming out of his mouth.

"Alisa, I want you to unbutton your blouse right now." It was a demand. I heard him gasp.

"Brent, I'm in the public!" I said with a giggle. "I am heading toward my car now. The way you make me feel—it's too much for words." I unlocked my door and slid into the front seat. Thank God the parking lot was empty where I parked. I didn't want the conversation to stop here. He continued, "I'd start a trail of kisses from your neck down your chest before circling your nipples with my tongue."

My fingers began to mimic his words, slipping under my blouse to rub my now pebbled nipples.

"While I took your breast into my mouth, I'd let my hand explore down your body, running over your curves. Your skin is so soft, Alisa." I heard his zipper in the background.

"Yes, please. Don't stop," I said, panting in between each word. His voice lowered and became raspier as things kept heating up.

"My hand follows your folds to find a spot that makes you arch your back. I feel you grab my cock and fist it and begin stroking me up and down. We're now looking into each other's eyes as you feel my two fingers slip in your wet, slick, entrance, and pump in and out. You lean down and take my hard cock in your mouth, your lips wrapping around my shaft, licking it as it throbs." He lets out a moan and sinks deeper into the fantasy.

"You continue to suck me up and down. We match rhythms as I pump my fingers inside of you, and your insides tighten around them. I can feel your moans vibrating on my cock."

"Brent, I-don't stop." I was in the same position he was describing, but it was my fingers doing the job.

"Tell me you're feeling this, Alisa. Are you with me? Are your fingers in you because my hands are stroking up and down on my penis. I am so hard for you, princess."

It was my turn to pick up where he left off.

"Your cock fills my mouth and slides down my throat while I play with your sac. Your balls are so full of cum for me. I can't help but moan every time your fingers pulsate inside of me. We begin to speed up, and I can feel myself on the edge of climaxing."

I nuzzled my phone between my shoulder and ear so I could have one hand caressing my nipple while the other was rubbing my clit. I was panting, struggling to stay on track with dirty talk when I was so close to orgasming.

"You take your thumb and place it on my clitoris, rubbing as you slide in and out. It sends me over the edge, and I orgasm, soaking your fingers. I look up at you and gargle your name, and you moan out mine before you explode in my mouth."

My thighs clenched, and I was overcome with an orgasm. I couldn't keep myself from whimpering into the phone.

From the other end, I heard, "Oh fuck, only you can do this to me."

The phone went quiet; all that's left from this phone sex session were gentle groans.

"Alisa," he whispered.

"Brent, I've never…done that before," I confessed, trying to get my breathing under control. It was true, I've had phone sex but never until completion. I'd usually just be twirling my hair in sweatpants when I was on the phone with Jimmy.

"When can I see you, Alisa?" I heard the desperation in his voice.

All I wanted to do was be wrapped in his arms, glowing in this incredible ecstasy. But as my mind began to uncloud from my monumental O, I realized we once again chose our lust for each other over tying up the loose ends of the past.

"Brent, wait a minute. Before this goes further, I need to know why you left me that day all of those years ago. It broke my heart. And while I love whatever this is right now and how it makes me feel, I need to heal that wound."

He fell silent. I couldn't believe I just ruined the moment. I wanted to kick myself, but this was the closure I needed. I heard him gulp and take a deep breath.

"Alisa, this is something that I need to tell you in person. For now, just know that now that I've found you, I won't leave you again."

I wanted to believe him. I was annoyed he couldn't just close the chapter.

"Well, I'll be in Port Jeff for a while," I said, not hiding my disappointment in his decision to keep his explanation from me. I was dying to see Brent, but I needed to choose my dad first.

"No worries. I will come to you. Tomorrow, Alisa, tomorrow." I loved the sound of his voice.

"Brent—," I said before being cut off.

"Alisa, I will come to you tomorrow evening, six o'clock. I'm off the next day, I promise we'll talk about everything. I'll answer all of your questions. I owe you that. Alisa, I mean it when I say I won't lose you again. I have to go for now. You came back into my life so unexpectedly, and you're all I can think about. From the moment I wake up, until I lay my head down to sleep, you're the only thing on my mind. The best kind of distraction. Text me your address. See you soon, princess." He hung up before I could say goodbye.

I reclined my car seat and began to think of what words could possibly fix the broken heart I'd been living with for so many years. I was under a spell too. He had shaken my life up since the moment I saw him on the news. I liked the way my heart fluttered when I heard his voice and how my stomach tightened when he touched me. The phone rang and I sprung up. It's the hospital.

"Alisa, can you bring me some provolone and grapes? Oh, yeah, and that bread from Giuseppe's."

Looks like my dad is feeling better with these demands. If I'm not mistaken, each of these items were on the "restricted foods" list from his nurse.

"Dad, are you allowed to have all of that?" I asked with a smirk. Keeping him from his favorite snack? This will get a rise out of him.

"Alisa Marie Rossi, are you treating me like a child?"

"Yes," I said sarcastically.

"Alisa, please. I can't eat the garbage here. You want your papa to eat garbage?" he said, begging, and I couldn't help but giggle.

"Dad, I'll call the nurse. If she says it's okay—"

He blurted out "*A fanabla!*" and I could picture his hands flying into the air showing his frustration.

"Dad, really?"

"They say I'm going to be here for at least three days. Do you want me to starve?" When my father got angry, his Italian accent thickened. It was nearly impossible to understand him so you were forced to read his lips and assume the context from his hand gestures.

"When are you coming to see your papa?" he asked.

"I'll be there in thirty minutes, and I'll bring some pastina."

"Gee, thanks," he said with a sigh of relief. "Oh, make sure you put cheese on it." Yep, there's the hard head I know and love. Little does he know I had already checked in with the nurse's station on this meal. Hopefully they don't punish me for the addition of cheese, but it was worth avoiding a major culinary meltdown.

"Ciao, Papa. See you soon."

CHAPTER 13

Brent

"Thanks, Tom, I really appreciate it," while exhaling with a sigh of relief. He's been my best friend since high school. He always had my back. Tonight needed to be perfect, and I knew I could count on Tom to make it go off without a hitch. I'll only have one chance to show her that waiting for me was the right decision.

"You're welcome, man," Tom said cooly. "It will be anchored by the dock at McAllister Park. Don't forget, low tide is at 10:30 p.m."

"No problem. I'll put those Mets tickets in your mailbox."

My Mets vs. Yankees Subway Series tickets were the trade-off for his help. I wanted to go with him, but this was more important.

"She must be special, man, for you to give up those tickets. You've been waiting for that game all season," he said in disbelief. Before he started questioning me about Alisa, I cut him off.

"Tom, we'll talk more soon. I have another call coming in."

Driving on the Long Island Expressway was frustrating. You always needed to account for an extra twenty minutes of traffic. Getting off her exit wasn't any better. I turned the corner of her block. She lived two blocks away from where I grew up. I was calm;

no nerves, just pure excitement. I was turning into her driveway, I noticed that she stayed true to form, adding a little Italian flare to her high ranch home that would otherwise be identical to the others in her neighborhood. I circled a water fountain that was stationed in the center of her driveway, and slowly the nerves started to set in. As I made my way to the front door, she slowly opened it, and the vision I saw was breathtaking. I have never seen a woman more amazingly beautiful before.

"Wow. Alisa, that dress is…wow."

She blushed.

"I'm sorry. You're just so beautiful." Her dress was a halter front that dipped to her navel of her back, bare, with just a clasp at the top and two hanging teardrop crystals.

"Thank you," she said. "Do you want to come in?"

"Alisa, if I come in, we may not come out." Her giggle was music to my ears.

"Come with me, my lovely lady," I invited, with a smile now engraved on my face. I couldn't help but place my hand on her lower back to guide her to my car.

As I opened the car door, she said, "Oh, how charming. What a gentleman."

I closed her door and noticed that her dress was another Versace. The second Versace dress. Ironic after our phone call last night.

"Where are we going?" she asked.

"Not telling," I told her, acting like a child with a wicked looked on my face.

"Brent," she said with a pout, hoping to get it out of me.

"Alisa, this night will be for both of us. I promise that you will love it. Something we will both cherish," I reassured, barely able to contain my excitement for what was to come.

"Brent. I'm not good with surprises, but I'll stop pestering you for now." She giggled again. I was going to make it my life's mission to make her laugh every day.

We took a tour through the multimillion-dollar homes of the Belle Terre community, otherwise known as the Golden Coast of Long Island, heading toward Port Jefferson Marina. Rumor had it that countesses and actors live there. I turned down the street that led to McAllister Park, a secluded little spot on the other side of the marina. I parked the car, I hope Tom packed everything. Why was I so nervous? I've never felt like this on a first date. I shook off the nerves and leaned over to the beautiful woman next to me and left a tender kiss on her cheek. I heard her take a breath, maybe she was just as anxious as I was. That notion calmed me, and I began to gain confidence that I was exactly where I needed to be—with her.

"Where are we? McAllister Park?" she asked, and I pretended not to hear her as I searched for the docked boat. *Bingo.*

"I don't think I'm wearing the right shoes." She looked at me with those hazel eyes, the fear of ruining her shoes on her mind. No way was I going to let ruined shoes be the first thing she remembered about tonight. I got out of the car and swooped her out of the passenger seat. I grabbed underneath her knees; she wrapped her arms around my neck, and I carried her to the boat. It was impeccable. The twenty-four-foot striper named Happy Hour would take us on our first adventure. She thanked me with a kiss on my cheek and giggled as her feet touched the deck.

"Brent, where are we going?" she questioned again.

I tilted my head, raised an eyebrow and gave her a smirk before I shook my head and said, "Patience, princess." She rolled her eyes and let out another giggle.

I watched as a smile slowly began to spread across her face as she looked out onto the Long Island Sound. The vision of her and the breeze, brushing her hair off her shoulders was picturesque. I searched the mini cabin and checked to see if everything was there— basket, flowers, blow-up bed, satin sheets, and champagne on ice—it was perfect. Tom never failed me.

I stood behind her, kissed the crook of her neck. "You are beautiful," I whispered in her ear, grabbing her hand and turning her around. "You want to steer the boat with me?"

She nodded her head in agreeance.

I placed her in front of me, moving her hair to the side, exposing the nape of her neck. She smelled so good, like sexual innocence—jasmine with a hint of sandalwood. I started the boat, put it into gear, and steered toward Conscience Bay, a quiet inlet that was home to sand bars during low tide, perfect for what I have in mind. Everything was falling into place, the sun was beginning to set, revealing hues of salmon and lavender in the sky. Alisa relaxed her body into me as we made our way to shallow waters. I anchored the boat and leaned down to whisper, "Do you trust me?" She turned slightly to look me in the eyes.

"Are you going to make me regret saying I do?" she countered, now raising her brow and smirking.

I smiled and gave her a kiss underneath her ear. She moaned quietly. Another mission I promised myself to do every day, make her moan by my touch.

"No, I won't make you regret anything," I said, winking as I grabbed the blindfold and tied it around her head. Her body tensed, and I leaned in to kiss her lips. I could feel her begin to relax with my quiet reassurance.

"Brent! What are you—" You can tell she did not expect that.

I leaned in again to steal another kiss.

"I have to admit, Brent, I'm a little freaked out," she said, biting her bottom lip.

I know how she feels, I'm freaked out by my true feelings for her. I needed her, craved her, yearned her.

"Alisa, I want you to feel like the princess you are. Allow me to do that for you, sweetheart." With that, I jumped off the boat. The basket, bed, flowers, and champagne were in tow as I headed toward the sandbar. I laid the bed down and made it with satin sheets, pillows; placed the champagne over the ice and created a little spread of snacks for us. Perfect. Time to get the last piece. I grabbed Alisa's hand, lifted her off the boat, and brought her to our man-made oasis.

I gently put her down, stole another kiss, and took off her blindfold. Her eyes gained focus of the picture in front of her. Her reaction alone made something inside me move. I did this right. She turned around.

"What! How did you do this?" The expression on her face was one that I will need to see again. Gorgeous.

"For you, I would do anything," I whispered, before kissing her forehead. I meant every word, and damn, it felt good. I grabbed her hand and led her to the bed.

"Brent, this is amazing," she said in disbelief.

The expression on her face reminded me of the very first time we met.

"Alisa, I meant it when I said I will treat you like a princess." I really didn't want to lose her again. I poured us champagne and handed her a glass, unable to keep myself from laying another kiss behind her ear, lingering a bit longer to caress her neck with my tongue before pulling away to cheers. She looked beautiful. The sunset highlighted every feature of her face. *Patience, Brent.* I was on the verge of snatching her up and taking her. Before we can indulge in the flesh, we have to clear the air. She moved toward me.

"All this for me," she said in her raspy voice that made it harder to keep my cool. I nodded yes. She wrapped her arms around me and laid her head on my chest. I felt the weight upon my shoulders. It's time to explain the reason why I was in the stairwell that day. Why that was the last day she saw me. Why I never came back for her. The day that I found my soul mate.

"Alisa, let me tell you what happened that day when we found each other." The words were out. She laid down on the bed and looked up at me with unwavering eye contact, patiently waiting for me to explain. *Gorgeous, absolutely gorgeous*, I thought to myself. I took a deep breath and prayed she'd forgive me or at least understand.

"I had been mesmerized by your beauty since the moment I first laid eyes on you. I waited for you that day on the stairwell. I needed to know more about you. I knew didn't have much time left at the school, but I couldn't help myself."

She looked confused.

"I was on a case, undercover. I was a detective for the NYPD. We were on a special assignment. I was twenty-two years old, and you were seventeen." I let out a nervous laugh. This was only the beginning, and I could feel a lump in my throat.

"The day of our kiss was also the day we concluded our investigation and arrested the teen suspects." I could tell she was trying to think back and assemble the events.

"That was Joey and Richie, right?"

I was in complete shock that she knew who they were, I nodded.

"I remember that day. I was talking to Sharon, my best friend, about our kiss and how I couldn't wait to find out what your name was."

I could tell she was hurt as she bent her head down. I lifted her head up and kissed her forehead. All this time she had no name to go with our kiss. I never realized that would be a big deal.

"I'm so sorry, Alisa. I didn't want it to happen that way. After the arrest, I was put in the witness protection program." She stayed quiet, her face was becoming hard to read.

"We were able to get the main guy. It was dangerous for me if they knew who I was." I paused for a moment with a thought on how she found out my name. I mean Doherty did mention her father was part of that crime family.

"Wait, how did you find out my name?"

"I was watching the news about the robbery in my restaurant. When the reporter was talking to you, my eyes were glued to the TV. At first I thought it couldn't be. But then I looked into your eyes. I knew. The feeling I had was the same one I had ten years ago."

Her eyes began to fill with tears. I leaned down so I could kiss those soft lips, and tears began to fall down her face.

"Alisa, what's wrong?"

"Nothing, I—"

"Tell me, princess, you can tell me anything."

"The next week after that day I waited for you. When you didn't come back, I began asking around to find out who you were. People thought I was crazy. I thought you were a ghost, make-believe. But that kiss was real. I felt it every day. I dated guys, but not one kiss came close to the kiss that we shared, and I didn't even know your name. I guess there are just a lot of emotions going through me right now." She shrugged her shoulders, looking away from me collecting her thoughts.

"Did you even try to look for me?" she asked, her voice cracking.

"Yes," I said confidently.

"I was in the protection program for two years. I didn't know your name either. I looked on the internet for your high school yearbook. I found you. Alisa." I reached into my pocket and took out my wallet. I pulled out a photocopy of the picture I saw in the yearbook.

"I laminated it so it would never fade."

The expression on her face was priceless. She grabbed the picture and stared at it for a moment to ensure the picture was of her. She shook her head. She leaned over, placed her hand on the side of my face, and kissed me. The kiss grew deeper. The energy between us was getting heated. Her arms wrapped around my neck, and her hands began to tug on my hair. The night was still young. I didn't want to ruin what I had planned. Reluctantly I slowed down. I gathered my thoughts as I looked into her eyes. I got up and took her hand in mine.

"Dance with me." I kissed her hand to ease the heated connection. She grabbed my hand, walked toward me. Once we locked eyes it was as if we were the only people on the planet. Everything else melted away. I wish I had more time with her back then. But then again, it was for the best. I didn't want her caught up in everything that was going on.

"I'm going to take you to the prom tonight." We both laughed.

I grabbed my phone and put on Bruno Mars, it was time to act out our phone call and then some. She snuggled her head against my chest. I'm sure she could feel my heart pounding out of my chest. My hands were on the small of back, enjoying the feel of her silky skin and playing with the crystals on the back of the dress. I waited for my favorite part of the song, reached up and unclasped her dress. She lifted her head and kissed me softly. She untucked my shirt from my pants and pulled it over my head, and on cue, her dress hit the floor, completely exposing her perfectly round breasts. I swept her up and carried her back to the bed lined with rose petals. I tried to control my desire and take my time. I didn't want to be a minute man her first time making love.

"You're mine, Alisa. You are all I have been dreaming of. You will never be lost again. You're forever in my heart." I was now convinced she owned me. I have never said those words to any other woman. The ironic part was that I know I will only say those words to her—only her. This woman will consume my thoughts for the rest of my life.

"You're mine, Brent. My heart has been waiting for you to find me." She bit her bottom lip. It's so damn seductive. As I gazed into her eyes, my hands began to explore her body. Slowly starting at her neck, my fingers feathering toward her chest, caressing her breast and running my fingers over her hardened nipples. My wet tongue guided her breast into my mouth. A low moan came from her lips as she arched her back.

"I'm going to make you feel so good, Alisa. I'll worship you till the day I die," I whispered as I continued my exploration of her body. I tried to pace myself building upon the anticipation of our connection.

"Take me," spilled from her mouth.

I gave her a trail of kisses down her torso as I continued to caress her breasts. I started at her hip, licking and sucking. I was hungry for more. My tongue continued on its journey to the ultimate destination. Pulling down her panties with my teeth below using my tongue to spread her lips and enter the core. She was so wet for me. The noises of ecstasy escaped from her mouth, and her thighs began to shake. I couldn't stop. I have never tasted anything so sweet in my life. I tasted her juices all over my tongue, dripping down my chin. I worked my tongue back up to her clit and slid two fingers in and out of her. Her moans continued to grow louder. The walls around my fingers tensed up, she was about to shatter. My tongue did its magic, and I hit her G-spot.

"Brent," she called. "Brent!" She exploded, first of many more tonight.

She grabbed my hair and pulled me toward her and attacked my mouth, kissing me as if her life depended on it. She was tasting her own juices. This made me greedier than ever. She reached for my belt, but I beat her to it. I pulled down my pants and threw them aside.

She looked up at me and whispered, "My turn." Her eyes turned the gold color I remembered on our first kiss. She started stroking my cock, going up and down. She started her exploration with her mouth down my body and licking me the way I did to her. The feeling of her lips on me, her tongue caressing my length, I could barely control myself. I propped myself up on my elbows to watch her head bob up and down. She looked up at me, her eyes telling me she was making me hers as she took me deeper into her mouth. This woman owned me from the beginning.

CHAPTER 14

Alisa

I couldn't believe this was really happening. I've been waiting all this time for this very moment. I stroked him with one hand and caressed his sack with the other. He's so huge, I hope I can fit him. I kissed along his chest and down his torso, with my hands still wrapped around his member. I licked his mushroom tip and ran my tongue over the slit. I put his cock in my mouth, and his hands moved to my hair. "Alisa, don't stop," he begged. I massaged his sack, and he lifted his hips. His cock was at the back of my throat. I continued to move up and down, circling the head of his member with my tongue every now and then. I felt his cock throbbing with every stroke of my tongue. I heard a faint whisper of my name, and he lifted me off him, withholding his release. Within seconds, I was on my back. He gripped my hands above my head.

"That was amazing, princess, and tonight I will make you mine. Is that what you want, Alisa?"

My response was instant, "All I've ever wanted is to be yours."

His eyes frosted over. A moment of silence, and a slight smile formed on his lips.

"Me too," he whispered.

I believed every word he was saying to me. Feelings overwhelmed me: happiness, excitement, passion—love. He pushed the hair out of my face and kissed me with a purpose. He pulled away and looked deep into my eyes as he reached for the condom and rolled it on. His eyes were intense and I continued to fall deep under his spell as they changed to a crystal blue. All of my dreams were finally coming true.

"Alisa, let me show you what you mean to me. I've been wanting to do this to you since that day ten years ago. Are you ready, my princess?" he asked in my ear, followed by a soft kiss, making me weak.

Without any hesitation, I nodded yes. The anticipation of his next move was driving me crazy. He started to trail kisses down my body. His hand glided down feeling my wet entrance. He groaned, realizing I was ready for him. He slid two fingers in, moving in circular motions. The need for him was overwhelming. I looked down and saw him stroking his penis. I was getting so close to erupting, every muscle in my body began to tighten. He slowed down right before I was ready to indulge in my second orgasm of the evening.

"I want to be in you when you come. I won't hurt you, Alisa, but it will bite for a second, and I promise I will make sure this is memorable for both of us."

The light from the moon put a glow on his face, and I kissed him feverishly. The movement of his tongue in my mouth worked me into a place I never wanted to leave. I felt his erection in between my legs. He teased me by rubbing it up and down the outside of my entrance. I couldn't help but arch my back and cry out wanting another orgasm.

He smiled and whispered in my ear, "Tell me what you want, Alisa."

"I want you to worship me and show me how bad you want me to cum with your cock inside me." I was starting to sound desperate and dirty, but the anticipation was driving me mad. I needed him *now*.

"A princess always gets what she wants."

Our tongues were frantic. I lifted my hips to show him my need for him, to show him that I was waiting for him to enter me. Gently he lowered me down, the tips of his fingers flowing down my torso; the feeling made me tingle. He slid down my body in a slow motion and blew across my breast before sucking on each nipple until they perked. The breeze hit me and chilled me to the bone, making me lose complete control of myself. He worked his way back up, and his penis was lying between my legs in position to enter. He held the sides of my face and slipped his tongue in my mouth. He penetrated me—it stung for a second. The sensation of him in me was more than I expected. I bit his shoulder. He filled me, and it felt so good.

"I got you, Alisa. I am never letting you go," he said as he rocked me slowly and seductively.

We both moved in unison, like we were made for each other. He groaned in my ear, "You're perfect, princess. We are meant to be together."

I felt every inch of him. He continued thrusting and caressing me as if I was his precious possession.

"We were made for each other, Alisa," he said, kissing that spot again. A moan poured out of my mouth.

His body was moving faster. My body started to quiver. He kept hitting this one spot that numbed my body. The feeling was so intense, igniting heat from my toes to my pussy. I started to arch my back again. His pounding was bringing me to another sexual explosion.

"Brent, I am going to—"

"I want to see you, Alisa. Open your eyes. Look at me, princess."

His look told me he really cared about me. I stared into his eyes and let him know I felt the same way. The chemistry had changed. My legs were wrapped around his waist. He looked into my eyes telling me he was ready for his release but ensuring I had mine. He slammed into me a couple of more times.

"Come for me, Alisa. Let it go, princess," he said in a low, raspy tone.

In that very moment, he pinched my clit. My body spasmed, and he roared before exploding. He kept thrusting into me to finish his release. The vibration hitting my G-spot spiraled me into another orgasm. A groan erupted from his mouth as I clenched on his cock. He fell on top of me then off to the side. I wanted him to stay inside me, for this feeling to never end. He caressed my cheek and kissed me softly on the lips.

"Thank you, Alisa, for never forgetting me. For allowing me to make it up to you the way I wanted to." He smiled at me as the moonlight haloed him.

We just sat there and held each other for some time. It felt so good to be with him. I felt the mattress dip and looked at him. He got up and held out a hand. I grabbed it and walked with him into the water. Once the water hit the middle of my calf, he lifted me, cradled me. He walked me out into the Long Island Sound. We were still silent, listening to the sounds of the waves crashing, I swore I could hear his heartbeat. We were connected now more than ever. He sank into the cold water. I wrapped my legs around his waist and laid my head on his chest. He lifted my chin up so we were eye to eye.

"I have never felt this way, Alisa. You take me to a place I never want to leave." I could tell he meant every word. I always wondered what it would be like the first time I shared myself with someone. He made it perfect.

"I know what you mean. I feel the same way," I said, I had never felt so transparent. It scared me.

We sat in the middle of the sound holding each other, talking between long kisses. After what felt like hours, he grabbed my hand, and he led me back to the anchored boat.

"Princess, in the cabin, there is a box for you. I think you'll like what's inside. I love to see you in that dress, but what I have for you will help make you a little more comfortable. I'll be right back, I have to clean up before the high tide."

I hurried to look inside the cabin and saw a light pink box. Inside there was a pair of black leggings and an oversized sweatshirt. I slipped it on and returned to the deck to watch him finish cleaning up our little piece of paradise on the sand. He went through all the trouble of creating our own private island just for me.

This couldn't have been a more perfect first time, I thought to myself while staring at the man before me. His shirt was off, his body was so fit. He looked like an ancient sculpture in a museum. Oh, how I wanted my tongue to explore every groove of every muscle... again. I was surprising myself how ready I was for round two of my Mr. Destiny. My imagination was going wild until—

"Princess!" Brent called out, snapping me out of my daydream. He handed me the untouched picnic basket and jumped into the boat. Still anchored, he took the blanket and led me on the bow. I sat in front of him, and he wrapped his legs around me, leaned his chin on my shoulder. We looked at the stars over the water while he told me about his childhood, growing up in Stony Brook, playing on high school sports teams and working for the local supermarket. He went to college with his best friend Tom. He even remembered going to my father's pizza place while in high school and ordering the baked ziti pizza. I wondered if I ever waited on him. My father brought me to work on Saturdays to learn the business. That's how I got interested in cooking and learned what it took to run a restaurant.

He told me more about the witness protection and a good friend he met. He had to start over. He admitted he was scared, not sure what the repercussion would be capturing the criminals. He didn't come out and say it, but I think the mob was involved. I told him more about Sharon and how we were friends since we were in junior high. I shared how I started my restaurant after being a sous chef for a Michelin three-star chef in Manhattan. I even shared how Michael was my lucky charm, and influential he's been in Sicilia's growth, thanks to his connection with the A-list crowd.

It was getting cold. Brent noticed me hiding my hands inside the sweatshirt and started to rub them for warmth. We made our way inside the cabin. It was small, with just enough room for a pull-out bed. He set up the picnic basket, spread out the rose petals all over the bed, and poured two glasses of wine.

"Mr. Collins, are you trying to seduce me again?" I gave him a curious look.

"Maybe," he said with that look he gives me.

"Well, I have news for you—you have." My lips turned up into a megawatt smile. He kissed me and lifted me onto the bed. It's getting late. I scrunched up my forehead.

"Are we sleeping here?"

"Mmm-hmmm," he answered as he nipped my earlobe.

"Brent, what happens if—"

He put his fingers on my lips. "I gave the hospital my cell if anything happens." He continued his exploration of my body. I didn't even know what time it was when we fell asleep. My dreams would be good ones. I really needed a good night's sleep. I felt so different, protected, cared for, free even. He makes me feel good, maybe even complete.

I woke up hearing the water hit the side of the boat. His arm was over my waist, and I felt his breath on my neck I turned over slowly to look at his face. He was sound asleep, I couldn't take my eyes off his face. He was one gorgeous man. I leaned in to kiss him softly on his chest; the hairs tickled my lips. Something came over me, and I couldn't just stop there. I left a trail of kisses going down his stomach toward his cock. My lips reached his morning erection. Who was this woman I have become? I swallowed him whole right there. I felt his fingers work his way into my hair, and he started to moan himself awake.

"Good morning, princess," he greeted as he moaned when I licked the tip of his cock. I could tell he liked his wake-up call when he started to help me get him to his release, his hips thrusting forward making his cock hit the back of my throat. I started to gag but controlled myself by swallowing. I felt him start to lose control.

"You're going to make me—" He lifted me up and in seconds flipped me on top of him.

"Ride me, Alisa."

Still being sore from last night, I slowly made my way on top.

"I've never…" I stopped, shy about my inexperience.

"Just like you're riding a horse, up and down, whatever feels good to you." He guided me, and I've never felt so full. It was amazing at first. I went slow. The feeling was coming back, the one that told me I was where I needed to be. My pace quickened. I started to grind down on him.

"That's it, princess, ride me. Feel me filling you." He arched his back, encouraging me to be erotic and daring. I felt comfortable around him, allowing myself to be sexually expressive.

"Brent!" I cried out. I started to tighten. The intensity was going to make me explode.

"I feel you squeezing me, baby. Go ahead, let it go. I'm with you."

"Cum for me. Show me how much you love my cock in you, show me how good I feel." Those words hit the spot. At this point, my eyes locked onto his, and I came so hard I saw stars. The universe had a whole new meaning to me. Brent lifted me off him and exploded. His load shot up onto my stomach across my breasts. Shit, no condom. We were skin to skin, nothing between us. His cum was all over me. He started to rub it in my skin, like was marking his territory. Normally I would object, but it felt good, I *am* his. He leaned up and started to kiss me. He stopped and looked up.

"You're mine and only mine. No other man will have you, Alisa," he said, pausing to run his hand through my hair. "You ruined me for any other woman, Alisa. Please tell me you feel the same way."

He looked deeply into my eyes searching for my answer. I wanted to tell him I was in love with him. It's too soon. I didn't want to scare him away. Plus, I wanted to make sure this was really love not just lust. I reached up and grabbed the back of his head and pulled him toward me. I kissed those tender lips, looked into his eyes, and breathed out.

"Yes. I feel it too. This is real." I was telling the truth even though it's scaring the shit out of me. He looked into my eyes and smiled. He brought me to his chest and kissed the top of my head.

"Princess, this is one journey I am happy to be on." He held me tighter. He exhaled and lifted up my chin so he could kiss my lips.

"Me too," I said, giving him a kiss right back. We just held each other and took each other in. I felt his heart beat fast. Maybe I wasn't the only one who was scared.

CHAPTER 15

Brent

After last night I could finally picture myself being with someone for the rest of my life. The best part is, the woman next to me feels the same way. Is this love or infatuation? I never want to be without her, but part of me worries that this spark is burning too bright to last. The scales of our relationship are weighing heavy in the physical, but there's time to learn and grow in the emotional. How can I complain? My morning wake-up call was glorious.

"What are we doing today?" I asked, still holding her close.

"We…I love the sound of that. It's perfect. I have to see my dad, and then—"

"Good." I picked her up, walked her on the deck, and jumped into the water. The expression on her face was a pure delight.

"Brent!" She playfully laughed. She swam away from me. I caught up to her, grabbed her waist, and we were forehead to forehead.

"I'll always find you, that I promise."

"Good, because I just found you again. Losing you is a nonnegotiable for me." She pried herself away from me and swam in the opposite direction. Giggles came after her performance that made me smile from ear to ear. My girl liked to play games.

We got back on the boat and headed to shore. I'll be thirty-three next month, and I feel like I got the prom queen by my side. I felt as giddy as a schoolboy. I quickly came back to reality.

"Brent, hello? Did you hear me?" she said, waving her hand in my face. She looked at me and smiled.

"Sorry, princess, just daydreaming." A smile appeared on my face. What was going on with me?

"Really, what about?" she asked with a smirk.

"Stop, Alisa. If we start that again, we'll never see your dad today."

"What time do you need to be in East Hampton?" she asked, looking down at her hands, fiddling her fingers. This time on the boat ending meant going back to reality—she wasn't ready to let our little private bubble burst.

"Not until tomorrow morning," I reassured her. Believe me, I want as much time as possible together, too.

"I can deal with that," she said, looking toward me and smiling before licking her bottom lip. I think I created a sex fiend.

We arrived at her house and quickly had our coffee and some breakfast. We wanted to get to the hospital as soon as we could. I knew it was weighing on her mind, and I wanted to show her that as much as I'd love to spend the day in bed together, I was more than happy to make this trip. To make sure we actually made it out of the house, we showered separately. Thirty minutes later, we were at the hospital. Alisa's dad was out of the ICU and was transferred to a private room. Alisa's friends, Sharon and Louie, were already there visiting. I didn't remember seeing them at Sicilia's grand opening, my detective brain was back in action. Louie looked familiar. I made a special note to check on him. I suddenly remembered that Doherty mentioned Louie Vaccaro. Could that be him? Could he be a pawn in the mob? I wanted to make sure Alisa was around people I could trust. This worried me.

Alisa made the introductions. She held my hand and stroked her thumb across my knuckles. A small gesture that meant so much. As if she was trying to calm my nerves.

"So what do you do, Brent?" Alisa's dad asked.

"I'm the police commissioner of East Hampton, sir."

"Impressive, son," he said, shaking his head with approval.

"Thank you, worked very hard to get there."

"No doubt."

The small talk continued and I heard more about Sharon's career as a photographer. Louie was unusually quiet. I knew he came from Queens and that the two met on a party cruise. Something about a bachelor party Alisa didn't elaborate, but I appreciated the abridged version. I really didn't need to know the details of the woman who will ultimately be my wife spending the weekend with fourteen men. Alisa kept looking at me to gauge my reaction. I was bothered but that was part of her past. I'm her present and her future. I gave her hand a reassuring squeeze.

Hours passed and I was beginning to get restless; I wanted alone time with my girl. The doctor came in to let her know her father was well enough to come home the next day. As we said our goodbyes, Sharon and Louie invited us to join them for dinner. Simultaneously, Alisa and I politely said, "No, thank you." Sharon and Louie both looked at us as we looked at each other, laughing at our response. We walked hand in hand; she slipped her arm through mine. This felt so right. Her phone rang. It was Michael.

"I have to take this," she said with an apologetic look.

"Hey, Michael," Alisa cheerily greeted before her smile began to sour and her look went to one of worry.

"What's going on?" she asked before putting the call on speaker phone.

"Well, I went in this morning, put the cash in the vault, and turned around to find a note on your desk. I called Detective Doherty."

"What did it say?" Alisa paused and looked at me. I leaned closer to the phone. Beginning to get frantic, she asked Michael again, "What does it say? You're scaring me."

He sighed and read,

> Hickory Dickory Dock.
> It's time to stop the clock.
> Kim's necklace I hock.
> Your pop is lucky to have his cock.
> Your life, tick tock, tick tock.

Alisa's face went pale. I took the phone from her.

"Michael, it's Brent, the commi—"

He stopped me. "Thank god you're with her."

"Where is Detective Doherty?"

"Right next to me."

"Please get him on the phone." At this point Alisa was crying and shaking. I hated to see her like this.

"Doherty."

"Commissioner."

"Do you have any clues about this yet?"

"No, boss. I wanted to question Alisa on it."

"Okay, continue looking for clues. Doherty, my office, tomorrow, 9:00 a.m."

"Yes, boss, 9:00 a.m."

Alisa was in shock, and began mumbling, "Why me? What did I do to deserve this?"

"Let's just get back to your house."

She nodded, and she didn't say a word as we made our way to the parking lot. I stopped her once we got to my car and turned her toward me.

"Alisa, I am not going to allow anything to happen to you," I reassured as I held her hand.

"I don't know, but who would want to do this to me?" She paused.

"Tick tock," she said to herself.

"Okay, were there any disputes with anyone recently? Vendors, construction crew, socialites, people in East Hampton who didn't want the restaurant open?"

"No, Brent. Not at all."

I bit the side of my cheek. "Old boyfriends?" I just had to ask. I really didn't want to know about them.

She looked at me. "No, no one that I could say would want me dead."

"Okay, well, I am staying with you tonight, and you are coming with me tomorrow."

"I can't." She looked at me. "My dad."

"Alisa, see if Sharon can—"

She cut me off. "No, Brent. It's my dad."

Right then and there, I realized that her father was her number one priority. The look I received assured me she was not changing her mind about this. Her arms were folded across her chest, I must come up with a plan so I know this stubborn girl will be safe.

"Okay, Alisa. May I offer a compromise? I am going to have two of my guys come and—"

"No, Brent."

"Alisa, you are my responsibility now, and always. Until I find out more information, you are either going to be by my side or you will have detail on you."

She smiled. "Someone has a crush on me." She hugged herself and swayed from side to side. I really liked the playful side of her.

"Alisa, I'm serious."

"Okay, Commissioner, I'll have detail." She saluted me in response.

I smirked at her, trying not belt out a laugh.

"Princess, get over here." I grabbed her and brought her into my chest. "It's more than a crush. I know you feel it too."

"Yes, I never felt like this with anyone, Brent, and that is the truth," she said with tears in her eyes as she looked back up at me.

"I'm scared, Brent," she confessed as she hugged my waist tighter. I felt her tremble.

"I'll protect you. Just make sure you never leave your detail or never leave my side, for two reasons."

"Two reasons?" Alisa looked up at me with a curious look.

"Well, for one, so I can protect you, and secondly, now that I have you, I want you, and I mean really want you by my side always." I sounded like such a sap.

If my buddy Tom heard me, I would never hear the end of it. I heard it now. Something like "Man, you are one whipped son of a bitch" or "She really must have some voodoo pussy." I let out a soft laugh under my breath.

She got on her tippy-toes to give me a kiss.

"Well, Commissioner, shall we go for another round of incredible sex?" The woman was insatiable, a real sex minx, but how could I refuse a princess's wish?

I nearly peeled out of the parking lot heading to her house. We raced to the door and once unlocked, we began stripping off pieces of clothing headed to the bedroom like breadcrumbs from the front door. Stripped down at the foot of the bed, she attacked me as if I was her prey. I love that she thinks she's the one in control.

She smiled with her finger on her lower lip and whispered, "Princess wants to ride her pony."

"Ready to hit double digits in orgasms?" An ambitious goal, but it felt like I had an endless gas tank with her. So many new things to try together, new positions to explore and pleasure to unlock.

She gave her my one-eyebrow smirk. "Promises, promises, my dear prince," she said, waving me off.

"I never say anything I don't mean. It would be wise to remember that," I taunted as I grabbed her waist, threw her over my shoulder, and bit her ass.

"Ow! You beast," she yelled with a laugh.

"Alisa, you have no idea. Now ride me, you wench," I playfully ordered before smacking her ass.

This journey is everything I've ever dreamed of...and more.

CHAPTER 16

Alisa

The sun was peeking through the curtain; Brent was already up and showered, sitting on the bed with my coffee. I slept so well. I didn't even hear him get up.

"Good morning, princess," he greeted with a smile as bright as the sun.

"Morning, my knight."

"Knight?"

"Aren't you going to slay the dragon for me?" I asked playfully, prompting a laugh.

"Yes, princess. My guys are outside, Officers Price and Daige. Call me if you need anything, Alisa, and make plans to be with me this weekend." He kissed my head as if I were a child. Cute but not what I was looking for.

"Brent," I whined, with a what-the-fuck expression on my face.

"Alisa, please, I have to go," he said reluctantly.

Noticing my now exaggerated pouty bottom lip, he rebounded with a passionate kiss. He pulled away with a smirk and shook his head.

On his way out I could've sworn he said "voodoo pussy" under his breath.

We reached new levels of bliss, countless orgasms, sometimes back-to-back. He created a sex-craved woman. I needed to feel him on me—in me. It was like I had tapped into an entirely new side of myself. I mean, after all, I was a virgin just a few days ago.

I rolled over to the other side of the bed and I could smell him on the pillow. I sunk my face in to smother myself in his smell. I could lie here forever.

My phone vibrated, it was my dad texting me begging me to pick him up from the hospital as soon as possible. He wanted out, and I couldn't blame him. It was more than just the food, although he wouldn't admit it. What really bothered him was the fact that we had spent so much time in the very same hospital when my mom was sick. Memories of her suffering, the late-night emergency room visits, I'm sure it was getting to be too much to bear now that he was conscious. Why would anyone want to hurt such a sweet man? Yes, he was hard-headed, but he would bend over backward for those he loved, and he'd go to the ends of the earth to protect them. Why were they after my father to begin with? What could I have done? I wracked my brain, trying to figure out who I could have pissed off so badly that they would want me dead.

"Ms. Rossi. Officer Price. Do you know this man?" Startled, I saw one of my details was holding Louie by his upper arm.

"Yes, Price, that is my friend Louie," I assured him. Louie was confused, and his face said it all I couldn't help but laugh. Price removed his hand. Louie rubbed his arm and walked with me.

"Alisa, why did that man frisk me? He took my license, patted me down, looked in my car, and practically harassed me with questions," he huffed, getting that all out with on one breath.

"Well, they found a threatening note in my office in East Hampton. Brent sent them to protect me," I replied, shrugging my shoulders.

"A note? What did it say?"

"It was written to mimic a nursery rhyme, basically threatening to kill me. It must have been the guys who went after my dad." Louie's eyes widened. I think he knows more than he is willing to tell me.

"They mentioned my father and Kim's necklace. Wait, Sharon's not here, why?" I was frantic that something might have happened to her.

"She said something about having to do a last-minute layout for the magazine," he said with a shrug. "So she sent me. She said if I didn't come and help, I wouldn't get any for a week. I would've done it without the threat!" he said with a laugh. "She'll meet us back here in a bit."

I laughed. "Okay, Louie, let's go."

The ride to the hospital was entertaining. Louie was telling me stories about Sharon's bowling technique. This hobby was news to me. Maybe she kept it from me because in the past, this was something I'd never let her live down. Instead, I thought it was cute, Louie made her happy. If the roles were reversed, I knew she'd appreciate that I was trying something new.

As I approached my dad's hospital room, I was relieved to see that he was back to himself. I listened to him flirting with the nurse, making her blush. I smirked and shook my head.

"Dad, leave her alone," I reprimanded him.

"What, Alisa, I need someone to take care of me when you're not there." His arms were out on either side of him. The nurse was laughing as she walked out.

"Vin, I'll send Jose to your house, don't worry," she said, then she winked before walking out. My dad pouted.

"So are you ready?" I asked.

"Yes. The doctor needs to sign me out. Wait, who is that?" my dad asked, pointing to Officer Daige who was now behind me.

Louie chimed in, "Her bodyguard!"

"*Porque?*" my father asked.

"They found a letter in the restaurant, and Brent wanted to make sure I was safe until they investigate it," I said nonchalantly. My dad grabbed his heart.

"The drama he has—I'm okay, Dad," I said calmly, letting him understand I was not scared and that Brent was being overbearing in his decision of me having a detail team.

"What did it say?"

"Dad, it doesn't matter, The police are taking care of it." I saw my father look at Louie to see if he knew anything about it. Louie looked at him and nodded to confirm he had no clue.

"*Bella*, come here. Tell your papa." This man knew how to get me.

I didn't want to burden him with this. The attack was too fresh. I tried to change the subject, but he was shooting daggers at me waiting for the truth. I sighed and read him the note:

Hickory Dickory Dock.
It's time to stop the clock.
Kim's necklace I hock.
Your pop is lucky to have his cock.
Your life, tick tock, tick tock.

"Well, they're right. I still have it!" he said, lifting up to his sheet playfully. We all needed that laugh.

"Good poem, but who did it?"

"I don't know pop, hence the bodyguard," I shrugged pointing at Daige.

"Your new guy got you a bodyguard?" he asked again, confused.

Up until this point, my father was my sole protector. I wasn't sure if he was pissed or pleased.

Louie smirked and tried to reassure him, "Vin, he has the resources. At least you know he cares."

"Louie, you're right, but times have changed, and this is my baby girl. She's my responsibility."

"Everyone, stop. Everything is good," I said, slightly annoyed. I was not a damsel in distress.

Thank god, Dr. Pappas came in.

"Mr. Rossi, I am happy to say you're free to go home, but no major activity for a week. I'm having Jose come to check on you with that nurse outfit you requested," he stated with a serious voice.

Coffee flew out of my mouth; my dad's face was bright red. *Good one, Doc.*

"Sorry, Doc, just having fun, didn't mean any disrespect."

The doctor laughed.

"I'm only kidding. No worries, Mr. Rossi."

The only thing that makes him that red is his homemade wine.

My father was discharged, and Louie helped my father in the car. They have created a close bond as of recently. It made me feel good. I always thought my father wanted a son. Louie was definitely filling that part these past couple of months. When we got back to the house, I made lunch for everyone. My dad kept saying "*Mangiare*" as if they knew Italian; they just kept eating and eating. I made three pounds of penne arrabbiata. Price and Daige may have eaten a pound each. Clearing off the table and washing the dishes, my mind wandered recounting the last twenty-four hours. I missed him—his smell, his touch. Is it odd to get so attached so soon? I decided to call Brent just to check in and he filled me in on the latest details of the investigation. They were putting the note through forensics for fingerprinting and asking the neighbors if they saw anything.

The tone of his voice changed when he asked if I had arranged to see him this weekend. I told him I was still working on it. An awkward silence came over the phone.

"I miss you," spilled out of my mouth before I realized what I was saying. There was silence on the other end. Oh no, mortified I went too far. He probably thought—

"Princess, I know. I miss you too."

The dead air was filled with words we weren't ready to say about feelings were weren't quite ready to admit.

"See you this weekend," I said with excitement.

"Alisa, you're staying with me this weekend," he said it like a command.

"Are you sure? I could stay with Michael. He has a spare bedroom for me." I began rambling, I didn't want to seem high maintenance. I really wanted to stay with him.

"I meant what I said about wanting to take care of you, wanting to protect you. You're staying with me…it would ease my mind," he reassured in a softer tone.

"Yes, sir," I said playfully, wanting to lighten the mood.

"I like the way you said that, princess."

I sensed the smile I was trying to get.

"I'll call you later."

I went back into the kitchen. Louie, Price, and Daige went into the den. My dad was sitting at the table waiting for me. He put down the Italian newspaper I bought him.

"Alisa, what is going on?" I knew that tone.

"Dad, I told you."

"No, I mean with Brent. You just met him, and now he thinks he can just put two guys on you. I'm not an idiot, Alisa!" He was looking for answers. He knocked the table with his knuckles in anticipation of my answer.

"No, Dad, you're not an idiot, and I didn't just meet Brent!"

"What do you mean? Have you just been keeping him from me?" he asked, surprised I never mentioned him before.

"No, Dad, let me explain." I told him about our encounter in high school. He was upset that I would show a public display of affection at that age. I was glad I was not seventeen again; otherwise, my ass would be a wonderful shade of pink right now. Then I told him about the morning after the robbery, when I saw him on the news, then in the precinct. I was not going to elaborate any more.

"And he thinks he can take the ownership of protecting you? I'm your father!" he yelled out, knuckles hitting the table again.

"Dad, I love him!" I said, blurting out those three words without even realizing what I had just confessed.

"*Lui e il mio destino,*" I said in a lower tone.

His eyes widened and he stood up putting his hand to his forehead with frustration. He was most likely hoping he misheard me. "Alisa, what do you mean he's your destiny?"

"I can't explain it, Dad. You always told me when you met mom, you knew she was the one within five minutes."

"*Ci.*"

"Well, I guess that's how I feel also," I said, my hands out in front of me, looking for his acceptance on our relationship.

"Okay, so I need to find out more, Alisa, if you are serious, and he seems to feel this way for you, too," he lowered his voice, his hands in front of him, fingers entwined.

"Alisa, I'm going to do some—what do you call it—snooping on him," he said, being serious but I couldn't help but smile. He was so cute, wanting to make sure Brent was good for me.

"If I have no choice, you do what you need to do, Papa, but don't be surprised if you don't find anything," I reassured, confident that there were no skeletons in Brent's closet that would make my dad think differently about him.

"How can you be so sure?"

"Because I just know."

"Alisa, Rossis need to think with their head, not their heart, capisce?"

If he only knew I had plans to stay with him all weekend.

"I understand, Papa, but sometimes the head and the heart are on the same page. Trust me, Papa, he is a good man. You do what you need to do. You will see I made a good choice."

"Alisa, you know you are my life. Eh, come give Papa a hug."

I was so lucky to have a dad like mine.

CHAPTER 17

Alisa went in to sit with the guys in the den. All these years keeping this part of me away from her can fall apart. I texted Louie to come in the kitchen as I came up with a plan. Something to help me finally free myself from the Marino crime family. I was just about to get to my freedom, and all of this was starting to blow up. Alisa's boyfriend was going to put another brick on my back to handle. I was happy she found someone. I saw in her eyes she was smitten with him. He will be good for her, but damn it, the timing was off. This guy wasn't just a cop; he's the fucking police commissioner. There has gotta be a way I could use this to my advantage. Louie came into the kitchen as I slammed my fist on the table.

"Hey, Vin, everything okay? How are you feeling?" He couldn't tell; this one wasn't that smart.

"Louie, I need your help." That's right, another test of his loyalty.

"Yeah, boss, what do you need?"

"Alisa is really into this commissioner. I need to find out more about him. I know Marco is still upset. He might go after her to get to me." He probably wrote the note or had one of his minions do it.

"About that, boss, I found out my brother's friend is a soldier for Marco. I think Marco may have been giving us a warning," he said as if it were a novel idea. This kid is going to be the death of me.

"Son of a bitch. If he is coming after my daughter, he's a dead man. Louie, get Carmine and the boys to snoop around, see if they can find out anything. I want to make sure what you're saying is a fact, if it was done on purpose." My knuckles hit the table again. Alisa came into the kitchen, looking at both of us as we abruptly cut our conversation.

She looked at me with the bottle of pills in her hand and ordered, "You need to take your medicine."

"You always take good care of me, *bella*," I said before kissing her hand.

"Papa, who else will? Plus you do so much for me. Times like this I get to give something back," she said with a smile and placed a kiss on my head.

I went to take a swig of my homemade wine, and she swiped it away.

"Papa, are you kidding me?"

"Let me have my wine."

"Yes, you can have your wine in seven days."

"*Porque?*"

"When you're done taking all your medicine," she said sweetly while handing me a Pellegrino and smiled.

"Alisa, you can let Brent know I could take care of you. We don't need to use his men. I'll tell your cousin to come over. He can handle anyone. He's a bouncer. I'll pay him to protect you if Brent feels you need a bodyguard."

"Dad, why? Anthony is annoying."

"Alisa, I don't know these guys," I told her as I finished peeling my clementine and put a piece in my mouth.

"Dad, they're officers," she said, shrugging.

"Exactly. Why should the taxpayers of East Hampton have to pay for your protection?" That was a quick response she couldn't argue with. I raised an honest hardworking girl—one who doesn't abuse the system—the opposite of me.

"Good point," Alisa said reluctantly.

"So it's settled then. Send the boys home and I'll call Anthony," I said trying to mask my relief. My nephew was dumb but strong, and I wouldn't have to worry about him snooping around my business.

The immediate distraction was gone. Anthony I trust; he's my own flesh and blood. Price and Daige, they could screw things up for me. I hope this commissioner doesn't interfere. It won't be good for him.

There was this feeling I got from Brent—something about him that was familiar. I knew Louie would do a thorough check on Mr. Brent Collins. I needed someone like Louie to be by my side during this time. He turned out to be a great asset; he told me everything. I mean he was dating my daughter's best friend, who I cared for like one of my own. The poor kid, always dating the wrong guys. I couldn't tell you how many times I needed to take care of issues that arose. No, I didn't kill them, but they may have shat their pants when Anthony took them in the alley. So Louie was no exception. I needed to make sure he wouldn't cause any problems. The informants told me he was like the artful dodger, pickpocketing, stealing the donation jars, in and out of juvi—perfect for what I will need him for. My little assistant, sometimes a distraction for the enemy. I mean I like the kid, but he was expendable.

Realistically, the only one who mattered to me was my daughter. I was really proud of her accomplishments. Her mother would have been proud too. She always strived for what she wanted and did what she needed to do to get there.

If Alisa ever found out what I did for a living, she would be very disappointed in her old man. She knew I owned the pizza place but what she didn't know was that the restaurant was given to me as a front for Mario to launder money. Alisa was also in the dark about the drama with my brother-in-law, Carmine, who changed his last name to protect himself. Mario thought it would have been best for Carmine to use my last name. So when I was made in the family, I gave the restaurant to him. Now he goes by Carmine Rossi, next in line to become the head of the family once Marco is removed.

I knew Marco would be angry. I had no idea he would go as low as to bash my head in. I'll be home for a couple of days. I should get my defenses ready for the retaliation. I needed the information on Brent from Louie. I needed to make sure he would not cause more danger for Alisa. She was good at hiding her true fears, but I knew she was scared. Normally she wouldn't have fought off having protection. Especially her cousin Anthony. Marco was going to pay for this. If he was the one who left the note, threatening my daughter's life and having her live in fear, he's a dead man.

CHAPTER 18

Brent

"Doherty, thanks for the update. See if you can get a clearer picture of the suspect."

We got a huge break in the case when the florist came forward with footage of an individual entering and leaving the restaurant between the window Michael gave us.

"No problem, Commissioner, I'll get right on it."

I heard the radio station play "Versace on the Floor." My thoughts wandered back to the other night. Alisa looked fabulous in that dress. The way the light from the moon hit her face. The way she felt in my arms and the look she gave me when I entered her—a moment I will never forget. The way we could effortlessly talk for hours, it just felt meant to be.

Once I snapped out of my thoughts, the day just flew by. I looked at my watch; it's seven o'clock in the evening. My cell started to ring. Alisa's phone number flashed on my phone.

"Hello, Alisa."

"Oh, sorry, I must have the wrong number. This can't be my sweet Brent, could it?" Oops, looks like she didn't appreciate my emotionless professional tone.

"Hello, princess," I said, trying to restart the conversation.

"Much better. Am I bothering you?" She giggled.

"No, just ending the day. What can I help you with?"

"Well, my dad is uncomfortable with Price and Daige. He is sending my cousin over who used to be a bouncer in some Manhattan club over to protect me."

"Alisa, my guys are trained. I feel safer with them protecting you while I am not around."

"Brent. What happens if it gets out that the East Hampton commissioner is overstepping his power to protect his lover?"

I couldn't help but smirk at her comment. "Lover, huh. How about the woman I deeply care about, enjoy her company, and will always be my princess?" Where the hell did that come from? I was convinced that I was whipped for sure. There was an awkward silence.

"Alisa, are you there?" I said, making sure she didn't hang up.

"Yes, you mean that much to me too."

"I know, *bella*." I hope I said it right.

"Taking up Italian, Romeo?" She giggled.

"Actually, just brushing up." And the awkwardness dissipated.

"Good news, we recovered some footage from the florist next door of the suspect leaving your restaurant. Are you available to come tomorrow to look over the enhanced footage and answer some questions on the record?" *Please say yes.* I missed her soft lips.

"Sorry, Brent, I can't. Dad can't leave the house for a couple of days."

"Remember, you're coming this weekend" I anxiously reminded her.

Please don't disappoint me. I can barely hold myself together. I just wanted to jump in the car and go to her. I am 6'5", 250 pounds of muscle; people in the force call me "iron man," but here I was being a delicate flower around this woman. Oh, what has this woman done to me? There was a time where I thought I would buy a house, get a dog, and on the weekends, fish and golf. A man of simple pleasures. The past couple of days I've been thinking more about having a family, a house with a swimming pool, and coming home every day to Alisa. She would have dinner waiting for me, and I would have her for dessert later on at night. I wanted her with me all the time. I mean who wouldn't want the one they love to be with them? *Love.* I know I'll never lose her again and that no other man will have her.

"Yes, I'll be there. Anthony is going to stay with my father."

I was waiting for her to tell me who will be escorting her considering Anthony was with her father. Did she really think I didn't catch that? Okay, I'll play this game.

"Does that mean you'll be without an escort on your journey? Hmm?"

"True, Brent. Do you have enough room for me, you, and Anthony in your bed? Hmmm?"

"Point taken," I said as I shook my head. That was a quick defeat.

"Brent, I can drive to East Hampton by myself," she said, huffing like a child. I knew she was crossing her arms over her chest.

"I don't like it, Alisa. I will pick you up." I figured I'd try.

"Brent, you're working Friday, and I'll be in the restaurant. After work you can meet me at Sicilia's. I'll make you dinner, and then you can bring me home to your place."

I liked the sound of that. She was so demanding and feisty.

"Fine. Princess, you're very demanding, you know."

"You know, I could say the same about you, Mister My Men Are Trained."

Touché. I smirked. "You're—"

She interrupted me, "Watch it, the next thing you say—"

"Perfect, princess," I spurted out.

"You're not so bad yourself, my knight. Do you think you can keep me locked up in the castle?"

"Would you have an issue with that?"

"No, at least for the weekend anyway."

We already had the best banter. Her giggle was my new favorite sound. It's so contagious.

"Babe, I need to get to the restaurant in Port Jeff before it closes. Sophia needs my help."

"Alisa, I think I like you." I didn't want to stop talking to her.

"I think I like you too, Brent, really. Get off the phone."

"Oh, that hurt," I said, holding my chest.

"Big baby." She kissed me through the phone and then hung up.

I was looking at my phone when Jen walked in. "Special Agent Stewart Vogel is on line 1."

"Thanks."

"Detective Doherty says he got a clearer picture," she informed me, looking at me with a smile.

I just nodded back and noticed she missed quite a few buttons on her shirt.

"He's putting it through the New York system to find a match," Jen said as she dropped her pencil on the floor in front of me and leaned down to pick it up. Confused, I picked up Special Agent Vogel's line and ignored the fact it was taking a little more time than usual to pick up the pencil.

"Anymore leads on the robbery?"

"Well, we actually have more activity at Sicilia's. My people tell me you're dating Alisa now."

What the hell, and the way he said it made me so angry. He did not even say hello first.

"How?"

"Tell me about the letter, Commissioner."

He knew about the letter. Who were his people? This was ridiculous.

"Okay, Vogel, it's time to let me know what you know."

"Not over the phone, Collins."

I should have known better tha to ask over the phone.

"Tomorrow?" he asked.

"Yes."

"Meet me in Southampton at the McDonald's on North Sea Road at 8:00 a.m."

"McDonald's, 8:00 a.m.," I repeated.

Stewart Vogel, what a character, but he's holding back. He knew something that was a big key to this investigation. I guess I will just need to wait until tomorrow. I have a list of questions for him. How did he know about me and Alisa? Any background knowledge on

Louie? Something about him just didn't sit right with me. I hope Vogel was ready to shell out some valuable intel.

I walked out of the office, turned the corner, and heard the commotion. There was a crowd around the front desk. I heard Jen talking in excited tones to someone. As I approached the station, there she was—Kim Killian walking toward me with her entourage. This actress sure did play it up. Five foot four, maybe one hundred pounds soaking wet, needed four bodyguards and her personal assistant.

"Commissioner Collins, do you have a couple of minutes to talk?" She reached out to grab my arm. I really wanted to get something to eat and go to the bathroom. It's 8:30 p.m., and I hadn't eaten all day, but…

"Of course, Ms. Killian."

"Thank you, Commissioner Collins."

"Right this way." I motioned my hand toward my office.

"Please take a seat."

"No, thank you, this shouldn't take that much of your time."

I sat back down before asking her to fill me in. If this does take a while, at least I'll be comfortable.

"My insurance company needs a police report and a status on the investigation. You see, Commissioner, the necklace was one of a kind. I bought it from a museum. It is dated back from the 1800s. It was once part of the royal family jewels of France," she explained before pausing, expecting to see my jaw drop to the floor. I knew I had to play it up to match her energy. These celebrities are so predictable.

"Wow, Ms. Killian, you don't say!" It was all I could do to not roll my eyes.

"Mr. Collins, I have a very radical and expensive taste. It's worth $2.5 million," her eyes darted back to me for my reaction.

"Well, Kim, Ms. Killian, we have not found it. But the case is developing and after some events that have recently occurred, we put out a memo to all the pawn shops. There was a letter found from who we can only assume is the suspect claiming that they have hocked your necklace. While I cannot guarantee the necklace will be found, we believe there is a strong chance of finding who may have stolen it."

"Commissioner, that's bittersweet news."

"Why would that be bittersweet?"

"Well, I won't get paid out until the investigation is over. Sure, I love the necklace and want to find it, but I don't want to get it back destroyed either. The necklace will be worthless, depreciated in value."

I understood her thought process. It still left me confused. Did she want it back? "Well, I will write up the report and investigation remarks and have it ready for you by Friday." That was the best I could do.

"Well, I intend to still be in town. I need to discuss the effects of the robbery with my partner. Have you met her yet. Alisa Rossi? You know she is single?"

"Yes, I have met her. I have an appointment with her in the upcoming days."

"I hope the robbery did not have a negative impact on the restaurant. She has worked so hard. She is one of the most business-savvy women I know. Brains and beauty, a man's dream come true, Mr. Collins."

"You are correct, Ms. Killian."

"Please call me Kim. Please come by the restaurant this weekend. Dinner will be on me. With all your hard work, that is the least I can do."

"Thank you for your offer, Kim. I will try to make it. I do have plans this weekend."

"I will have my personal assistant come by Friday to pick up the report, Mr. Collins. Hope to see you again."

"Please call me Brent. I will have everything ready by noon on Friday."

"Thank you for your time, Brent." She sashayed out of my office as her entourage followed in precession. I smiled at the thought of her trying to set me up with Alisa. She was right about one thing. Alisa was beautiful and smart. Smiling, I cleared my desk and headed home.

I was famished. I looked in my refrigerator for something to eat. It was completely empty. In all of the excitement from last week I hadn't had the time to go shopping. My housekeeper, Mary, would usually pick up my groceries for me, but I completely blanked on sending her a list.

Luckily, Alisa isn't the only one who can put something together in the kitchen. I tossed together some leftover pasta with oil and garlic and some broccoli and headed into the living room to watch some television.

Flipping through the channels, I saw headlines of Kim Killian's Jewel Heist on TMZ. I lingered to listen to the tabloid's hairbrained theory. They thought it may be her actor boyfriend Jamie Worman, something about jealousy of fame and fortune.

I leaned back on the couch with my eyes closed and realized that Alisa would be staying over this weekend and a sense of panic washed over me. I sprung up and I looked around the house thinking about what she would think of it. The house cleaner was coming Friday morning, so no worries there. I needed to text to let her know I was having company over this weekend. I know she will apply her feminine touch and stock up on anything that will make Alisa feel more at home.

> Mary,
>   Having a house guest, trying to impress, please add special touches—flowers, candles, chocolates, champagne. No limit, just add it to the monthly bill.
>   Brent

I realized it's 11:00 p.m. I hope I didn't wake her. Looks like she was up because less than one minutes later:

> Brent,
>   Female guest, I suppose if she could be the one. I'll make it romantic and extra clean. Red or yellow roses?

She was always on me to find someone. She even tried to set me up. It was her niece's friend. I think she was once a truck driver with that mouth. She used any curse word as an adjective. It was f—— beautiful. No f—— way. Unbelievable, no wonder she was still single. I mean she was really pretty. We had a good time and all, but not someone you'd take home to Mother. I texted Mary back.

>   Yes, Mary, she is special. Red roses please.
>   Please fill the fridge up with fruits and vegetables.
>   Thank you.

My mind was once again consumed with thoughts of her. I wanted to hear her voice, but then again a midnight phone call might wake her up. Hm, a text is a temporary fix for my craving.

Sweet dreams, princess!

You're still up. Big kiss, my knight.

Put me in your fantasies tonight.

Haven't stopped since I was seventeen. Dream of me. XO

Knowing that I'm on her mind was enough to send me into a slumber, dreaming of all the tomorrows ahead with my princess.

I was waiting for Special Agent Stewart Vogel at the McDonald's. I haven't been in a McDonald's in years. The coffee wasn't that bad. He came in wearing a cap, looking like he was going to play a couple holes of golf.

"Collins."

"Vogel. What do you got for me?" I cut straight to the point. I needed this case solved and Alisa safe. I wanted to put this all behind us and start our lives together without the mafia breathing down our necks.

"Well, my guys tell me that the attack on Alisa's father wasn't what they say it was. It looks like Marco Futzelli had something to do with it.

"Mark, I mean Brent." Vogel just stared at me.

I tried not to look as shocked as I felt. How did he know my given name? I had to change it for my safety years ago. I furrowed my brow and asked, "You know about me Vogel?"

"Yes, you are known back at the agency, Mark. You took the baby steps to get the big fish. You're legendary. Your courage is admirable," he said, nodding his head out of respect.

"Do your guys know who I am?" It was a question I needed to ask.

"Yes."

"Tell me who it is." If they know me, I should know them.

"Mark, you know I can't."

Yes, you can.

"Vogel, my name is Brent Collins. Under the current circumstances, you can understand that the name Mark Tilman cannot be used." All I needed was for someone to put the face and the name Mark together.

"Understood. Brent," he said, silently apologizing.

"How deep is he in?" I thought it's Louie who was his informant. He was the closest to Vinny and was always around.

"We are about a month away from taking down the whole family."

"You're referring to the Marinos?" I was amazed by the ambition. This family felt nearly untouchable when I was on the case all of those years ago.

"Yes," he said without following up with further explanation. Typical FBI, one-word answers, trying to leave me in the dark as much as possible.

"Tell me more."

"Not this time, Mar—Brent."

"You find out who wrote the note? Stewart, is Alisa safe?" I asked plainly. *Please tell me yes.* I can't have anything happen to her.

"Just keep a detail on her even though her cousin is coming. Marco isn't happy." He knew about Anthony.

"Understood. One week from today, same place."

Vogel nodded and got up to leave.

"Vogel, thanks."

"Brent," he said as he lifted his cap.

I needed to know more. Alisa was in danger. Her dad, he had to be connected somehow. I wondered who Vogel's other cover was. I assumed one of them was definitely Louie; he knew about the cousin.

Trying to connect the dots as I made my way back to the station, I realized the antique store was on the way. I remember spotting a little locket when I strolled through a few months ago. It caught my eye, but at the time I didn't have anyone to buy it for. During my impromptu pitstop, my phone buzzed. Someone's ears must've been ringing.

It was a text from Alisa that sent me into a laughing fit, prompting the cashier to laugh along at the spectacle.

It was a photo of a knight climbing to reach the top of Rapunzel's tower pantless, followed by, "I did dream of you last night," the text read. She sent me a picture, or GIF, of Rapunzel and the knight climbing up to get her.

Only you would find this picture. I like your caption. You're mine now, Alisa.

Yes, yours, Brent, always. XX

Yes, all mine.

See you tomorrow, my knight. XX

Counting down the seconds. XX

With the freshly wrapped locket in tow, I thanked the saleslady on my way out. She told me Alisa must be a keeper because I couldn't stop smiling. She was right.

I headed back to the station and put the gift in my desk drawer. For nearly thirty minutes, I sat there doodling trying to come up with the right words. I didn't want to come on too strong, but my affection for her was pouring out of me. The list of options scribbled on my desk included the following:

> Love, Brent
> Your Brent
> Brent XX
> Hopelessly devoted, Brent

Why was I making this so difficult for myself? I was scared shitless of my feelings for her. Yes, everything was moving quickly but I felt like I've known her for years. We just fit together. I decided not to play any games. She would appreciate the truth. I bit the bullet and in pen signed the card "Love, Brent."

CHAPTER 19

Alisa

My cousin Anthony arrived an hour ago. He already made himself comfortable. I passed by the bedroom that I set up for him. Clothes were scattered on the bed, four bottles of cologne on the chest, and a box of trojans. It didn't end there. It seemed that Anthony had helped himself to my once fully-stocked refrigerator. Looks like I'll need to be ordering groceries to be delivered before my dad uses this as an opportunity to order pizza. Add that to the to-do-list before I can make my way to East Hampton to spend the weekend with Brent.

I shook my head as Anthony approached me with a smirk on his face. Anthony was like a son to my father and a pain-in-the-ass big brother I never wanted. When we were growing up, he always pestered me. Sadly, things have not changed in terms of his maturity level. He still acted like he was sixteen—messy and loud with an endless amount of perverted jokes.

"Get away, Antonee," I said, using my Queens accent.

"Uncle Vin said I can't leave your side." He shrugged his shoulders with his hands out.

"Really? I doubt he wanted you to go to the bathroom with me." I love my cousin. I really do, but he can be such a dumbass. No wonder he couldn't find a good woman to take care of him. He would be a lot of work.

"Umm, no, Alisa," he replied slowly.

The light bulb went off, ladies and gentlemen.

"Okay, back off. Let me use the bathroom in peace."

"Okay, but—"

I cut him off. "Listen, I'm going back to East Hampton tonight, and you are not coming, got it?" I stated explicitly, giving him my stink eye.

"Ohhh, I'm going with you. Uncle Vin said—"

I twisted his ear like our grandma used to do when we didn't listen. I laughed so hard; he started laughing too. He started to tickle me like we were twelve again.

"Stop or I'll pee all over you."

"Okay. Do you remember Atomic Anthony, cuz?"

"No, Antonee, don't you dare. I swear I will—"

He lifted me over his shoulder and body-slammed me on the couch. I couldn't believe he just did that. I couldn't stop laughing. With all the commotion, my father walked in.

"Anthony, you are supposed to protect her from other people." My dad looked around and put his hands on his waist. Here we go. The lecture.

"Are you two pretending to be wrestlers again? Last time you two did that, you both had bruises all over you. Anthony, do you remember when Alisa pulled down your pants in front of your *nonna*?" he reminded him as he shook his head and barked out a laugh.

Anthony and I used to watch professional wrestling all the time when we were kids. I'd put him in a head lock, and he would lift me and slam me on the couch. We both looked at each other and laughed even harder. One time I was so mad that he was winning, I pulled down his pants. My *nonna* came in and saw Anthony's hairy butt. She told him he looked like a gorilla and to shave it immediately.

"Dad, how are you feeling?"

"Good, like new," he exclaimed, beating his chest like Tarzan.

"I'm going to East Hampton tonight, and I am staying with Brent. I don't need Anthony."

"You're driving in? Anthony will drive you to Brent's, then call him when you're ready to come home."

I knew this wasn't going to be easy. He was so stubborn.

"Ah, no. I'll drive. I need my car. I have to go to the restaurant. Don't worry. Brent will have people watching me once I'm in East Hampton."

"Alisa, just have Anthony follow you to the restaurant or Brent's house. Just make Papa happy, would you? Don't make this difficult." There was a twinkle in his eye.

"Dad, if it makes you happy, I guess I have no choice."

I didn't need him to follow me. Anthony playfully stuck his tongue out at me. I couldn't help but laugh to see a 6'2", 285-pound grizzled man with a trimmed goatee stick out his tongue as if he was five years old.

"Antonee, we are leaving in an hour. I have to stop by Sicilia's in Port Jeff first," I said calmly, trying to be cordial about the whole thing.

I started to pack my suitcase. I just realized I will be at his house for the weekend. I hope he was not one of those typical bachelors. He didn't seem to be that way, the type of person to keep a dirty home. I looked through my closet for some sexy underwear and different outfits for work. I should bring some everyday clothes and my bathing suit. I'm not sure what he has planned. I packed my makeup, toothbrush, and other toiletries. I thought about bringing an extra bag of things to keep at his house with how things are progressing, but I didn't just in case it scared him off.

Finally in my car and headed to the restaurant, I was so pleased to see the Port Jeff location alive and well. A loaded parking lot, crowds of families making their way in. Weekends were always a hit. Friday nights were for the tourists and the college kids. Many of the locals came to have their dinner and take a walk around the marina. Tonight, the actor from *Karate Kid* was bringing some friends to the restaurant; he's a loyal customer. I have his autograph lined up with other movie stars and celebrities who have visited.

I walked in, and Sophia was talking to a silver-haired fox, and I mean a real damn good-looking man. She was glowing, hanging on to his every word as he spoke. He was built like a twenty-five-year-old but must've been in his mid-forties. They looked very familiar. She turned her head and saw me.

"Hi, Alisa, this is my friend Stewart." Her hand was on his arm.

"Hi, Stewart, Alisa Rossi," I said, reaching my hand out. "I hope you enjoyed your meal."

"Yes, I did. I was just asking Sophia if we could have some dessert together, later." I knew that smirk.

Before I realized this might be a mutual flirt, I blurted out "Oh, I see. Unfortunately, I think Sophia is working until 10:00 p.m. tonight." Yes, he was hot, but there looked like there was a major age difference between them. I would guess Sophia is about thirty.

"Oh, Alisa, I am willing to wait," he said, winking at me.

Sophia's eyes widened, and I felt the heat between them. He reached over to kiss Sophia's hand. He strode by the bar and took a seat. Sophia followed him with her eyes. She liked him. I interrupted her train of thought.

"Sophia, are we ready for Ralph's reservation?"

"Yes, he called to confirm. Oh, and Kim will be in East Hampton to go over the books."

"Good. I will be in East Hampton later if you need me."

"How's your dad?" she asked, tilting her head waiting for an answer.

"Good, thank you." She was so sweet. "So are you having dessert later?"

"Yes, he is, well, Alisa, he might be the man for me." She started to blush.

"Good. My mother used to tell me that a good woman will always find a good man. I am happy for you."

"Thank you. One day you will feel the same way."

I headed into the kitchen as I saw Stewart get up from the bar to go to Sophia. She looked happy. How stupid I was making him wait to have dessert with her. *Ohhhhh, dessert.* I giggled to myself, now I got it.

I thought about me and Brent. I guess you could say we were in a relationship. Brent was one of the most thoughtful, good men I have ever met. Destiny had brought us back together. His words were ingrained in my head: "I will never lose you again."

Those words were more than words but a promise. I didn't want to lose him either. I wondered what destiny had planned for us. I grabbed my phone to text him that I was leaving.

I'll be leaving in fifteen minutes to see the most amazing man. Your Alisa XX

He didn't reply right away; it's not like him. Maybe he was in a meeting. I got into my car and saw Anthony was behind me. The Mustang roared, and he gave me the thumbs-up. He has always made me laugh, the biggest dumbass teddy bear I knew.

We were on the Sunrise Highway, and the traffic began to die down. It was time to get my freedom from all this "protection." My father and Brent would be furious if they knew what I had up my sleeve, but I don't need someone to shadow me to my destination. A group of cars had just exited the highway, and there was plenty of room to roam. I saw an opportunity for me to use the speed this car had to make my escape. I waved to Anthony in my rearview mirror and gunned it. I was two exits ahead of him, what a thrill. I looked in the rearview for a second time, and I couldn't help but notice there was a Maserati on my ass. It happened all the time. Macho men couldn't help but want to race me—a certain need for speed, I guess. I was riding high from losing my tail—what's another race? I moved closer to my steering wheel and pushed the pedal to the floor.

"Screw you, Maserati," I said to myself with a playful smile. Suddenly my car jerked forward. I looked back, and that son of a bitch hit me. My temper ignited. My foot was on the gas. I looked in my mirror again to see if Anthony caught up to me. He was nowhere in sight. I may have made a mistake. Anthony would have been helpful to have right now. The Maserati was weaving in and out of lanes to get to me again. What the hell! My senses heightened and I was in full panic mode. My eyes kept darting from the road to the rearview mirror, watching him gain on me. I felt helpless. Not even triple-digit speeds could lose this guy. He pulled up to the left of my car, and slammed into me, making me lose control of the wheel. My car flew off of the highway and crash-landed into the Pine Barrens Reservation. I felt my body slamming against the steering wheel and the pressure from the airbag, followed by complete darkness.

CHAPTER 20

Brent

I was going over quarterly budgets in my office. My least favorite part of the job. These boring reports would consume entire days. When I finally was able to come up for air, I realized the sun had set, and it was dark outside. How could it be nine o'clock? It had been hours since Alisa told me she was headed my way. I reread "Your Alisa" several times and smiled. She should have been here or at least texted me that she was safe. I didn't even have a missed call. An uneasy feeling overcame me. Maybe they were swamped at the restaurant, and she couldn't sneak away to give me an update. Trying my best to not think the worst, I called up Sicilia's to get some answers. Michael picked up after four rings; they must be busy.

"Welcome to Sicilia's," Michael's cheerful voice comes through the phone.

"Hey, Michael, it's Brent. Commissioner Collins," I said, not sure which name to use.

"Hey, Brent. It's kind of busy. Can I call you back?" This was a good sign; she probably didn't call me because she's busy. Relief.

"It's okay. I need to speak with Alisa."

"Brent, she is not here. She was supposed to cover my shift tonight. I have a date. Plus, Kim is waiting to talk to her."

My anxiety kept building.

"What time did she tell you she would be there?"

"Seven thirty. I knew she was coming to see you first, so I thought maybe you two just lost track of time…you know," he said before, whispering "shit" under his breath.

The realization that something was off hit the both of us. After that note in her office, this could be something really bad. She could be in danger. I slammed my fist on the desk, sending the pencils and reports flying and scattering across the floor.

"I know. I'm concerned too. If she gets there, have her call me. Call me if you find anything out." I gave Michael my cell number.

I went to call her phone; maybe she broke down. I tried to think logically about this. If she would have just let Price and Daige pick her up and drive her here. I shouldn't have let her send my guys home. Who was I kidding? She's a fighter. I would have lost the battle. I tried her cell; it rang only once before going to voicemail. The panic continued to build. My next call was to Sicilia's Port Jeff location.

"Hi, this is Brent, Alisa's…" I paused. I was not sure what I was to her. I knew she was mine, but…"boyfriend," I said it fast.

"Oh, hi, Brent. This is Sophia." Oh, that's right, the manager for Port Jeff. She seemed to know who I was, maybe Alisa has been spreading news about the man in her life.

"Is Alisa there?" I asked, trying not to sound panicked.

"No, Brent, she left around five thirty, I think. She texted you before she left. Is everything okay?" Her voice sounded concerned.

"No one has seen her yet." I was freaking out. *Calm down, Collins* was now the mantra blaring in my head. I slammed my fist on my desk again. The remainder of the reports fell to the ground.

"Is Anthony there? Anthony was following her around," she questioned.

"She drove herself?" I was now confused; that was not the plan. Why would she not follow the plan?

"Yes, but Anthony, her cousin, was following her."

I felt a little relief; at least he followed her. Why didn't she call me to tell me about the change in plans? Maybe they went out for dinner. Wishful thinking.

"Thank you, Sophia. I am going to give you my cell number. Call me if you hear from her."

"Will do. Have her call me too so I don't worry. This is not like her."

I gave her my cell number and put my head on my desk. Where the hell was she? I called her house, hoping someone picked up. God damn voicemail. I called my connections in Southampton, Riverhead, and Suffolk County. I knew I had to wait twenty-four hours for a missing person, but if I had the resources, why not use them? Each station patched me through to their commissioner, which were all great friends of mine. They knew this was serious. I described her car, BMW Spyder; her look, petite with brown hair and hazel eyes. I was filled with dread. Whenever I work on a missing persons case, it ends in one of two ways. My heart couldn't take it if things went wrong. I leaned back in my chair, and I began to plot out my next steps. I had to take my emotions out of it; if I didn't treat this like a case, I might miss a clue.

The phone rang and took me out of my thoughts. Sicilia's Port Jefferson restaurant's phone number popped up on my phone. A sigh of relief came over me.

"Alisa, thank—"

"Brent," a man's voice came on the line.

"It's Vinny, Alisa's father." My heart stopped.

"Sophia said that Alisa isn't there yet." I heard the concern in his voice.

"No, sir, she is not."

"*Shit!*" he screamed into the phone.

"Anthony came back home because she was so far ahead of him that he just turned around and came back here." He sounded pissed.

"What exit, Vin? What time? Why would he do that?" My heart was beating so fast. I knew this was a bad idea having an untrained security on her.

"Not sure. I will call you back, Brent. I'll get more information from my nephew. Call me if you hear from her. I'll be at the Port Jeff restaurant."

He hung up, I hurried to clean up the mess I made on the floor. I had bigger worries than these reports. The mayor would just have to wait until next week. Jen had already left for the day, so I had to shoot her a text letting her know I'd be out tomorrow unexpectedly. Once I locate Alisa, I won't be leaving her side for days.

> Jen,
>
> Something came up. I will not be in tomorrow. Reschedule my appointments for Tuesday. Have a good weekend.
>
> Brent

> Brent,
>
> Is there anything I can do to help? The reports, do you need me to send them? What time do I meet you for the Riverhead Town picnic on Sunday?
>
> Jen

The Riverhead Town picnic? I shook my head, I never agreed to go with her. I told the entire team that I would be meeting them there. Anyway, I had already told the commissioner that I would not be able to make it since I blocked out my weekend to be with Alisa.

> Jen,
>
> I will not be going to the picnic. Enjoy yourself with the team. I will take care of the reports next week. Thanks.
>
> Brent

I thought—okay, see you Tuesday. Jen

I got in the car and just started traveling out west. I must find her. I told her I would protect her and never lose her again. I never go back on my promises.

I needed to start thinking positive. Negative thoughts brought negative outcomes. I smirked, remembering what my father told me when I was trying out for the football team in high school. He was right. Think positive and positive actions will follow. I started to calm myself. She probably had a flat, and roadside service was changing it. Her phone was on "do not disturb." She needed to clear her mind and went to the beach to walk around. All these thoughts entered my mind.

Looking on either side of me driving down Montauk highway, the radio was playing oldies, and Justin Bieber's "One Less Lonely Girl" started to play.

"Don't need these other pretty faces like I need you and when you are mine in the world," I sang along and realized that was exactly how I felt. I put that on my playlist. I decided to hit the streets to look for her car. The moon was now high in the sky, and the stars were twinkling bright. I had a little smile knowing that we were looking at the same moon.

Pessimistic thoughts crept back into my brain. What if she's out there scared, or hurt, or worse? A tear rolled down my face. I quickly wiped it away, not allowing those thoughts to overwhelm my mind. I squeezed the steering wheel tighter and with a knot in my throat said, "I'm coming for you, princess."

CHAPTER 21

Alisa

I woke up with a chill on my face. *Where the hell am I?* I looked down. It's pitch-black outside. My head was pounding, and I felt sore. I stretched out my hand and felt around to give me some sense of where I was. I felt dirt, leaves, and sticks. I touched the ache on my head—blood. *What the hell happened?*

I tried to remember what I was doing. I looked around trying to understand my surroundings. It's so dark, and I couldn't see a thing. I noticed my right leg was bleeding. Excruciating pain was shooting throughout my body. I ripped a piece of my shirt and wrapped it around my leg to try and stop the bleeding. I was in a wooded area surrounded by trees that were so thick, their branches wouldn't let the moon shine through. I heard the leaves rustling with the wind and soon the air was filled with sounds of crickets chirping.

I found a rock, sat, and tried to gather my thoughts. *What the hell happened? How did I get here, and where is here?* I was getting frustrated. *Where's my bag, phone, car?* I felt around to find it so I could call someone. I got up from the rock. Pain started to shoot up and down my body. This was not good. I let the pain subside and tried to remember how I got here.

I remember taking the Long Island Expressway and then hopping on Sunrise Highway with Anthony close behind. I remembered making a break for it and speeding off ahead. Things were getting blurry after that. I remember feeling scared and in danger...oh my god, the Maserati! That friggin' Maserati surged right into me. A chill went through my body. That wasn't your average case of road rage. It must've been connected to that note on my desk. I looked up into the dark sky and did the sign of the cross to thank God that I was still alive. I tried to get up again, but my head started to spin. Maybe I should stay put for a while. It would be safer to find a little shelter and wait until sunrise.

I have never felt more alone. Here I was, in the darkness, stuck with my thoughts. My head was foggy, and it hurt trying to think about how this could've happened to me. Survival and finding civilization needed to be my priority. Not licking my wounds. Someone must be looking for me.

"Brent!" I called out.

He must be freaking out and not too happy about the way things have played out since shaking my details. I laid my head back against the tree and rested my eyes to help diffuse the pounding in my head and started to fall asleep.

The dawn lightened the sky and the sun's rays peeking through the pines woke me. I looked around to get a better understanding where I was, if there was an obvious way to an exit. All I saw were trees and brush. I looked down at my leg; it stopped bleeding, but it hurt. I touched my head and had some scratches and bruises, but I felt okay. I found a branch and used it as a cane. Those *National Geographic* shows were coming into use as I headed toward the sunrise. It's a slow pace, but I managed.

The thought came to mind I must be in the Pine Barrens. I looked around to try to find my car or any of my belongings. This was frustrating. I shouldn't have ghosted Anthony. I must have walked fifty feet when I stopped abruptly. I heard noises. Someone was coming. They were looking for me. A wave of relief washed over me. I started to scream for help and stopped. All I had was this branch. What happens if the driver of the Maserati was trying to finish the job? Panic returned and I started desperately looking for a place to hide. I went behind a bush; the noise was coming closer. I could hear footsteps crunching leaves on the forest floor. *Take a deep breath, Alisa. Everything will be fine.* The footsteps continued to grow closer. I looked around for a rock to use as a weapon and tightened my fingers around it until the tips turned white.

I was scared out of mind. My back was against the tree, and my eyes were closed, listening for movement. Everything went quiet, so I peeked out from behind the tree, hoping to spot someone or something nearby. I started at the forest floor and worked my way up. My heart was pounding out of my chest with anticipation. Did I have the strength to defend myself? I guess I would just have to find out.

I panned over to the left and squealed. It was a deer. I let out a deep breath and nearly fell to the ground in relief. The deer was unphased by my fear and continued her travels, stopping every now and then to eat the vegetation in front of her. I got my breathing regulated, shook my head, and wiped a tear that fell down my face and continued my journey.

It seemed I have been walking for miles at this point. I didn't see my car or my belongings. I couldn't make out a path that would lead me out of the forest I was trapped in. I was starting to lose hope. The pain in my leg started to tingle, and my stomach started to grumble. I hadn't eaten since yesterday morning. I started becoming hyper aware of my body. My mouth was dry, and I started to feel my body get heavier with every step, getting weaker with every passing minute.

Raising my head, the aroma of smoke was in the air. I saw smoke ahead, hoping the car was the cause. I brought myself up to my feet and headed toward it.

My legs were giving out, so I sat for a second to reenergize. I used this time to think. Brent was probably looking for me. Out of habit, I reached in my back pocket for my phone. Empty. My dad, he must be in a panic too. And poor Michael, I never showed up to cover his shift, which is so unlike me. I know they're all worried sick, but once they find me I know they'll be wagging their fingers at me for acting childish. My thoughts went back to Brent.

He must be going crazy. I knew he cared for me. This thing that was between us was strong and was scary that it was going so fast. The steps in a developing relationship should be slow. That's what my dad says, but for us, it's at asteroid speed. I knew I was in love with him, and after this near-death experience, I needed to tell him. First, I needed to get the hell out of this forest. I straightened up and furrowed my brow. I had a mission—get to safety and confess my love to Brent.

I started to move again toward the smoke. I reached where there was a ditch with white powder everywhere. What the hell? I looked and saw my BMW plates on the ground. Holy crap. My car, it must have exploded. How did this happen? My body tightened, I started to hyperventilate. Oh my god! Everyone must think I was dead. I started to feel faint, gasping for air looking frantically for my phone in the debris. I looked down at my leg and watched the makeshift bandage I made soak with blood. My steps grew smaller, I started to feel weak, but I heard cars. I couldn't be that far off from the main road. I heard faint voices coming from the tree line. I screamed for help but because my throat was dry, it came out as a raspy whisper. It was painful, but I desperately needed medical attention. I kept calling out, waving one arm, hoping to be spotted and ushered to safety.

Suddenly, everything around me turned black.

CHAPTER 22

Brent

It's been some time since I heard from Vinny. I decided to call him at midnight, not giving a shit if I woke him up. He needed to understand I will always be a part of his daughter's life. I called Alisa's house phone and rather than Alisa's sweet voice on the other end, it was Vinny.

"Vin, what did Anthony say?" I asked, annoyed.

"He lost her on Sunrise Highway. He can't remember what exit."

"Shit!" I cursed.

"Why didn't he just follow her?" My temper was rising.

"Alisa made a comment to him last night and thought she would be fine by herself. So while he was following her, she sped up and lost him. You know the traffic going out there. There was no way he would have caught up, so he turned around and came back here." I could tell he was still trying to wake up from my disturbance. Well, tough shit.

"Son of a bitch. I've been driving all night trying to find her, Vin." He's sleeping, and I was fuming with frustration.

"Call me when you find her."

No shit, Vin.

"Where is Anthony now?"

"In Queens taking care of his father's business."

My jaw clenched tighter, saliva was dripping from my mouth like a bulldog.

"Go back to bed, Vin. I'll call you when I find her."

"My daughter is missing. You think I'm sleeping? I've been up all night, waiting for a phone call to tell me where she is. You think so little of me that I could sleep when my daughter is missing? You have some nerve thinking that way." I heard a fist slam the table and some words spoken in Italian. By the way he was screaming, I could tell they were not nice.

"I wasn't implying you were not concerned about your daughter, sir. I will call you if I find out anything. Good night, sir." I ended the call, realizing I just woke up the bear within him.

I drove on the side streets of the Hamptons working my way toward Sunrise Highway, every so often dropping in a coffee shop or store and showing them a picture of Alisa I took. Her beautiful face. The man at the gas station recognized her from *Dean's Paper* as the restaurant owner of Sicilia's where Kim Killian's necklace was stolen.

I hopped on Sunrise Highway, listening to music trying to keep awake. The sun started to rise when I saw activity on the eastbound side of the road, flashing lights grabbed my attention. Could all of this commotion be about Alisa? I quickly took the exit and pulled up to the bushel of police cruisers. I took a deep breath to gain my composure, got out of my car and headed toward the officers. I flashed my badge to pass the yellow caution tape.

"What do we have here, Officer?" I asked in my work voice.

"Looks like a hit-and-run or an out-of-control vehicle. We received a call from a driver that witnessed the car flip over."

Please don't let it be her car. My heart was racing. "Where is the driver?"

"When we got here, the car was in flames. We are still trying to identify the vehicle."

I just looked around and continued to tell myself, "It can't be her. It can't be her." I walked up to the remnants of the car, trying to figure out if it could be hers, looking for any clue to put my mind at ease. I slowly turned around to find Dan, the fire marshal of Southampton, looking at me.

"Commissioner Collins."

"Dan, tell me," I said, hoping for good news. I met Dan when I became commissioner years ago. He must've been on the force for decades now. He was a staple in the community.

"It's a BMW i8 Spyder."

Shit, shit, shit!

"How are you sure?" I was in a state of disbelief.

"We found a tire about five hundred feet away from the scene. It must have flown off on impact. The impact of the hit was, well, let me put it this way—the vehicle must have been going one hundred miles per hour or faster."

"No!" I swore. My heart sank. Tears welled in my eyes.

"Yes. We are still looking around for evidence of the driver."

"Marshall." A firefighter was walking toward us with something in his hand.

"Yeah, Keith."

"We found a cell phone."

I looked at it. My worst fear was a reality.

They turned it on, and both looked at me. "Brent, is that you?"

I just stared at it, the picture of me and Alisa on the boat with the sunset in the background and me kissing her forehead. The look on my face must have told a story I wasn't ready to divulge. I turned around and put my hands on my knees to get my shit together. I found my strength and turned around and began nodding, if I opened my mouth, I knew I wouldn't be able to hold back tears.

"Yes, Dan, and that is Alisa, my girlfriend."

Dan looked at me and took a deep breath. I could tell he was struggling to find the words. He exhaled and put his hand on my shoulder, before delivering the heart-wrenching news.

"What do you know, Dan?" I asked, trying to stay calm.

"The caller said he saw the car go into the Pine Barrens flipping over several lanes. Brent, the car must have been about one thousand feet away."

"The car was on fire when we got here, and thank god we came when did, or else it probably would have caused a wildfire, like the one in 1995. I was just a rookie back then," he said, putting his hand through his blond hair.

"You sure kept this under wraps, never brought her to the biweekly dinners," he said, trying to lighten the mood. I've been alone for a long time and never met anyone I felt was worthy of meeting my work family—until Alisa.

"Not long, we just found each other again." I changed the subject before my emotions took over. I didn't need Dan see me break down and tell everyone.

He continued to tell me other items his men had found. Some of the items may not have been from this accident. The only item I wanted to find was Alisa. Dan could not tell me if Alisa was in the car or not. He needed to go to forensics with the remains of the car and some of the soil around the scene. We continued to go over other details. I was exhausted, and I needed to release the tears that burned my eyes.

"Dan, call me if you find anything."

I took her phone with me and just sat in my car. I thought about the last time I saw her. That night before was so special to me. I looked at the picture on her phone again. Without even feeling the tears run down my face, I wiped them away.

I had to call her father. I hit the redial button. The phone was picked up before it ever rang.

"Brent, did you find her?"

"Vin." The tone of my voice set the tone for the conversation.

"What happened, Brent?" His words were shaky.

"Vin, not good. She's—"

"No, Brent, don't tell me." This was his worst fear.

I felt the welling of tears in my eyes.

"Vin, there was an accident. They found her phone and her car. The car was torched. I'm so sorry." The tears were coming down even harder now as I clutched her phone.

Vinny fell silent before letting out a gut wrenching roar, "Nooo!"

"Do you want me there, Vin?" I asked, trying to console him.

"Brent, why?" he said, hearing the tortured feelings he had.

"I don't know much right now. They are not confirming anything until forensics review the remains." The hope she was not dead still lived inside me. It had to.

"Brent, find that bastard who wrote that note," Vinny demanded.

"I will, Vin. You know there still might be hope she is alive." I prayed.

"Hope that she is still alive? You told me the car was torched. She was in the car. Brent, I pray to God you are right. I won't give up hope when it comes to my daughter. From your lips to God's ears."

With that, he hung up the phone. I wanted to go see him, but right now I needed to be by myself. I started to drive back to East Hampton at a slow pace. I stopped in the middle of the road while a family of ducks crossed.

Why didn't I just tell her I loved her? I wanted to tell her the night on the boat that I was falling in love with her, but I was a coward. Will I be able to live my life, knowing she never knew how I truly felt? I was going to tell her this weekend. I wanted to kick myself for waiting.

Her phone was all I had of her; it was now glued to my hand. I couldn't stop the tears from flowing down my face as I headed to the liquor store to grab a bottle of anything that could help numb the pain.

I opened the door to my house and immediately remembered that Mary, the cleaning lady, had been here to romance the place; satin sheets, rose petals, a bottle of champagne on ice, and candles were everywhere.

I got the bottle of Jack Daniels and just started chugging it without even getting a glass. The buzz couldn't come quick enough. I looked through her phone, scrolling through her pictures she had taken. I never saw her take these pictures of us. There was one of her and me at Conscience Bay, another of me with the sunset behind me, and us on the bed with the moonlight in the background. I scrolled to the next; this one grabbed my attention. We were naked in her bed with a sheet around our waist and her arm around me. I was sleeping, and she was kissing my shoulder. The look of devotion on her face. I sent the pictures to myself, wanting this to be a memory I will never forget. Emotions overwhelmed me. I didn't want to cry again. Flashbacks of the past haunted my mind again, that first kiss all those years ago, finding each other again—I really believed it was destiny; it had to be destiny.

"But fuck destiny if fate brought us to this day, the day that the God above took her away from me," I said out loud, squeezing my eyes shut so the tears remained inside me, bashing the glass table beside me. The alcohol was starting to take effect. I laid back on the bed and imagined her next to me, staring deep into those hazel eyes. I wanted to run my hands through her hair and tell her how beautiful she is, how I don't want to go a day without kissing those lips. My body ached for her. I just wanted to wrap my arms around her, cocoon her in my love, and keep her safe. Tears kept flowing from my eyes. I wanted her warmth, to hear her giggle. Instead, I was alone, in silence, left with my own thoughts, rolling on the bed in agony, hoping the pain would end. But how could it end without her?

Will I ever see her again?

Don't lose hope, Collins.

CHAPTER 23

Alisa

I heard people talking. My head hurt, and my eyes were so heavy I couldn't open them. Someone was calling my name. I didn't recognize the voice. Beeping noises went wild around me, people spouting out numbers, and orders were being called out. My eyes still didn't budge. I didn't know where I was. The first thought came to my mind was they had me. Those people driving the Maserati found me. I heard the voices again. I strained my eyes to open.

"Alisa, Alisa, are you awake? Can you hear me?" I didn't speak. I noticed a man now standing above me.

"Oh, thank God, her eyes are fluttering. Someone call Brent. I think this is the woman he is looking for," I heard him say.

"Hello," I said. "What happened?" My eyes were prying open. I was so tired. I could hardly hear myself speak.

"A miracle," the man said. "I'm Dan, the fire marshal of Southampton, and you, my friend, are someone who survived a really bad car crash."

"I know," I whispered.

"You are in Southampton Hospital."

I was in the hospital, not with the assholes. Feeling of relief, I breathed easier.

"What happened? How did you find me?" I moved my lips, hoping he heard me.

"We were on the scene of your accident. A witness called it in. Your car is destroyed. My men were looking for parts and clues to what happened. Keith, one of the firemen, was deep into the woods. He found your phone and gave it to Brent. He is your boyfriend, correct? We saw the picture on the phone. He was looking for you. While we were heading back to the trucks, Keith heard noises. He went back into the Pine Barrens to see if it was you calling out. You were hitting a stick across the leaves. When he approached you, you looked up at him and passed out. We took you here. It's four o'clock in the afternoon. We've been waiting for you to get up," he explained, stroking my arm trying to keep me calm.

"Thank you," I said, nodding my head.

Another person walked in when the fire marshal left. He was looking at my chart in plain clothes.

"Hi, Alisa, I am Doctor Hughes. I'm just going to examine you. Can you move your hand for me? Good. And wiggle your fingers. Good. Your toes. Great! So, Alisa, you have a concussion and some lacerations. We had to put about ten stitches in your leg. And you are badly bruised. I want to keep you overnight to keep a close eye on you, because you bumped your head pretty bad." He waited to see if I had any questions.

"My dad," I managed to get out, "need to call." I was still struggling to talk with all this pain. Why don't I remember it hurting so bad?

"Yes, the fire marshal is calling Brent, and he will get in touch with your dad too. You will probably be in and out for a while and feel really tired because your brain is recovering from the concussion and trying to heal." He was holding my hand trying to console me.

I must have fallen asleep. I woke up to the smell of roses. I heard my dad on the phone.

"Call Louie. He'll find out who the fucker was. Yeah, yeah, got to go." He rushed off the phone.

"Alisa honey, it's Daddy. Daddy is here, honey." He kissed my forehead and rubbed my hand. "Oh my god, honey!" He kissed my hand. Tears were running down his face. "We thought we lost you."

I could tell he was scared. He was talking to me as if I was ten years old and I fell off my bike.

"Dad, who were you on the phone with?"

His eyes were still on me, and he still looked concerned.

"Nobody, honey, just your cousin Anthony, making sure you are okay. He feels terrible," he said, stopping himself from lecturing me about my recklessness.

"Dad, it's not his fault," I said softly. I deserved my ass being handed to me, not Anthony.

I looked around the room, and coming through the doors was Brent. He just stared at me. My father excused himself. Brent looked as if he just saw a ghost.

"Alisa, you're awake." He ran to my side and kissed me on my lips with such affection.

There was a moment of silence between us. He was holding my hand tightly as if he never wanted to let it go. "I love you," he said as he stared into my eyes. I could see little pools of tears in his eyes quivering, begging to be released.

"Brent, I love you," I confessed, setting loose the weight on my chest. It felt so good leaving my lips.

He kissed me again, but this time it was different. It was as if it had locked those three words in between us. This moment had eclipsed all moments that came before. Anything that happened leading up to this moment didn't matter because now he was mine and I was his. Nothing could break this bond.

"Alisa, I can't even tell you what was going through my mind the past twelve hours." His eyes were tired. He looked run-down, but he was still gorgeous. He gave me my phone. How did he have my phone? They must have found it. I remembered the fire marshal telling me something about that. I hope they have my purse too.

"I called everyone and told them you were okay."

"You thought I was dead, didn't you, Brent?"

After I saw the crime scene on Sunrise Highway..." He paused and shook his head continued, "They only found your phone and the car was burnt to ashes, basically nonexistent, and you were nowhere to be found. I—" He stopped again and grabbed my hand. "I never want to go through that ever again," he said, kissing my forehead. I felt a tear run down from his face onto mine.

"I'm here, baby. I'm not going anywhere." I looked into his tired gray eyes. His tears fell from his eyes onto my hands. I could tell something was off. I could smell the alcohol coming from his pores. He had definitely been drinking.

"Alisa, I never want to live through that again. You're moving in with me."

I think he just lost it. He asked me to move in with him. I really must have bumped my head hard.

"Brent, you can't be serious."

"Tell me you will move in with me, Alisa."

"Brent, I—" It was too fast, too much.

"Alisa, I need you by me. I need to make sure you're safe."

There was a look of desperation in his eyes.

"Brent, can we please talk about it when I get out of here?" I wanted to, but I was not sure I should be taking this seriously yet. He was scared, and he was drinking. He may want to take it back.

"Sure. I know it is happening fast, but—" He stopped what he was saying and continued with, "How are you feeling, my love?"

"I'm sore and tired."

He kissed my hand. "I know, princess. I took the next two days off so I could take care of you."

Whoa, maybe he was serious about me moving in. I scrunched my face in excitement. "Really?"

"Yes, why are you so surprised?" His head tilted to the side, curious as to what I am thinking about.

"Not surprised, excited," I reassured.

"I got you, princess, always. Your knight is here to rescue you from the demons." he said with a smile, staring into my eyes. He looked so tired, and the smell of alcohol on his breath was beginning to sour.

My dad walked back into my room.

"Okay, I called your aunt. She's coming over to help us out for a couple of days," he said, his hands out to the side of him.

"Dad," I interrupted him, "I'm staying with Brent."

He looked at me, then at Brent.

"He took off from work for me," I said with excitement. Brent kissed my forehead. Brent saw my father's expression.

"Yes, sir, I want to take care of her." He looked into my father's eyes to show him that he was now my protector. Yes, my knight in shining armor. My dragon slayer.

My father's old-fashioned ways were getting the best of him. He wanted to make a scene but knew he was in a public place.

"Alisa, don't you want your own bed? Your aunt is a nurse. She can—"

I stopped him again. "No, Dad, Brent will take care of me."

A nonnegotiable look appeared on my face. He mumbled something under his breath. I knew he was cursing; I knew he finally realized that I was twenty-seven and no longer needed his permission to do what I wanted.

"Alisa, what can I do? I'll call your aunt, tell her to pass by Brent's house to check on you." He knew he lost his battle. He's not happy. He just realized that there was another man in my life. One that I wanted in my life. I loved Brent, but I was still Daddy's little girl.

"Dad, it's okay. I am getting tired, and it's getting late. You have to travel back home. Visiting hours must be over soon. I will call you tomorrow. Good night." I needed some peace and quiet now that I was safe in a hospital bed. All I wanted to do was close my eyes and fall into a deep sleep. The painkillers were beginning to kick in.

He came over to the bed to kiss me good night. In Italian, he said he thanked God up above that he didn't lose me.

My dad went back into the hallway to give the nurses his number if anything changed. He looked back, smiled at me, and blew me a kiss. Brent turned on the TV and came into bed and pulled me to his chest.

"I think he took that well," Brent said with a laugh.

"Yeah, real well. You know I'm his baby. He never saw me choose another man over him before," I said, playing with the hair on his chest.

"I'm honored," he replied, with a megawatt smile on his face.

"Love you," I said sleepily, kissing him under his jaw.

"Loving you more." He put those tender lips to mine.

"Sleep, princess, I'm not leaving you," he whispered, holding me tight.

"Visiting hours are over."

"Yes, they are, but I am using my pull to not leave your side."

"Abusing the system again, Commissioner."

"No, it's payback for all the extras I do for the Hamptons." He smiled and cuddled closer to me. And just like that, everything was right in the world.

CHAPTER 24

Vinny

"Yeah, Josie, you don't need to come. Her new boyfriend is helping her," I said, rolling my eyes. The feeling of losing my baby girl was bittersweet. She seemed really happy, but I knew there wasn't anyone who deserved her. Yes, I needed her to live her life, but I needed to do my research. You never know how people are unless you have a private investigator check them out. And I was sure to have someone already on that.

"Yeah, Josie, I guess it's pretty serious. They just started dating. No wedding date yet. You know you can call her." She kept rambling. I don't know how Carmine deals with her.

She started telling a story about her and my late wife Rosalie. I didn't have the patience to listen, so I interrupted, "Is Carmine there?"

"Good, put him on, ciao."

"Ay, Vin."

"Carmine, we may have trouble."

"What are you talking about, Vin?"

"Alisa's new boyfriend, he is the police commissioner in East Hampton." Of all the fucking things to be.

"Oh, shit, Vin, what the fu—"

"I know. I have Louie checking on Marco. I think they put a warning out on us with Alisa. If they did Carmine, you know what we have to do?"

"Vin, understood. It's a miracle she is alive. We thought she was dead last night. Josie was in the funeral home in Howard Beach making the arrangements before you called and told us she was in the hospital. Josie just came back home from Saint Sylvester's. She's been saying her novenas."

"Yes, I know. I was scared, Carmine. I have kept everything from her for years. If anything would have happened to her because of me, you would have planned two funerals. I would have taken my life."

"Well, now time for paybacks, Vin."

"I know, but I want to make sure it's his family before we make our move." I had a little apprehension. This was the big setup. It would make the papers and the news.

"Vin, are we all set for Wednesday?" Carmine ignored my question.

"Yeah, Louie is making the final plans."

"This kid Louie, is he pure, Vin? There is something I don't like. I can't tell you why, but I don't like."

"Does it matter, Carmine? He'll be dead anyway."

"Vin, but Alisa's friend, isn't she in love with him?"

He had a point, but Sharon will get over him. I'm doing her a favor. She never attaches to anyone.

"Ah, she'll find another. Carmine, I still want Anthony to keep an eye on Alisa. If Anthony can't do it, I need someone else. Alisa can't know."

"This Brent guy, you now he might be good for Alisa, but he is a problem for me. You know what I mean?" Carmine was making a point. If he was going to be the new boss, it wouldn't look good if his niece was dating the law. This would cause problems in the family.

"You want Anthony to check on this guy Brent?"

"No, Carmine, not yet. I already have someone doing that. You know Alisa is my life. Not just anyone can take her hand. I want to see if we could flip him. If he does for us, we do for him. Capisce?"

"Good, Vin, I trust you."

"Carmine, remember the agreement. After this, I'm out, no more. I'm tired of this shit, and with Marco, you know dead, it'll be my chance to move to Florida and golf."

"Yeah, I know, Vin. You did more than you needed to do for my late sister. God rest her soul." I knew he did the sign of the cross. It's not like he's going to heaven.

"Carmine, we never talked about it. How much did we get for Killian's necklace?"

"Around $2.5 million," he said with pride.

"Good. Gotta love the underground market."

"Yeah, one million for you and one million for me, and the family gets the rest."

"Perfect." He better put the money where I told him to. I better make sure it's there. I changed the subject as I saw people come down the hospital hallway. That's all I needed was for someone to hear my conversation.

"Tell Josie I'm going to bring crates of tomatoes tomorrow. Time to make the sauce." It's our annual tradition. Fresh tomato sauce was always a good thing.

"Vinny, you freakin' kill me. You make this tradition a religious ritual. I swear you like it better than making the wine," he said with a boisterous laugh.

Normally, I would never doubt my brother-in-law, but lately everything was changing. I couldn't keep up with it. I couldn't trust anybody, not even the one guy I grew up with. I made one last comment before I hung up. I wanted him to know that family came first and I was not one to mess with.

"Carmine, never betray me. It's not worth the consequence, capisce?" I hung up the phone before he could reply.

I am glad I didn't tell him about the microchip I found in the necklace. He would want to split the profits. He and his family already took a lot from me over the years, including the life I really wanted for myself. I didn't know what was on the microchip, but someone would be looking for it. I wouldn't ask for much, maybe another million, which would be a prime addition to my retirement fund.

My Alisa, I can't believe I was able to keep this secret from her. Now after twenty-seven years, I was able to finally remove myself from this life I never wanted. There was a great possibility she may find out. I just needed two more weeks. I looked up to heaven to grant me this one wish.

CHAPTER 25

Brent

Alisa fell asleep watching reruns of *Friends*; she knew every word. It's amazing how natural all this felt. It's been less than a couple of weeks, and the magic between us continued to spark and create a bond that was laced with deep care and understanding. Gently I pulled my arm from around her, kissed her, and stepped out of the hospital room. With everything that happened in the past twenty-four hours and his informant spilling the beans on our relationship, a phone call to Special Agent Vogel should be no surprise to him.

"Stewart."

"Hi, Brent. How's your girl?"

"She's resting. She is being targeted. I feel it, Stewart."

"I have people that are still looking into it. Look, we found out Killian's necklace is untraceable. It was sold on the underground market. Someone paid $2.5 million. Alisa is not out of danger yet. There is word that Marco personally went after her. Carmine had his people out collecting anything they could find out, specifically if Marco had anything to do with Alisa's accident. Carmine was Alisa's uncle from her mother's side of the family. Alisa is now being used as a pawn, Brent. Also word has it that they are investigating her new boyfriend. I hope all the loose ends were tied up."

"*Shit!*"

"What are your plans for the next couple of days?" he asked.

"Alisa is staying with me. I took a couple of days off."

"Good. It's time to meet again. Monday, same spot, at 8:00 a.m.," he said before promptly hanging up.

I shoved my phone into my pocket and looked up to see Michael running down the hall with a sense of panic.

"Is she okay?"

"Yes, she's sleeping."

"Brent, there was a message on the restaurant's answering machine. I called Detective Doherty to let him know," Michael stated, annoyed about the never-ending bullshit. These threats were pissing him off too. Their friendship was more than I thought.

"What did the message say?"

"This motherfucker loves nursery rhythms." He shook his head with disgust. He recorded it, and he pressed play on his phone.

Ding dong the bitch is dead,
the bitch is dead,
off with her head.

"Fucking bastard. They think she is dead. I can understand why. The scene of the accident proves that she should be."

"Was it really that bad? I must admit I'm scared shitless. I hired two guards for the restaurant."

I knew he cared for her like a brother, I hope, but there was something that tells me if she ever made a move on him, he would not back down.

"Good call, man. Let me know if you need anything from me," I said.

"How is she doing? Can I see her?" he asked, looking into her room.

"Good, but she is sleeping."

"I'll wait. You look like shit. Go home and clean up. I'm here."

I looked down at myself and saw the disheveled clothing. I still smelled like Jack Daniels. As I was looking back up toward Michael, he just shook his head and smiled. I decided to take him up on the offer. Also, it will give me a chance to get the house ready for her.

"Michael, does Alisa keep spare clothes at the restaurant?"

"Yeah, why?"

"She is staying with me for a couple of days and would probably appreciate some fresh clothes."

"Wow, I would have thought you would prefer her naked," Michael said, winking at me.

I laughed. "Yes, but she may get cold." I laughed some more. "Can you please call the restaurant and tell them I will need to get into her office?"

"Sure thing, Commissioner." He paused and looked me in the eye. "Uhm, Comish, you do love her, don't you?"

"Absolutely," I said without hesitation.

"I can tell. I was you once. It's hard not to."

I looked at him curiously wondering what he meant by that.

"Another time, Comish. Go get ready for your lady."

Michael walked in and rearranged all of the flowers and put on E! channel. I used the opportunity to get ready for my lady. As I headed to the restaurant, I called Doherty to get some information on the robbery from last week. Kim's necklace, of course I know what happened to it, but which family had the in?

"Doherty."

"Hey, Brent, I heard about Alisa. I am glad she is okay."

"Thanks. Any more updates on Killian's necklace, or the phone message from today?"

"Yes, we found out that the call came from a burner phone purchased in Hampton Bays. How do you know about the call?"

"Michael came into the hospital to visit Alisa and told me about it." Who else?

"Boss, something is up with Michael. Something is off. I can't tell you what it is, but it's a feeling I have."

"How so, Doherty?" I didn't notice anything.

"Well, we went into the restaurant after Michael contacted us, and there was no reaction. He was very mellow about the whole thing, but with the necklace and note, it was the total opposite."

Strange.

"I'll look into Michael. How about the burner phone, any leads?"

"Right. The burner phone was purchased in Hampton Bays. I'm heading there tomorrow to look at the tape, hope. The merchant remembered the guy but couldn't give a good description. He only remembers an expensive car pulling into the lot."

He was good at what he did. I'm happy he was on my team. Most men would need to be told what to do.

"Good, so it was information that it could be anyone in the Hamptons with an expensive car. Well, at least we can narrow it down to seventy-five percent of the area. Anything else?"

"Yeah, the necklace has not been traced yet, but I think there might be another way they could have sold it. You see, I remember a case I studied in school about the underground market. It is like a second internet system for the wealthy—a blackhole. I mean the necklace was a treasure, right? Is there someone who can check into it, boss?"

"Doherty, I'll check into that. Not a bad idea. By the way, Doherty, I'm taking off the next two to three days. Call me at home if there is anything else."

"Got it, Commissioner. Enjoy your time off."

Within no time, I found myself in the parking lot of Sicilia's. I didn't even remember leaving the hospital. Taking a couple of minutes for myself to just breathe, realizing how lucky I was that she was still alive, I lifted my finger to wipe away a stray tear falling down my cheek. This was one emotional roller coaster for me. I had run the emotional gamut—love, anger, fear, loss. I checked myself in the mirror, dark circles decorated my bloodshot eyes. I ran my fingers through my hair to look more presentable. I was welcomed into the restaurant by a slender woman with blond bobbed hair and extra-long eyelashes, like furry spider legs dancing on her eyelids.

"You must be Commissioner Collins."

"Yes, I am," I said while flashing my badge.

"Michael said to let you go downstairs into Alisa's office. Is that correct?" We started walking downstairs. Every once in while she would turn her head and smile. The smile that I have seen women give me when they wanted hands-on attention. Normally I would appreciate and entertain the flirtation, but that was the old Brent, I'm a new man, loyal to my woman. And right now, I was taking care of business, no time for banter—innocent or not.

"How is Alisa?" She sensed the awkwardness.

"Good. I mean she is achy and has stitches on her leg, but she's alive." She smiled back at me with a brighter smile. Her back was arched in the door jamb displaying her breasts.

She waved me into the room. She didn't move but just stared at me. I couldn't help but smirk at the bold actions of this woman. I walked straight into the bathroom to get some toiletries. Glancing at the shower, a flashback of that night came. What a steamy session. She brings out this carnal desire within me.

"Did you find everything you were looking for?"

"Yes, I can see myself out. No need to wait here with me."

"Don't be silly. I mean someone needs to wash—I mean watch your back. Considering there is no one else here, I could do it. Speaking of wash, are you in the mood for a shower, Commissioner?" She approached me, walking her fingers up my arm.

"No, I am not interested."

I gave her a look signaling her to stop, no need to further embarrass herself. In a huff, she left the room, slamming the door behind her. Clearly, she's never been turned down before. I laughed it off and headed to the closet, which was packed with clothes, shoes, purses, and accessories. Did she live here? What a collection. I filled a duffel bag and was sure to pack a purse since hers most likely was lost forever in the crash.

Just as I was zipping up the bag, I heard static, like someone was crinkling paper behind me. Maybe blondie snuck back in after I spurned her advances. I looked around, I was alone, and as I moved closer to Alisa's desk, the noise grew louder. I glanced at the lamp and was in shock, someone had planted a bug to listen in on Alisa's comings and goings. I didn't touch it maybe Vogel planted it. I'll know for sure after our meeting on Monday. If not, I'll get Doherty on it.

Looking at the contents I put in the bag, I think I had everything. Climbing the stairs back to the restaurant, I saw the blond woman again.

"Thanks. I think I have everything for Alisa to stay with me for a couple of days."

Bingo, the light just flickered in her head. Yeah, lady, what do you think is going to happen when your boss finds out you were hitting on her man? Her smile disappeared, she knew she overreached, severely. I couldn't hide my smirk, sorry, not sorry, lady. I'm spoken for.

I headed back to the house expecting to open the door to the disarray I left it in hours before. My drunken anger got the best of me; I was like a destructive tornado leaving shattered glass and empty liquor bottles all over the house. Thankfully the housekeeper came and got rid of the evidence. I hit rock bottom last night but finding out Alisa was alive without severe injuries brought me back. I was now looking at the world through rose-colored glasses. She made me want to be a better man, a man who was worthy of her love until the end of time.

I was staying at the hospital with her tonight. I took a shower to get the alcohol stench off me and decided not to shave. I liked this look, and I was off today anyway.

I was in the car heading back to the hospital, realizing I never filled Tom in after my night on the water with Alisa. He really pulled through for me and helped make it special. Satin sheets? Brilliant. I owed him more than those Mets tickets.

"Hey, man, sorry for going MIA," I said after Tom picked up after two rings.

"So did everything work out?" he asked nonchalantly, trying not to be too obvious of what the real question was.

"Yeah, it did, thanks."

"So you got your dick wet."

Normally I would laugh at that comment, but it's Alisa. No one should talk to her that way. "Don't talk about her like that."

"Simmer down, boy, didn't realize she was that special. Geez, man. Didn't mean to insult anyone."

"Sorry. It has been a hell of day. I just wanted to say thanks again. You really did good. When I come out again, we need to get together and have a couple of beers. My treat." Tom knew me well. Actually, he was the one person I could always trust and rely on.

"Wow, thanks, and you're right, it will be on you. You know how much it took to get the basket from Ms. Hart. She was asking me fifty questions about who was the lucky lady. It wasn't until I told her it was for my mother did she stop asking questions. You should have seen her face. It was funny. You're in the car. Where are you going?"

"Heading to the hospital. The girl I wanted to impress is in there. I can't get into it right now, but next week we'll get together. You in?" I asked, trying to dodge the conversation. I knew he wanted more details but that would have to wait. Everything was still so fresh. I wanted to keep my macho persona intact. I knew I'd melt like butter if I talked about her accident.

"I'm going to let this one slide, Brent. But you didn't pull one over on me. Next week I want all the details. Give a kiss to that girl of yours for me. Make sure you use tongue." He laughed, knowing that just pissed me off.

"You are such an ass, man."

"I like it all—pussy man, tits man, and an ass man."

I hollered out a laugh so loud I almost pissed my pants. Such a comedian. "Never change, bro. I really needed that laugh."

"I've known you too long. I know something is up. You'll let me in when the timing is right. Just don't close me out."

This was exactly why he's my best friend. He knows when to back off and when to pry and right now, I just needed some support.

"I won't. Just need a little more time. Call me next week."

"Got it. Just let me know if you need me. You know I will be right there."

"No doubting that. Same here."

The call ended knowing we would always have each other's back. We always did.

I was driving down Sunrise Highway toward the hospital, taking in the scenery around me. Everyone was enjoying the last weeks of summer. I couldn't wait just to take a walk with Alisa on my arm, just like the couples walking around town. Reaching the hospital parking lot, I took out my phone and looked at the picture I sent myself from Alisa's phone. It brought a smile to my face every time.

CHAPTER 26

Alisa

I woke up to those green eyes and a big smile right in front of me. The man I called my friend, my rock, and my brother.

"What's up, baby girl?" Michael was holding my hand and had tears in his eyes.

"What's wrong, Michael?"

"Other than you in the hospital or that I thought you were dead last night?" He rolled his eyes.

I started to laugh, and he laughed with me.

"Oh, and you made me cancel my date with that wannabe actress last night. You owe me big time," he said playfully with his arms crossed against his chest while he was tapping his foot.

"Well noted, Michael. I'll just yell at the car who ran me off the road to wait a day next time," I said with a laugh that was followed with a shooting pain in my ribs forcing me to squeeze my eyes shut and grip my side. *Too soon for jokes, Alisa.*

"So tell me what happened." He grabbed a chair and sat by my bed and held my hand.

"Not much. I remember a Blue Maserati hitting me and then waking up in a wooded area with a headache and a cut on my leg. I kept going in and out of consciousness. Thankfully I found my way to the road before passing out and I woke up here."

"Where's Brent, my father?" I asked, questioning why he was here alone.

"I sent Brent home to clean up, he looked and smelled horrible. You could tell he was drinking last night. After he freshens up, he is set to swing by the restaurant to get you a change of clothes."

He stopped to look at me as I had a smile from ear to ear. The smile grew on his face as wide as mine.

"You guys are serious, huh?" He already knew the answer.

"Michael, I told him I loved him." His eyes widened.

"Really, baby girl, I've known you how long now, and your v-card, is it still intact?"

My eyes went down and then I looked back up at him. I was not ashamed, just happy.

"You're kidding me. Already, you slut?"

There's a first. Someone calling me, Alisa Rossi, a slut. I started to giggle. "Ah, yes, he was all man.

"Michael, what is wrong?" I asked, I knew there was more going on. I could see it in his eyes that something else was bothering him. He was trying to mask it, but I knew.

"When I heard you went missing, I was terrified. I couldn't help but think about the day I lost Maria. I know it has been five years, but she was my soul mate, Alisa. *No one* will ever replace her." He bowed his head and pulled my hand toward his lips to kiss it. I hated seeing him suffering again. The loss of Maria hit him hard and he hasn't fully recovered from the loss. Knowing I brought back those memories hurt me.

"Oh, Michael, you can't blame yourself. Fate said it was her time, babe." I rubbed the tears off his face.

"But if I just went with her, then maybe—"

"Michael, you have been doing this to yourself long enough," I reprimanded him of his thoughts of what happened that day.

"But—"

"Michael, you would not have been able to do anything. She had a convulsion while she was driving and went through the—"

"I know, Alisa," he interrupted. The image of her hitting the guardrail and flipping over the cliff of the Pocono Mountains was too graphic for him. She was going to see her college girlfriend in Pennsylvania for her bridal shower and spa day. She never made it.

"Okay. I don't mean—I just need you to stop blaming yourself. It was an accident. You had no bearing on the results of the accident." He had been suffering for way too long. He needed to talk to his therapist again.

I felt something that jolted my insides. I was getting that feeling of electricity running through my body. I looked up, and there he was at the door. He was absolutely gorgeous and all mine. The scruff on his face added a rugged edge. Fitted T-shirt, black gym pants— delicious. I mean *finger licking good*, as Sharon would say.

Michael stared at me at me and puffed out a laugh and rolled his eyes. "With that look on your face, I don't think I am needed anymore." He kissed my forehead, waved his hand off, and said goodbye.

"I'll call you later, baby girl." He shook Brent's hand as he left the room.

"Did he say something?" I hardly heard him as Brent entered the room. Brent bent down and gave me the softest, most delicate kiss on my lips. I got wet between my legs just by his touch. The power this man holds on me was dangerous.

"Alisa, should I be jealous...'baby girl'?" He had on the infamous eyebrow smirk reaction.

I swear I can't get enough of it.

"No," I said quickly. "You are the most beautiful man I have ever seen, Brent Collins." Where the hell did that come from? I swear he has some sort of spell over me.

"I'm all yours, Alisa."

"This scruff you have going is the sexiest thing. I'm already wet." This spell he had casted over me was in full effect. Who am I?

"Well, let me see," he said as he put his hand underneath the sheet.

He leaned over to the bed, gave me a more than enthusiastic kiss, and I felt his hand head toward the folds in between my legs. Two fingers went in, and I was in a state of euphoria.

"You feel so good, Alisa. Oh, if you weren't all hooked up to these machines, I would—"

My monitor beeps grew louder as my heartbeat picked up. If this continues much longer a nurse will be busting through the door to check on me. I couldn't help myself, I put my hands on his shaft and caressed it nice and slow.

"Alisa, the door is wide open."

The spell was working overtime. "I'll stop if you stop."

He crashed his lips to mine, pumped in and out, and all the monitors started to beep faster.

"Stop. Stop, Brent, the nurse is—"

With a gargled moan, I exploded. That was quick. The machines were slowing down, but I continued to caress him. The excitement of trying not to get caught was boosting my courage to do something I wouldn't ordinarily do. I put my head to the side of the bed and leaned down. I untied his pants and grabbed his cock and slid it into my mouth. Thank God for his gym pants.

With a gasp, Brent said, "Alisa, I am not going to last long."

I sucked and stroked it like a straw trying to get to the bottom of a delicious milkshake, and I needed every last drop. I heard him groan as he continued to grow in my throat.

"Alisa," he whispered as I felt him on the verge of exploding. His body tensed up and I quickened by pace to take him over the edge.

"Princess," he said as a faint whisper.

Just as smooth as a shake, his cream ran down my throat. I watched as he soothed himself down from the pleasure I inflicted on him. I loved feeling like I was in complete control. He pulled his pants back up, and I was wiping my mouth with the back of my hand. The nurse popped her head in just as he was tying the string to his gym pants. Perfect timing.

"Ms. Rossi, it's time for your medication." Boy, was that close. She looked concerned as she read the monitor. Did it expose our moment?

"You must have kissed her," she said frustratingly, looking at Brent.

"Your blood pressure went up, Ms. Rossi," she said, winking at me.

She was onto us, I could tell. Maybe she waited outside the door the entire time. I couldn't help but giggle at the thought of it. Brent squeezed my hand. He must've been thinking the same thing. As she left, she asked Brent if he would be needing a pillow and blanket.

Oh yes, please.

"Well, looks like I'm sleeping here tonight, princess. I'm not leaving your side," he said giving me a no-nonsense look. This is a battle I won't win, but what's the harm in having a little fun before I give in?

"You don't have to. I mean, I am in the hospital. There are security guards everywhere," I said half-heartedly reassured.

On one hand, I would love for him to stay, but I wouldn't want for him to be uncomfortable, or feel like I was an obligation. This relationship thing was still so new to me. I wasn't used to being this vulnerable. I couldn't picture any of my exes going to the great lengths Brent had taken over the last few weeks.

I remembered my mom saying the beginning of the relationship was always the best. If he offered to do something for you, always let them. If you expect them to do something and they don't, cautiously choose the battle you want to argue. It could be the one that will make you lose him forever. Her words stuck with me.

"I know, but I don't know if you realize this. I care about you, Alisa. I never want to see you scared or hurting again," he said, rubbing the back of his hand on my cheek, looking deep into my eyes. I saw that he truly loved me.

"Putting cuffs on me?" I giggled as I broke seriousness between us.

"Well, I think we should wait until you feel better," he teased with a wink.

I slapped him on the chest playfully. "Pervert." I love our dynamic.

"That's why you love me," he said with a grin.

What we had between us was strong and we still had so much to learn about each other. So much potential.

"You're correct, Mr. Sexy Man," I said while batting my eyelashes.

"I love you, too, Alisa."

Things felt so comfortable. He was like my missing puzzle piece. If it didn't work out, my heart would shatter, and I was not confident I would recover. I decided to clean myself up a bit, when I returned from the bathroom, he was sitting in the chair looking at his messages and returning some calls. I looked in the duffel bag he put on the bed. He packed me clothes and PJs, even some makeup and a toothbrush. What man does this? He's amazing. If there was one characteristic about this man that shone through was that he was the most compassionate, caring man I have ever known.

My phone rang; it was my dad checking up on me.

"Bella, come ti senti?" My dad was asking me how I was feeling.

"Still sore. I'll be fine, Papa."

"I know, you are strong like your father," he said while trying to hold in a laugh.

"How are you feeling, Papa?" Hard to believe my father and I were in the hospital within the same week.

"I'm good, I had my wine and provolone. Don't worry, I had my fruit—grapes."

I barked out a laugh. Brent looked up from his phone to make sure I was okay.

"Dad, you're not supposed to eat that. Your cholesterol."

"Ah, you still care about me. I thought you would forget about me since you have a new boyfriend."

"Dad, you make me laugh. I will always take care of you. You just have to get used to sharing me with the one I love."

Brent's head popped up listening to the conversation. The smile on his face lit up the room. The conversation continued with my dad. He was telling me he'll help with ordering for the restaurants. He said he checked in with Sophia at the Port Jefferson restaurant; they were short staffed and offered to give a helping hand if she needed him to. He then switched gears to update me on my Aunt Josie and

Uncle Carmine. As he was talking to me, I could tell something on his mind and couldn't figure it out. Ever since Mom died, something changed. More recently, it's become more noticeable. He's somehow more protective...to the point of paranoia at times. I'm sure my accident only piled on. After that fiasco, I realized I needed to spend more time with him. Between the new restaurant and Brent, we haven't had our Sunday dinners.

Brent was still on the phone looking into his emails. I loved the look of concentration on his face, his strong jawline, and the crease in his forehead was the sign of him thinking. A smile upon my face formed. I was really happy. He sensed me looking at him and lifted his head and smiled at me.

"Is everything okay with your dad? Does he need help with something? I could ask my friend Tom to pass by."

"Brent, you are the most selfless man I know." I shook my head. He does want to take care of my needs and now my dad's.

"You bring it out in me, princess." He winked.

He got up and sat on the side of my bed. He lifted my chin up and kissed my lips. Looking into my eyes created our deep connection, one that told me this was it. He was the one.

"It's been a while since I tasted those lips." Sweet talker.

I looked over his shoulder to Sharon at the door. She had a freshly gift shop purchased balloon and a teddy bear sporting a bandage on its head.

"Thank God," she said with a sigh of relief. "Move, Mr. Commissioner, that's my best friend," running to my bedside for a tight hug.

"Don't ever do that to me again."

Brent looked at her and laughed.

"I promise, okay?" *I hope I can keep it.*

"Hello, Sharon, nice to see you, too," Brent said, smiling.

"Hi, Brent. Can you do me a favor and give me and Alisa ten minutes? Louie is in the cafeteria getting me a latte. Alisa wants one, too."

"Sure, I'm hungry anyway. Do you want anything to eat?" he asked.

"No, babe."

Before he left, he kissed me passionately, leaving an impression for Sharon to ask me more questions about our relationship.

"I'll be back soon." He winked at me and headed out the door.

Girl talk with Sharon was always longer than ten minutes. She waited until he left and gripped my hand.

"I love him," she shouted.

"Good. I hope it's Louie, not Brent."

She laughed and hit my arm. "Ouch."

"Sorry, how are you feeling? You're silly, girl." She never answered my question.

"Okay, until you hit me," I said, rubbing my arm.

"He took me to Russo's on the Bay on Cross Bay Boulevard and told me how he could see us happy together in the future and how he cares for me in a different way than he ever did for anyone else.

"Then he told me loved me and gave me this!" she said nearly all in one breath before throwing her arm in front of my face to reveal a bracelet with X's and O's. The O's were diamonds.

"Wow, Sharon, that's beautiful," I said, nearly blinded as the diamonds sparkled in the fluorescent hospital lights. I'm not sure what Louie did for a living, but this must've put him back at least a couple hundred dollars.

"And it's not even my birthday or an anniversary," she said with a squeal.

She was still playing with her bracelet with a huge smile on her face. I had never seen her so happy.

If there was anyone who deserved a good man, it was my friend. Suddenly her smile dropped to a frown and she lowered her head.

"What's wrong?" I asked while raising her chin to see her now tear-filled eyes.

"Nothing really," she sighed.

"Sha...what's bothering you?"

"I love him, Alisa. I'm scared. I believe he loves me and all, but he's always leaving me or changing our plans and heading back to Howard Beach for something. What if I'm not the only one?" She looked to me for an answer.

"Doesn't he usually take my dad with him? No funny business there," I reassured, which prompted a small smile.

"Sharon, he would not spend money like that on a fling," I said, shaking her wrist.

On cue, Louie and Brent came in. Brent sat next to me. He brushed his fingers through my hair and gave me a kiss. He handed me a cappuccino.

"Not sure if it's any good. It came from the vending machine." It's those small gestures that show me that he truly does care.

We were all in my hospital room getting to know each other better. Sharon kept talking about the photos of Cardi B and Lady Gaga outside Jones Beach for the Hot 100 Concert. She was the best storyteller, so animated, she had Brent laughing. I looked at all of us. This right here has never happened. Sharon and I had boyfriends, sure, but never at the same time. Especially ones that had stolen our hearts.

Louie was rubbing Sharon's back while she was still talking about the photoshoots she had booked for the end of summer. Louie's eyes were glued to her, he was smitten. This was us, and I couldn't wait to see what the future had in store for the four of us.

Visiting hours came to an end, and Sharon and Louie left for the evening. Brent closed the door and put on the TV. I lifted the sheets on the bed for him to come in.

"No, princess, you'll be uncomfortable."

The look I gave him said get your ass over here now.

He took his shoes off and slid in. It's a tight fit but exactly what I wanted. My head was on his chest; he's playing with my hair.

"Alisa, you know last night when I thought you were dead, I drank myself to sleep. You have brought a purpose to my life, Alisa. I never knew I was so lost. I had never been in love before...before you."

I ran my finger down from his forehead, over his nose to his lips, and gently tapped them. This man is my soulmate. Thank you, God, for making this happen. A day that started with fear and pain ended with a promising future filled with unconditional love. My fingers cradled his face, and my lips reached his, and we melted into each other with a silent promise of never parting.

"*Destino,*" I whispered.

I put my head on his chest. "I love you, my knight."

"Good night, my love." He kissed the top of my head and snuggled into me.

CHAPTER 27

Brent

I felt her chest go up and down in rhythm with my own; we were so in sync with one another. I was still playing with her hair. I truly couldn't imagine life without her. She possessed my heart and mind. I meant what I said to her last night. She was the only woman I truly loved. She was different in so many ways. I could sit and stare into her eyes and know exactly what she was thinking. This woman owned me. She could break my heart for good, because I could never love anyone other than her.

Twenty-four hours ago, I thought she was dead. Losing her last night wrecked me. I thought about who wanted her to hurt her and why. The blue Maserati running her off the road, the nursery rhyme notes and the voicemail at the restaurant. What did she get herself involved in? All I knew was nothing like this would ever happen again. I would handcuff her to me for the rest of her life if that meant she'd be safe from harm. *Oh, she'll be handcuffed to something.* The thought made me smile.

I remembered the conversation with Doherty. He thought Michael was withholding information. I realized that her dad was also acting strange. I tried to remember who told me that Carmine was her father's name. The last couple of days proved that Vinny Rossi was her father. There were so many loose ends. I started to get paranoid.

I was meeting with Special Agent Vogel on Monday. He may give me some more clues, but right now, I was going to enjoy this moment with the true love of my life.

The sun was peeking through the shades of the window. I looked down and saw those hazel eyes gazing up at me. Pure beauty. I caressed her face and drank in the most breathtaking view, memorizing every freckle, the softness of her cheeks, and the soft blush color of her pouty lips. She kissed me softly on the lips and whispered in one breath, "I love you like I never thought I would every love anyone. Destiny brought me to you, and fate will never let me lose you. I only want forever with you."

I'm not sure what I did right to get this woman. Those words meant so much to me. I sealed it with a kiss.

At that moment I knew she felt something nudging the side of her thigh because she slowly reached down and began stroking me. Her eyes turned the gold color that told me her libido had awakened and was ready to be naughty. She lifted herself up.

"Alisa, what are you doing?"

She put her fingers on her lips, and she straddled me. This woman was insatiable, on the verge of a nymphomaniac. It's like after twenty-seven years of not having sex, she was trying to make up for lost time. She lifted my shirt off and felt my chest as if she was trying to remember the grooves and valleys. Careful not to touch her injured leg, I aligned my cock to her entrance. I knew she was wet because I felt her juices on my torso. She put her hands on my chest and lowered herself and began to ride me as if she was part of the Southampton Horse Classics. Scratch that, like she just went to Belmont Raceway and wanted to win the triple crown.

I took a quick glance to check the door was locked. My groans started to get louder as I got deeper into her body. I began to rub her clit. One touch, her head flew back, and I felt her tighten around my cock. I watched her as she moved faster and grinding me to the root. I was about to explode. The intensity and feeling of her riding me drove me to my breaking point.

"Brent, cum for me," she moaned out.

"Together with you, as one," I said, looking into her eyes.

Her head fell, her hair was draping over her face, and our eyes were locked. I was holding back, and it was getting impossible not to release. Feeling where she was at, she grinded into me one more time as I pinched her clit. The sensation of the walls of her pussy gripping my cock was overwhelming. In unison, we both released our orgasm. She kept grinding until she calmed from the intensity we both felt. It's one for the record books. After a moment, we both looked into each other's eyes, and as if it was orchestrated, we both said, "I love you." I just held her in my arms. The intimate moment we had was one I never had with anyone else.

The smile on my face turned into panic. I tried not to sound fearful. *What was I thinking?*

"Alisa, I just, uhm, no condom."

She looked at me, watching my forehead pulse.

"It's okay, calm down. I'm on the pill."

My shoulders relaxed, and a sense of relief washed over me. Why would she be on the pill if she never had sex before me? I know I popped her cherry; I had to throw away the sheets from that on the blow-up mattress because I couldn't get the stains out. I chose not to ask that question. One day the two of us would have a family—if all goes according to plan. I'm just not ready to give up the one-on-one time just yet. We still had so much to do together, learn about each other; we had countries to see, concerts to attend.

I got out of the bed, got all cleaned up when the doctor came in. Alisa was still in the bathroom getting herself together. He examined her one last time and confirmed that Alisa was going to be released today. I got excited knowing she was coming home with me. I had her all to myself. Me and my little minx.

The nurse came in to give her prescriptions and instructions. They put her in the wheelchair to exit the hospital. I got a head start to bring the car around. I couldn't help the giddy feeling I was getting. The nurse assisted her to the car, and it looked like they were sharing a laugh, and off we went. I left a note for the housekeeper to stock up on certain things—bandages, ibuprofen, and flowers, peonies specifically, since Michael told me they were her favorite.

I realized that I needed to know more about her, know all her favorite things, her hopes and dreams. She needed to know more about me. She needed to know who I was back then; I was more than just an undercover detective.

We pulled into the driveway, and the housekeeper was heading out. She looked at us and waved.

"Who is that?" Alisa asked.

"My housekeeper, Mary." I looked over. Her face was—

"You're jealous of my housekeeper," I said with a smile.

"Don't be ridiculous."

"Alisa, look at you—you're jealous," I teased as I hit my signature eyebrow raise-smirk combo. She got caught being jealous.

I got out of the car, walked around to her side. I opened the door, cradled her in my arms, and kissed her cheek. My housekeeper was laughing.

"This is the love of my life, Alisa."

Mary smiled. "Hello, Alisa, I'm Mary," she said, waving at us again.

Alisa was so embarrassed she turned her head into my chest. I walked her into the house and set her down on the couch. I went back out to get her medicine and clothes. When I came back in, Alisa was looking around the house with her back to me. She looked out the windows at the ocean past the dunes.

"The view is the main reason I bought this house," I told her.

I wrapped my arms around her waist and kissed the crook of her neck. "Are you hungry?"

"Yes, ravenous."

"Good, Mary made pasta." I picked her up and carried her to the kitchen and put her on one of the stools. I stuck one napkin in her shirt, and then took another napkin and tied it around her eyes.

"Brent, what are you doing?" she asked, making that giggling noise I loved so much.

"Being romantic," I purred into her ear.

"Oh." She giggled and continued her conversation. "You know, the nurse saw us this morning. And—"

I placed butterfly kisses down her jawline and down to the crook of her neck. "I really didn't care if anyone saw us. I want what I want, when I want."

"After dinner, I am going to fuck you like you want me to—hard and erotic."

She grabbed me by the face and kissed me intensely.

I pulled back. "Patience, my dirty girl, first we eat."

I took a sip of wine. I took another, went to kiss Alisa, and poured some of the wine into her mouth. Not expecting it, the wine poured out. I took my tongue and licked it up.

"Brent," she whispered.

"Patience," I said.

I took a bite of the pasta—perfect! I put more on a fork. "Open your mouth, princess." I put the forkful in her mouth.

"Mm," she purred.

"Good, right?"

She nodded.

I fed her a couple of more forkfuls. The moans from her mouth woke up my insides. My hand was grazing her inner thigh. I could smell her arousal; I was hoping I could last. After five minutes of tormenting myself, I started to tease her with my fingers. I grabbed the ice cube and rubbed it along her neck and cleavage.

"Ready for dessert?" I grabbed the strawberries and cream set out for us. "Open, princess."

She bit it and licked her lips clean as she moaned, practically begging me to take her right there.

Still blindfolded, I took her to my bedroom that was thoughtfully decorated with lit candles and peonies all around. I laid her on the bed and took off her blindfold. She adjusted her eyes to the light and looked around.

"How did you know peonies were my favorite?" she asked, in awe. "Brent, this is beautiful."

"It's nothing compared to you."

She took her pants off and slid down her panties, then her shirt. She slid her bra straps just off her shoulders.

"Open your legs and show me that pretty pussy. Now, Alisa." I liked control in the bedroom. You could tell she liked the way I was talking to her. She lay back on the bed. The bed was full of peony petals. She ran her hands across her body and spread her legs. Making sure that I didn't touch her stitches, I grabbed her leg and kissed her inner thigh to tease her until I hit my target. She started to moan. The pink folds in between her legs were glistening. The sweetness of her core was turning me on more and more. I become addicted to her taste. My tongue was going in and out of her, eating up all I could get.

"Brent, oh god, Brent!" she called out. Those words only got me going even more. I grabbed myself and stroked my cock. I felt the walls of her vagina tense up, and her hands were in my hair as she grinded my face into the apex of her thighs.

"Oh yes, princess, yes," I mumbled with her honey covering my tongue. I picked up the pace and slid in two fingers, hitting her G-spot. I was relentless. I couldn't get enough.

"Oh…oh no, not again. Brent!" she shouted as her back arched to the ceiling and she flung her head deeper into the pillow.

Two down. I couldn't help it. I turned her around, smacked her ass, and plunged my cock in that warm, wet pussy.

"Tell me you want me. Alisa, tell me what you want."

"Fuck me, Brent," she ordered. *Oh, my little minx was talking dirty.*

"I can't hear you," I said in a low, stern tone. I wanted to hear it again.

She turned her head to look at me and called out, "Fuck me hard, you beast!"

I roared and started pounding her pussy like an animal. We started to move together; she felt so good. She started to moan again.

"Harder, Brent, fuck me harder."

I lost all control. I felt her release. My sac got tight, and the floodgates opened. I held her head back and kissed her as I continued with forceful thrusts. I slapped her ass and collapsed on top of her.

The sensation of that orgasm was still running through my body. My breathing started to even out. I looked toward Alisa.

"Well, that was quite the welcome home party," she said, still breathless.

"I love you," I said, "and I will never stop telling you that." I meant it with all my heart. It's settled. I was whipped.

"Ditto, bronco rider."

I took the pillow and hit her with it and teased, "You know you're getting more demanding in your dirty talk, young lady. Fuck me harder?"

She slapped my chest. "Shut up," she replied.

I swear I could hear her laugh all night.

We just sat there and talked. I got to know all her favorite things, and I told her mine. We talked about our childhood and our friends throughout the years. She told me stories about the countries she has visited and the ones on her bucket list. Every now and then she pulled her fingers through my hair and gave me a kiss. I had to tell her about my stay in witness protection program. I had gotten to know her better, but she didn't know who I really was. I didn't want to ruin what we had right now. Instead, we watched more reruns of *Friends*, which I have come to learn is Alisa's favorite comedy series while we ate lunch in bed. Everything seemed like it was supposed to, comfortable, easy, and effortless. I wish I could bottle this day and whenever things get hard, or confusing, or scary, I would just uncork it and relive it over and over again.

Her phone rang; it was Louie. It wasn't long into the conversation before she was slack jawed in disbelief. I stopped chewing so I could hear what Louie was saying. *What is happening now?*

"What, when, Louie? Okay. Call my uncle. He might know," she said with her hand raised to her temple.

"What is going on, Alisa?" I asked, concerned about her recovery from yesterday's fiasco.

She started to cry uncontrollably, tossed her phone across the bed, and put her head in her hands. Through the tears she muttered, "I can't take this shit anymore."

"Alisa, let me help you. What did Louie say?"

"My father is missing."

I looked into her watery eyes.

"Sophia told Louie and Sharon that someone came in looking like an actor from *Goodfellas* movie, grabbed my father, shoved him into a car, and took off." She put her head on my chest looking for comfort "Brent, who could be doing this?" She couldn't stop crying. "I have to go find him. He is all I have."

"Did they call the police?" I asked, trying to make her think logically. I could tell her mind was everywhere right now.

"I don't know. I would think so."

"Okay, let's go. We'll go to Port Jeff and stay at your place tonight until we find out more. Do you need to call Michael, your uncle, or cousin?"

"That sounds good. I'll call everyone in the car." She seemed more settled. Her eyes were less red.

I drove Alisa to the restaurant in Port Jefferson. There was crime scene tape roping off the entrance. Sophia was talking to the detectives. Other officers were taking photos and collecting fingerprints. I looked over my shoulder and saw Special Agent Vogel. He was staring at me. He put his fingers to my lips signaling to be quiet. What the hell was he doing here?

Alisa grabbed my arm to go with her to talk to the detectives. She seemed calm, but I knew underneath her collected demeanor, she was just ready to break down again. I really didn't blame her. She definitely has had her share of bad luck. I was just happy I was here to help her through it. Even happier that she wanted me to. She explained what happened to her the past couple of weeks. She went over the robbery and informed them I was the police commissioner in charge of the investigation. She proceeded to explain how her father was jumped by a couple of thugs in Queens. She informed them that Louie would have more details about the incident being that he was present before telling them who to contact for that specific investigation. She started to go over her incident from two days ago. I saw the tears well up in her eyes. I told the detectives to sit down. I sat in the chair and had her sit on my lap. I was rubbing her back; she put her head in the crook of my neck. I immediately felt the tension dissipate.

"Well, Ms. Rossi, it looks like the car plates that were given to us by a witness tracked to a man by the name of Marco Futzelli. Do you know a...Marco Futzelli?" the detective asked, adjusting his thick-rimmed glasses to make sure he was pronouncing it correctly.

Alisa sat silently for a moment, trying to search her brain for the name before reluctantly saying, "No," with a shrug.

"Well, he is the head of the Marino crime family. Is your father—"

"No, he's not. He would never get himself involved with that embarrassment to the Italian heritage," she quickly replied, outraged by the thought.

"Okay, Ms. Rossi. We have our team on the lookout for the vehicle," the detective reassured.

"What was the vehicle that they drove away in?" Alisa inquired curiously.

"It says here a blue Maserati. Does that ring any bells?" he asked.

Alisa and I looked at each other.

"Officer, that is the same vehicle that ran my girlfriend off the road on Friday night. You may want to contact the Southampton Police." The puzzle pieces were fitting together.

I held Alisa tight to my chest; her tears quickly began to soak my shirt. She looked up at me in disbelief, unable to wrap her brain around all the traumatic events that transpired this week. I kissed her lips, which were salty from catching her tears. Over her shoulder, I saw that Vogel was trying to get my attention. Sophia brought Alisa a cup of coffee, and I excused myself and headed toward the bathroom. I looked into all of the stalls. Vogel came in.

"Okay, what is going on, why are you here?" I asked, demanding to understand why he was in Port Jeff at Alisa's restaurant.

"Not here, Collins," he said with his hands raised. "I guess you're staying at her house tonight?" *Obviously.*

"Yes," I said, slightly annoyed to share personal information.

"Tomorrow, 1:00 p.m. at Stony Brook's duck pond," he ordered emotionlessly.

He left the men's room. I saw him head toward the girls. He leaned in and grabbed around Sophia's waist and placed a kiss on her cheek. Question one has been answered. I would never put the two of them together as a couple, but who was I to judge?

We checked with the detectives if there were any other questions they needed to ask before we headed to her place. I put my arm around her waist. We were in the parking lot looking out into the sound. The reflection of the moon on the water was beautiful. Alisa turned around and kissed my cheek and whispered, "Thank you."

I kissed her back. "No thanks needed, love."

We headed over to her place. She was still very upset, rightfully so. We walked into the kitchen, poured a glass a wine for her, and got a bottle of beer for me. We sat on her couch; her head was on my chest, and I played with her hair while she tried to get some sleep.

I was so worked up I couldn't sleep. I went over the past few events in my head to try to put it together. The Marino family—not good. What could Vinny have with them? Marco was the brother of Joey and Richie; he must be about twenty-two years old, head of the family at twenty-two. The power at that age was dangerous. The other families will fight for the top spot, or the soldier will challenge his knowledge of the business and try to pull one over on him.

I reviewed the relationships Alisa had that I knew of:

> Sharon—best friend from grade school, photographer.
> Sophia—manager of the Port Jefferson restaurant, started off as a waitress two years ago; dating Stewart.
> Michael—old customer turned into a manager at the new restaurant. He was like a brother to Alisa. Doherty said something was off with him.
> Louie—lived in Howard Beach, boyfriend of Sharon, did spend some time with Vinny, and told us that whole story about his brother's friend hitting Vin. I made a mental note to learn more about him. I think Louie might know what was going on.

I will talk to Special Agent Vogel about it tomorrow. I wondered about Vogel. How he knew so much about me. After the two years in the witness protection, the agency did reinstate me. I did little cases, even some desk work. After a while, I didn't see myself in it anymore. I wanted to be more with the public.

Alisa began talking in her sleep. "I'm happy, love him, Dad. He's my forever."

Dreaming of me? My heart beamed with happiness. But things took a turn, she started twisting in the blanket, and a scared look came across her face.

"Leave me alone! You lied. You kept it from me all this time. Why?" she yelled out, her eyes tightly shut.

What was that about? I carefully tried to wake her up.

"Alisa, wake up, princess. Wake up. You're having a bad dream. Alisa, sweetie, wake up," I said sweetly caressing her face.

I kissed her cheek, traveled down her neck. I felt her hands grab my hair. She pulled me toward her lips and deepened the kiss.

"Now that's how I like to be woken up from a bad dream," she said with a giggle.

"You okay?" I asked, concerned.

"Yeah, fine now that you're by my side," she said with a kiss.

"Always," I whispered and nipped her ear.

"Ow! That hurt," she said playfully with a pout. "Kiss me and make it better?" she asked, mimicking my smirk-eyebrow raise move. This girl has me wrapped around her finger.

"Alisa, you minx," I whispered in her ear before gently running my tongue along her earlobe and sucking it into my mouth.

"Minx, hmm. I like the sound of that, but I just wanted to thank you properly for saving me from my nightmare."

"Oh, so you want to thank me properly. Curious for you to explain in further detail," I said, pulling her closer to me.

"I would, but I feel it would be better if I could just show you," she said, running her finger down my chest. She batted her eyes and held out her hand for me to follow her.

I grabbed her by her waist and lifted her in my arms and gently placed her on the bed where she proceeded to show me in detail how thankful she was.

I was one lucky man.

CHAPTER 28

Vinny

"You're a fuckup." I spat out as blood dribbled out of my mouth. This little remark prompted Marco to hit me again.

"Where is the necklace and the money, Vinny?" he asked, grinding his teeth and clenching his fist.

"Fuck you," I yelled, inviting another slap across the face.

"Vin, do want me to kill you?" he asked with a Cheshire cat smile. His breath smelled like he just ate of a garbage can or, worse, a hooker that didn't bathe.

"Screw you!" I called out, refusing to break. He was such a cocksucker. I hope hell was treating him like a pig on a spit at a slow speed.

"The good news is that your daughter made it out. Bad planning on my part, but I don't make the same mistake twice, got me?" he said pompously.

"I lost the necklace," I lied.

"Now fuck you, Vin," I said which was followed by a kick to the ribs, blood sprayed from of my mouth. Just then, I heard a familiar voice and looked up to see Louie. *Holy fuck, that bastard.* Louie was smiling at me, that son of a bitch double agent.

"I hear you were going to be getting rid of me," Louie said as he strode over to where Marco and his guys tied me up.

"Now look at who is shitting his pants. You're an old stupid dick, Vin. By the way, Vin, did I introduce you to my step-cousin,

Marco Futzelli?" Louie said now eye to eye with me. That's the worst of the disrespect that one could get in this business. That's the fuck you of all fuck yous other than sleeping with someone's wife.

"Okay, Vin, let's cut the shit now. Tell me where the goods are or Alisa gets it after you, then Josie, and I'll go down the line of the Massaro family," Marco said, fed up with the games.

Massaro family was my wife's maiden name. Due to unforeseen issues with the Marino family, her whole family took my last name. It threw off the police investigation that Carmine was implicated in. Some even think Alisa was his daughter. *What a bunch of dumbasses.*

"Vin, you were good to Louie, so this is what I am going to do. I will give you the night to tell me, but one false move and see those dogs over there," he said pointing, "they are trained to kill, so don't make me have to use them." The drool from the Pitbulls' mouths was falling to the ground. They looked like the man-eaters they were rumored to be.

"Good night, Vin, sweet dreams," Louie said as he turned around to leave.

"Fuck you," I shouted. "Fuck the both of you."

I couldn't believe I trusted that motherfucker. I told him things that could even get Carmine pissed off. I thought about what the hell I was going to do. I couldn't believe the shit I was in now. Alisa. I hated to admit it, but I was so happy her boyfriend was a cop. I prayed that he could protect her. This was going to go down bad. It didn't take long after the action ceased the dogs fell asleep. What a crack team. My head was throbbing with my hands tied, my only option was to tuck my chin to my chest to rest and come up with a plan.

Alisa was going to find out about me. The one thing I have held from her. I knew she was looking for me. This time I hope she doesn't find me. I don't want to think about the way she would react finding out the work I do. The disappointment on her face would put me to my grave. It would be worse than the beating I received from that punk Marco. Twenty-two-year-old head of the family because he took out his own uncle.

Louie, that prick. He confided in me about how much he truly loved Sharon. The bastard even asked me if, one day, when the time was right, he can marry her. I didn't understand why he asked me. He explained that I was the father figure in her life. She loved and respected me very much. Little did I know he was the one to put me here. He told Marco everything. I guess I was the dumbass. I am not sure how this would wind up tomorrow, but I prayed that I would come out of this alive, and if word got out about my affiliation, that Alisa would be forgiving.

CHAPTER 29

Brent

I turned over and stared at her sleeping. So angelic, flawless, perfection at its finest. I thought about the future for the first time in a different way, and it looked much happier with her in it.

My phone rang. I got up and moved into the kitchen. It was Detective Doherty.

"Boss."

"What's up, Detective?"

"The burner phone, it was Alisa's friend Louie who purchased it," Doherty shared.

I knew something wasn't right about him.

"So you were able to get a clear picture. This needs to be a positive match," I told him.

"Correct. It was a positive match, sir," Doherty confirmed. There was silence on the other side of the call. I think I hurt his ego by questioning his work.

He continued, "It gets better. We ran the fingerprints from the note found in Alisa's office, they belong to Louie. The only thing that we can't figure out is who took the necklace. Louie had an airtight alibi, he was stuck in traffic with Sharon. He was nowhere near the scene when the robbery took place."

That's why he was my number one guy. He wouldn't stop. He did what he needed to do to get the answers to the clues that he found. He always followed his gut, and it's been right so far. I wondered if he was able to dig up any information on Michael. I now knew he wouldn't have anything to do with the case, but something he said the other day made me question the way he felt about Alisa. He cared so much for Alisa. Jealousy was eating up my insides. I quickly brought myself back to the conversation.

"Good job. I don't want this out just yet. This could be connected to an event that took place last night. Doherty, do not discuss this with anyone. Understood?" I hung up. That motherfucker. Louie, there's something more to him. He had plenty of opportunities to kill Alisa. I dialed Special Agent Vogel. I needed to talk to him immediately.

I heard heavy breathing. "One minute, baby. Collins, this better be good."

"We have to talk. I got more info." I could tell he put his hand over the phone.

"Baby, this is important," he whispered, only partially covering the receiver.

"Collins, Ferry house, fifteen minutes," he ordered and hung up the phone.

I knew I owed him one for interrupting his morning glory.

I left Alisa a note on the nightstand, letting her know I would be back soon. I couldn't help to take a glimpse at the view before me. The sunlight peeked through the curtain. She was resting with her arm under the pillow, and the sunlight was hitting her face, highlighting her profile—the flawless skin, the eyelashes fanned out on her cheek, and the one curl that gently tickled her neck. The vision was one that was now embedded in my mind. I leaned down and pressed a simple kiss on her forehead, not wanting to leave. But I needed to find the answers to solve this puzzle. I had to protect her from the chaos that surrounded her.

I waited for Vogel. He drove up in his BMW. Getting out of the car, I couldn't help but smirk at his appearance. I saw a love bite on his neck and the sweat pants, Italian T-shirt, not to mention the bed head.

"Sorry to interrupt," I said.

"Well, spit it out then," he grumbled, Rage was brewing. He probably got shit for leaving that warm bed.

"My guy traced the phone to Louie and the fingerprints on the note to Louie as well," I informed him, looking at his face and amazed at his blank reaction.

"I know," he said.

"Well then, spill it, Vogel," I demanded. Now I was the one pissed.

"Louie works for us," he admitted.

"What the fuck, Vogel?" I spat out before remembering I was speaking to superior officer.

"Don't worry, Vin is still alive. Brent," he added, answering the question I had, "Vinny is the man we are watching. Marco put a hit on him. Vinny and his brother stole the necklace, and Marco wants the money for it." Shit, Doherty was right about Alisa's dad, just the wrong name.

"Who pushed Alisa off the road?" I needed to know.

"Marco. Brent, if you really love Alisa, then just keep her safe. We got this. Don't interfere," he warned.

"How do you know about the necklace?" I asked.

"Sophia, she is my girl. In and out of the bedroom obviously," he confessed with a smirk.

"I thought there was something going on," I said smugly with my arms crossed over my chest, I shook my head, and I looked out into the Long Island Sound.

"Vinny has an office downstairs, it's bugged, and Sophia monitors it. Oh, and there is one in Alisa's office in East Hampton," he reluctantly divulged.

"And Sharon?" I asked.

"Innocent, has no idea," he reassured.

Thank God. That would kill Alisa.

"Good. Well, the news about her dad will crush her. Stewart, please tell me Alisa—" I couldn't finish the question. It would ruin me if she was part of the robbery.

"You are good. Not a clue. She has been working on her success since high school. She doesn't even know her father is connected. I know it sounds ridiculous, but it's true. Sophia has been monitoring her for a couple of years," he reassured, putting my mind at ease.

My tense shoulders automatically relaxed knowing she had no clue.

"Brent, Marco is looking into you, but don't worry. Louie is the informant, so the information they are receiving is in fairy-tale dialogue," Vogel said, trying to dispel my fear.

Shit. He might know about me as the one who put his brothers in jail.

"From where we are standing, you're good," he said, as he patted my shoulder for reassurance.

"Trusting you on this. What do you need from me?" I asked eagerly.

"Nothing. I mean it, stay back and try to keep Alisa and Sharon occupied." I heard the urgency in his voice.

"Where is Marco now?" I asked.

"In Queens, the Ozone Bowling Alley. I have said enough," he said sternly, he was annoyed that he had already told me more than he should have.

"Brent, I mean it—don't interfere!" he ordered.

"Thanks, Stew, I won't," I reassured.

I headed back to the house. The lights were on, and I saw Alisa in the kitchen. What was I going to say to her? If and when she found out the news, it would destroy her. I put my head down on the steering wheel and smirked. How the past couple of weeks changed my life. Ironic how this crime family was part of our story so many years ago and even now as we turn into the best chapter yet.

I walked in searching for the woman who stole my heart. As I walked in the kitchen, Alisa had a spoon in one hand and Ben and Jerry's in the other. She's an ice cream for breakfast type of girl. I reached in and grab the spoonful that was in midair. She slapped my shoulder playfully.

"Where did you go?" she asked, followed by a little head tilt.

"I went to the police station. I had forgotten to tell the detective to get in touch with Doherty about the note and the phone call."

"Phone call?" she inquired.

Oh crap, I forgot to tell her. It must have slipped my mind, well, with me thinking she was dead two days ago that phone call didn't seem so important anymore.

"Michael received a phone call the night of your accident— another nursery rhythm," I told her, shrugging my shoulders. It's not like I'm belittling the call, but between everything else, it was moot.

She started to tear up. Everything was coming to be too much for her. I held her in my arms, knowing that this was just the start of the information she would be receiving soon.

"Why me? Why my dad? We are good people. We've never hurt anyone," she said in disbelief.

"I know, princess," I kissed the top of her head, knowing full well that her father was not as innocent as she believed.

"They'll find him," I reassured, brushing my hands through her hair.

"Alive," she said. "And I want whoever is responsible for all of the pain they've caused my family to pay dearly."

"Positive thoughts, my love," I said, trying to calm her.

She looked up and kissed me.

CHAPTER 30

Alisa

Brent was being very protective of me today—he knew something. Or was I just being paranoid? He wouldn't keep anything from me, would he? I hope not or else that would cause real problems in our relationship. Trustworthiness was a big part of my character. I couldn't be with someone who wasn't honest with me. Even worse, deliberately keeping information from me was another nonnegotiable.

A hand came around my waist, and Brent nipped my ear and gave me kisses along the nape of my neck.

"How are you holding up?" he asked, concerned about my well-being.

"As well as expected, I guess. Have you heard anything from your friends or the police?" I lifted my head and gazed at him with curiosity.

"No updates. I got off the phone with Detective Doherty a little while ago. He's reviewing the security tapes to pin down who left the message with Michael. Did anyone call you? Sharon? Louie? Sophia?" His voice sounded frantic. "Have they heard anything? Where are Sharon and Louie? I thought she would be here." He's anxious.

"I should call the detective. See if they have any idea where my dad is. Sharon hasn't called. Your right. I'm surprised that she isn't here. Although she knows I have you for support now." I reached up and kissed underneath his chin.

"Always, princess. I hope she doesn't think I'm coming in between you and her. I wouldn't intentionally do that," he said pulling me into him tighter.

"We aren't like that. In fact, the opposite actually happens. You saw her in the hospital kicking you out so she can spend time with me," I said, tapping him on the shoulder and starting to giggle, remembering his reaction. It was priceless.

"I love that sound," he whispered gently. "I promise you that I will make sure you laugh every day in good times and in bad."

I looked at him, realizing "the good times and in bad" was part of wedding vows.

We headed into the den and sat on the couch. I really didn't want to go anywhere. I was still not one hundred percent from the accident. Brent has been wonderful. He has been waiting on me, making sure I was taking my medicine, and he even cooked for me. Yes, it was a grilled cheese and salad, but the thought was there. He was so cute trying to impress me with his culinary skills. He could toss a salad just like any other sous chef. I laughed to myself.

His phone rang. He kept his screen covered and told me it was his friend Tom calling. I couldn't wait to meet him. I mean he has already met my friends, Sharon, Louie, and Michael. I wanted to learn more about him. He got up and walked into the other room.

I called Sharon and let her know what was going on with my dad. She was so upset last night.

"Shaz, where are you?" I asked, hearing traffic in the background.

"In Queens, looking for Louie," Sharon replied, sounding annoyed.

Confused, I asked, "Why, isn't he with you?"

"I wanted to surprise you and get you those cookies you love from Severoli's on 101st Avenue, the fresh bread and broccoli rabe, and sausage bread from Rosemary's," the New Yorker said all in one breath.

Mm. "I knew you were my best friend for a reason," I stated, sitting cross-legged on the couch.

"I know," Sharon mumbled with a laugh. She knew I appreciated her thoughtfulness.

The background noise changed to cheery music and what sounded to be like cymbals crashing together.

"I just walked into the bowling alley. It's Monday league night," she said, clearly preoccupied.

"I thought you bowl on Wednesdays?" I should pay attention a little better.

"We liked Wednesday's league so much we just signed up for Monday, too," she explained.

Wow, she must really love this guy.

"He's not here. Oh, wait, I see him. Call you later," she said before hanging up the phone.

Brent came back in after closing all the shades.

"Who were you on the phone with? Was it Sharon? Where is she?" he asked.

"Funny, I just called her. She is in Queens, looking for Louie."

He had the look of fear in his eyes.

"What's wrong, babe?"

"Call her and tell her to come home," he demanded, handing back my phone. I became alarmed.

"Why? Before I hung up, she found him at the bowling alley."

He took my hand. "Princess, you need to call her and tell her that you need her to come home now. Tell her that you need her."

"What the hell is going through your head?"

"Trust me, Alisa. Do it now, honey. I will explain later."

I must be missing something here. I didn't like feeling out of the loop. Confused but willing to comply, I called Sharon back and put it on speaker. Once she picked up, all I could hear were faint whimpers.

"Sharon?" I could hear her sobbing on the other end.

"He told me to leave and that I was crowding him and to stop being such a leech," she explained, nearly choking on tears.

That seems out of character.

Brent was trying to get my attention and mouthing, "Tell her to come home now, babe."

I relayed the message.

"I am," she said. She fell silent for a moment and then she whispered, "Oh my god, Alisa."

I suddenly heard gunshots. The bowling alley erupted in screams, and I heard her running.

"No, Louie, oh my god, Louie!" Sharon screamed.

"Sharon, run for cover. Go behind a pole or under a table," Brent yelled into the phone.

"Don't go near him! Don't go after him!" Brent's face was turning red from fear.

I yelled into the phone, "Sharon, run for cover now!" I heard a shot that sounded really close to the phone. I felt numb automatically. "Sharon, are you okay?"

"Yeah," she whispered. "I am under a table. Alisa, I'm scared." She was panting, struggling to catch her breath.

"Stay there," Brent screamed. The phone cut out.

I was enraged. I wanted to be there with her so she wouldn't be scared and alone. I wanted to hold her hand and we could find a way out together. Brent began pacing back and forth in the kitchen.

"Okay, what do you know? What are you keeping from me, my love?" I asked, trying not to completely lose my cool and giving him the benefit of the doubt. I felt my face beginning to turn red. Brent just stood there, dumbfounded, maybe he didn't expect me to dig deeper.

"I…I can't," he could barely get the words out of his mouth.

Wrong words, dear.

"You can't or you won't?" I asked venomously.

"I can't," he said, his hands out to his sides.

"Brent, this is not a good sign for our future. Tell me," I begged, beginning to cry out of anger and frustration.

He shook his head no.

"Get out!" I screamed.

"Alisa," he said, following me into the kitchen.

"Get out now! My best friend is in danger, and you can't—"

He grabbed me and pulls me into his chest. "No, Alisa, you need to trust me." He looked deeply into my eyes, begging me to trust him. Well, it worked both ways.

"You want me to trust you when you can't even trust me? get out!" I yelled as I pounded my fists on his chest.

"Alisa!" He pleaded.

I wasn't going to let up.

"Now, Brent. Get out!" I picked up the ice cream carton and threw it at his head. I sat right where I was and started to cry. It felt like the walls were closing in on me. My world was beginning to crumble just as things were starting to level out.

"Alisa, please, I don't want to leave you here alone." His hands were folded in prayer position, "I just need you to trust me."

"Why, why should I trust you?" I asked, knowing nothing he could say would calm me down.

"Because I love you, because I need to protect you," he explained, trying to reach out and hold my hands.

"I don't want to hear it anymore," I said, now shutting down, my arms folded across my chest.

He hasn't gotten a chance to see this side of me. I never thought he would. I could be one crazy lady, he was lucky I wasn't also on my period or else he'd really be feeling the wrath.

"Okay, I know you want to know, Alisa. I want to tell you—"

I cut him off. "*But* you won't. Is that what you are going to tell me, Brent?" We just stared at each other. There was a moment of silence.

"Alisa, I promise I'll tell you as soon as it's safe to."

My eyes went wide. "*Get out!*" I couldn't control my temper now. I held my head because it hurt. I went to get my pain meds as he wrapped his arm around my waist.

"Please, princess, I love you." I felt the desperation in his voice.

"Brent, I need you to leave. Maybe I'll call you later." I released his hands from around my waist and walked away.

"Is this what you really want, Alisa?" I saw the tears well up.

"For now. Yes. Please leave," I said, pointing to the door. I needed him out before I lost it.

"I'm trying to protect you!" he yelled desperately trying to convince me.

"You are here with me. What are you trying to protect me from? Leave now," I told him, waving him off. He needed to leave. I have to get to Sharon. I knew he wouldn't let me if he stayed.

"Just know I am leaving because you asked me to, but I don't want to. Alisa, I will always love you. I'll call you later to check in." He cautiously came over, kissed me, grabbed his gym bag, and left.

I slid my body down the wall until I landed on the kitchen floor and cried. First my restaurant then my dad followed by my accident and now Sharon? I've always been a tough one—cast iron pan tough—but Brent keeping stuff from me was the last straw. I had to do something. I couldn't keep sitting here helpless.

I grabbed the spare keys to my dad's car and called an Uber to take me to the restaurant. The cut on my leg started to bleed. Damn it. Taking an extra gauze, I rewrapped my leg and hopped in my Uber.

I walked into the restaurant, and Sophia ran up to me and began walking alongside me as I made my way to my office to snag the copy of my driver's license I had on my desk from when I applied for my liquor license.

"Aren't you supposed to be at home getting better?" She looked down at my leg. "Alisa, your leg is bleeding. Where are you going?"

I ignored her, not necessarily on purpose, but I was on a mission.

Sophia was at the door. "Alisa, did they find your dad? Are you going to get him? I can drive you. I'll have Brian take over until I get back. You really shouldn't be driving."

I knew she cared, but leave me alone. She continued to distract me. I found a spare credit card.

"Where is Brent? He should take you." All I heard was white noise. I was set on getting to Sharon. She needed me right now. The sounds of gunshots and screaming kept replaying in my head. I was pissed at Brent and didn't want to give him the opportunity to play hero after lying to me, and I certainly didn't want him to keep me from making sure Sharon was okay. I needed to check on her with my own eyes.

"Sophia, thank you for your concern, but I'm fine. Do you know where my dad's car is parked?" She reluctantly told me. I found the car and started to head into Queens.

CHAPTER 31

Brent

I couldn't believe that she told me to leave. I should have stayed. But the look in her eyes—I betrayed her. I couldn't tell her. I headed to the restaurant in Port Jefferson. I parked my car by the ferry house to think. I decided I was going back, but I had to give her some time. She needed to calm down.

As I was watching customers make their way into the restaurant, I realized I recognized a face walking out of the doors. Shit! I rubbed my eyes thinking they were deceiving me. They weren't. It was Alisa, hopping in a Mercedes and taking off. I immediately called her phone, as it rang, I quietly whispered, "Alisa, pick up the phone, pick up the phone," hoping it would prompt her to answer. No luck, I left a frustrated voicemail.

"Princess, I love you. Please call me. I promise I can explain soon—"

Beep.

I looked down at my phone—dead. I never charged it, great! I kept following her. My mind kept coming up with possible scenarios on how this could all play out. I was weaving in and out of traffic to catch up with her. Headed toward the Southern State Parkway, I realized she was making her way to Queens. Shit, this wasn't good. If my phone wasn't dead, I would've called in a favor to get her pulled over, allowing me to catch up and talk her out of it. I had no choice but to trail behind her. She shouldn't be driving, she's in no shape to be behind the wheel.

I was so mad at myself; I should have just told her. Looking at the clock, I hoped by the time she got to the bowling alley, it would be all over and the crime scene would be taped off with the news crews pulling up to cover the drama.

I felt calm and stuck to the plan. She turned off the exit and turned onto Cross Bay Boulevard to Atlantic Avenue and headed toward the Ozone Bowling Alley. My heart started to race.

Police cars were everywhere. I spotted Vogel, but I ignored him. I saw her get out of her car scrambling to find Sharon. I was following her. I looked at her leg; it was bleeding, and now she was limping. She was running toward someone or something. I saw her pace quicken, and her hand was now over her mouth. I turned the corner, and she was on her knees. She had her arms wrapped around her friend's limp body; tears were flooding her face. She kept looking around, screaming for help. Louie squatted down next to her. I slowly kept making my way closer, watching Alisa continue to sob and kiss Sharon's hand. Louie was touching Sharon's face and suddenly let out a guttural scream.

"*No*, no, Sharon baby, come back to me!" Louie cried. Sharon was unresponsive. I was now feet away and could see that her lifeless body was lying in a puddle of blood. She was hit. Those monsters took her life. It wasn't supposed to go down like this.

Alisa looked up and spotted me. I ran toward her; thinking she needed my embrace. She handed Sharon's body over to Louie, stood up and rushed toward me, blazing with fists pounding my chest, cursing in Italian.

"I got you, princess," I said, trying to wrap my arms around her.

"You get away, get away. You didn't tell me she was in danger. You couldn't trust me. Leave, you bastard!" she cried.

She was grieving, I knew she was angry, I tried not to take her words personally. "I'm here, I'm here," I reassured in a low tone.

"You knew about this. You should have trusted me to keep my best friend safe. Now, now she's…"

She went down to her knees. Tears were streaming down her face. The look of anguish and pain was evident. I bent down to her level.

"You helped them kill her! You should have told me she was in danger."

The yells began attracting attention, and it felt like all at once everyone turned away from the crime scene and began looking at us, watching Alisa's meltdown intently. They had no idea how much effort I put in trying to keep her and her family safe. From their standpoint, I'm sure I looked like the bad guy.

She had a look of disgust on her face. Nothing I could say in that moment would change her mind. I opened my mouth to explain myself, she lifted her hand to silence me and shook her head.

"Brent, you need to forget me because I don't want to remember you!"

A slap in the face would have hurt less. Taking those words I said to her ten years ago and throwing them back in my face with a different meaning, the same bullet that went through Sharon's heart just shattered mine. I looked into her eyes in disbelief.

"Alisa," I called her name.

Close by, a gurney was being loaded into an ambulance. She turned her head to get a glimpse and realized it was her father strapped in, unconcious, getting worked on by an EMT. She fell to her knees again and looked up at me.

"Did you know about this too? Did you?"

She was now looking through me, not at me and not with love. Before I could say anything, she got up and hobbled to his side as quickly as her injured body would take her.

"Daddy, I love you. Can you hear me, Papa? I love you. Don't leave me like Mama. I'll have nobody, Papa. Do you hear me?"

My heart sank. *I'm still here for you, Alisa, always.* I started to make my way toward her, and I felt a hand gripped my shoulder—it was Vogel.

"Come with me," he said, trying to calm me down.

I didn't want to leave her, but it was clear she didn't want me around. It was like a knife through the heart. I guess I needed to shift my attention and figure out what the hell went on here and figure out where it all went wrong.

"Is Vinny dead?" I inquired.

"No, but badly hurt," Vogel shared.

I couldn't help but to continue to steal glances of Alisa, who was leaned over Vinny crying. She must've sensed me and turned her head toward me. She was throwing daggers with her eyes like I was scum on the bottom of her shoe. My heart never hurt so much. I did the right thing, so why did I feel so badly about it? I hoped that this anger was only temporary. Maybe once the dust settled, Alisa would understand I was just doing my job all while trying to keep her safe. It felt like a double-edged sword. Lose the job or lose the girl.

She meant every word. I knew I did the right thing. I told Sharon to keep cover, not to move. I shrugged it off knowing that in a couple of hours, once the air settled, I could talk to her let her know why I couldn't tell her.

Vogel once again gripped my shoulder to lead me away. I walked with him toward the van sitting at the church on the other side of the bowling alley. It was your typical stakeout vehicle equipped with the cameras and media equipment. He sat me down and I finally got the case details, I just needed to wait until shit hit the fan to hear it.

According to Vogel, Marco kidnapped Vinny from the restaurant and demanded the money or the necklace Vinny stole from Kim Killian. Vinny didn't give a crap what Marco wanted. Marco's men beat the crap out of Vinny until he submitted to their requests.

Louie told Vinny's brother-in-law Carmine and nephew Anthony what was going on. Louie played the informant on both sides of the family. During the beating, Carmine and Anthony barged in the back room and guns were fired. Pure chaos ensued. Alisa's uncle and nephew sustained minor injuries and are now in custody on the way to the hospital.

Marco was dead; Carmine shot him in back of the head. Vinny was in critical condition from the beating he got from Marco. Alisa's friend Sharon saw Louie and ran toward him. One of Marco's guys figured out Louie was playing both sides, and shot Sharon to retaliate.

"Oh, man, Stewart. This got out of hand," I mumbled, my hand in my hands.

"Louie was torn up," Vogel explained. "Apparently he really fell in love. He planned on taking her when he went into protection."

Stewart looked down at the street camera and saw Louie by Sharon's side.

"He told me that he wished he never took this job. He found his forever girl. He actually asked if there was a way he could leave and be put in hiding with Sharon. He was denied." He shook his head.

Falling in love, being one of us, it's a rocky journey. That's why I dated the ones who really knew about this job. It was easier all the way around. Relationships were strained, and you needed to hide information from that person so they didn't get hurt.

"Stewart, I saw it. He did. Sharon and Louie were good together."

I remembered what he said to me in the cafeteria about Sharon. She knew how to calm him down, how to make him laugh, and how to comfort him. Just the way he described their connection, he was in deep. Their bond reminded me of mine and Alisa's.

"The sacrifice we pay to do the job we love at the agency. What's up with Alisa? She seems upset with you. You didn't—"

I just stared at him. I couldn't say a word. The feeling of loss was a hard thing, and this was the second time this week. There were no words to describe how I was feeling.

"She saw through me. She knew I knew something. I couldn't tell her, and now this has happened. Stew, I—"

"It's time to be patient. Look at what happened to her tonight. Don't make this about you. It is about what she is going through. She'll give you your chance to explain."

"How can you be so sure, Stew? She is feisty."

"You know she was part of the investigation too. Trust me. Destiny is a funny word, but when it comes to relationships and the information we found out about you and her, let's just say you keep on finding her, gravitating back to her—that's destiny."

He slapped my back knowing and searched my face to see if I believed him. I needed to this big brother moment. I wish I had these with my own flesh and blood.

I looked at Stew and smiled. "When did you become a romantic?"

"I may be in the FBI, but I still have a heart. Brent, does she really know you? Does she know who you really are? Does she know why you were in that high school that day you met? You know what I mean."

"No. She doesn't."

"Maybe that's something you should do when the timing is right. You know when you trust her and bring her into your world," Vogel suggested.

I took into consideration on what he was saying. Did I trust her? I knew I did. So why hadn't I shared this part with her yet, the real reason I left that day and never returned for her?

"You are basing your future with this woman on a lie or omission. She's right, Brent. You may not trust her. So the question is back to you, why?"

I just stared back at him; I knew he was right. I don't know what's keeping me from sharing myself with her. I looked outside the van and watched as Alisa climbed into the ambulance with her father. My heart ached that I couldn't be by her side.

"Where are they taking Vinny?" I asked.

"Jamaica Hospital. It's off of Atlantic Avenue," Vogel replied.

Stewart gave me the directions to the hospital. I knew she didn't want to see me, but once I realized she left the keys in her dad's car, I figured I should drop it off to her. One less thing for her to worry about.

Heading toward the hospital, I tried to figure out how everything that was done could have ended up much worse if I told her. She could have been the one on the floor instead of Sharon. I came to the entrance of the hospital and entered. I debated if I should bring the keys to her myself. So I can look at her and see if I could get a chance to just hug her, give her support. I stopped at the front desk and decided I should give her space.

I texted Alisa:

> Dropped the car off and left the keys at the front desk of the hospital. Car is on the corner of 89th and 135th Street.
> We need to talk.
> I need you princess. XX

I got an immediate response.

> Thank you for doing that. I need you to forget me, Brent. How can you need someone you don't trust?
>
> Goodbye, Alisa

It was like a punch to the gut. My past was still hunting me, keeping me from true happiness—true love. Defeated, I walked out of the hospital's main entrance and started to make a phone call to the department. From the corner of my eye, I saw Louie walking toward me all bandaged up. There we were, two broken men.

"Hey, how's Alisa?" Louie asked.

"I don't know. She is not speaking to me," I answered.

"She's not speaking to you? What happened?" he asked, confused.

"Louie. I spoke to Stewart—I know everything. I know who you are and respect you for it. With that said, I'm so sorry about Sharon. I heard you had true affection for her."

A tear fell from his eye. Within seconds, the tears streamed down his face. We walked toward the bench about one hundred feet away. I realized it was my turn to take on the position of big brother. I could feel the guilt emanating off of him, knowing he put her in the position to be shot.

"Brent, my last words to her were 'don't be a leech,' the last words before she closed her eyes. I watched them shoot her and couldn't do a thing about it." He hit the bench with such force it echoed. "I loved her, man, with everything I had. She was one tenacious woman, heart as good as gold. Spirit that makes you proud to be with a woman like that." He shook his head in disbelief.

"This job, what are you going to do?" It sucked, but I was not good with this type of talk, man-to-man sympathy stuff. He looked at me, and a slight smile appeared. He could sense I was being awkward and trying to say something to console him. It took him a minute to continue with the conversation.

"I have permission to go to the grave site, but as you know, with witness protection in disguise…as Chad Winters."

Oh, I knew witness protection well.

"I'm going to check in with Alisa. What can I do to help?" he asked as he grasped my shoulder. I appreciated the gesture, but I knew his efforts would ruin his cover. I couldn't put him in that kind of danger.

"No, thanks, this is my mess. I will figure out a way for her to listen to what I have to say. You know my side of the story." This was a disaster. A goddamn tsunami.

"Brent, let me tell her what I can. You two had a connection that was strong. I saw it. I can't promise you that she'll run back into your arms, but it may make her think about hearing you out. The rarity of finding someone who you love in this line of work and not being able to fully share yourself…" He paused, the words getting harder to say as his eyes welled with tears. His grip on my shoulder was tightened, and his eyes closed with agony, trying to gather himself.

"I should have told Sharon where I was going, told her what she really meant to me, and told her to put on a pretty dress and be ready for the night of her life. Instead of going bowling, we could have gone to Manhattan in South Street Seaport where we first met, and I should've proposed to her," he said as he reached into his pocket and showed me the ring. One tear he was desperately trying to hold back escaped and a river followed. He quickly wiped them away.

"Brent, just give her some time, but don't let her go until you tell her what you need to tell her," he said before he walked away.

My heart went out to him. He lost his love forever. I saw him enter the elevator, and as he turned around, we looked at each other and nodded. This would be the last time I would see him. He would be entering a new life.

At least my love was still alive. Not talking to me, but alive. I was relieved to know that someone would be with her. I thought of the one person who would drop everything to be by her side since I was in the doghouse. I dialed Michael to let him know what was going on as I entered the subway station to head back to my car.

"Michael, it's Brent. Listen, not sure what your day is like, but Alisa needs you." I leaned my head back on the brick wall. I felt emptiness inside.

"What do you mean? Where are you, Brent? Are you with her now?" Michael's fifty questions woke me up from the self-pity. I dreaded, knowing I had to explain what just happened. I braced myself on the wall behind me and told him what I could.

"There was this crime scene. It might even be on the news tonight. It happened in Queens. Alisa is not hurt, but Sharon died, and her father is at Jamaica Hospital in critical condition. There is so much to the story. I need you to go to the hospital to sit with her. I just can't go over it with you right now."

"You never answered the important question—*are you with her?*" The tone in his voice elevated. The worry was transparent.

"Michael, she doesn't want me around right now. I love her, Michael, but something I held back from telling her…" I paused to gather my thoughts. Before I could even finish, Michael jumped in.

"She feels that you betrayed her. Maybe even didn't trust her. Brent, that right there is Alisa's number one need with anyone she deals with, trust, either in business or a relationship. That's why she never stayed with anyone long enough to completely fall in love with them. She didn't trust them. If there is a good reason for why you did not tell her what you needed to, give her time to deal with what she needs to deal with and try again."

Michael was really close to her. He knew her better than anyone. He continued the conversation letting me know that he was on his way and that this conversation was not over. The protective brother instinct.

I reached the parking lot of the bowling alley. The area was all taped off, and the investigation was wrapping up. I was having flashbacks of the fatal crime scenes I've seen over my career—scenes I wished I could forget.

As I reached my car, I glanced over to the area where I saw Alisa lean over Sharon's body, begging for her to wake up. Wishing it was all some kind of nightmare she could shake her out of. My body tightened with grief for her.

I headed back to East Hampton. I was consumed with scenarios of how today could've played out differently. What I could've done differently. A sense of loneliness hit me head on.

I got home, put my gym bag on the counter and saw the dishes that Alisa washed before we left last night. What a difference a day made. Our connection was strong enough to get us through this. I had to give her time, take Louie and Michael's advice.

My body was worn-out, and my mind was fried. The shower was calling to me. The cascade of water up against my body was refreshing. I changed the nozzle to the pulsating setting to help loosen the tightness. I tried to make a list of my next steps.

1. Doherty needs to complete the case.
2. Call Stewart for any updates he could tell me.
3. Call Tom to get security cameras in Alisa's house.
4. Have Mary make room for Alisa's clothes in closet.

What am I doing? Here I go again. I breathed out and shook my head. This was really hard. Yet it's only been a couple of weeks of our relationship. I decided to take my friend Jack out from behind the bar and get reacquainted to the misery I went through a couple of days ago.

Time can be my friend and enemy. Ironic.

CHAPTER 32

Alisa

My mind was in disarray. I had no one to talk to. A tear flowed down my cheek. I started to giggle as I rubbed my eyes. I felt like I was losing my mind. I was yet again sitting at the hospital after my father was nearly beaten to death, still recovering from my own injuries from an attempt on my life. My world had been turned upside down. In twenty-four hours, I was with the one person who I thought I would be with for the rest of my life; to finding out my father was missing; to seeing my best friend, *my sister*, in my arms not moving; and then to see my rock, my father, beaten, gasping for breath. Why was all this happening? Looking up, I saw Louie come up the stairs. Silly to say, but a sense of relief overwhelmed me. He automatically wrapped his arm around me for a tight hug. His chin was on top of my head, and we stayed there for a moment using each other for some comfort after today's events.

"How's your dad?" he asked.

"He's in surgery," I said as I was twisting my fingers in front me. I really was nervous. I saw what my father looked like, and the thought of losing two people who were the closest to me freaked me out. I quickly changed the subject.

"Louie, just know that Sharon really loved you." We both started tearing up. Reality that she was gone hit me looking at him and seeing the hurt in his eyes.

"Alisa, you need to know I really loved her," he said, looking into my eyes so I could see the truth in them.

"Yes. I know. Louie, let me ask you a question. Did you say she was a leech to protect her? You knew she was going to be in the cross-fire, didn't you?" I tried to get the information I needed to understand everything that transpired. I needed to know what Brent knew and why he kept it from me. There were so many missing pieces to this puzzle.

"How did you find out?" He had this surprised look on his face. Did he really think that I was that stupid? What was it with these men?

"I have been here for an hour going over everything, replaying all of the events in my head. Sharon called me upset, because you told her to leave. She wanted to find you to surprise you. When I arrived at the bowling alley, I saw you talking to the FBI. I recognized the people involved. They were part of the mafia. Did my dad take Kim's necklace? He did, didn't he?" Louie looked at me stunned, as if I had inside information. I wish I did. I continued.

"Don't worry, I know you can't say anything. They wanted the necklace." I continued to just spurt things out just to get a reaction out of him. His arm wrapped around my waist as he guided me out the door.

"Alisa, let's take a walk. It isn't good to discuss this here."

I was still not sure if he was the good guy or the bad. There were police officers on either side of the hallway. The officers just nodded him through. He continued to walk down the hall into the visitors' room. Once we entered, he looked throughout the room and locked the door. I needed to know.

"I need you to tell me the truth. You're the good guy that had to be bad. The problem was that you fell in love with my best friend. You didn't know how to separate reality and your job." The look on his face told me his answer without even hearing it come from his mouth. His shoulders were slumped and he was looking at me with a blank expression. It took him a moment to gather his thoughts to speak.

"Alisa, you are right. I did fall in love. I never felt that way with anyone. You are also right. I can't tell you much, but I can tell you one thing because I trust you. I am undercover agent for the FBI. Your dad is not who you think he is, but he did a great job not getting you involved." He paused and shook his head thinking of the words he wanted to say to me. Right now my world was falling apart. Louie cleared his throat and continued.

"Brent had no idea until this morning what was happening. He was told to keep you and Sharon safe. Alisa, I know it's none of my business, but that man loves you, Alisa. He told me in the hospital in Southampton. I never met Brent until he was with you. He's a good man, Alisa, very well respected." He had his hands on my shoulders.

"Louie, thank you for telling me and trusting me, but I can't say the same for Brent. He should have trusted me just like you have. I understand now how important it is not to say anything you told me, for your safety and mine," I said, looking down at my fingers twisting, and shaking my head realizing that Brent could have just told me crumbs of what he knew. That would've been enough. Maybe Brent wasn't actually ready for a real relationship, one that is built on trust, not just lust. It felt as if my heart was in a million pieces for so many different reasons.

"Alisa, thank you. I also need to let you know the agency is very regimented. You can't be liberal with information. The next two years following Sharon's funeral I won't be able to contact you. I will always wish you the best. You have become a friend of mine. I need to go. Please text me the information regarding Sharon's services." He left looking over his shoulder as the NYPD went toward the ICU. A guard was now at the door to where my father's room will be. My mind was racing, I could feel a migraine starting to form.

My phone chimed; it was a text from Michael:

> Let's hope the worst is over.
> Brent called me.
> Be there for you tonight, baby girl. XX

> Thank you. I could use a friend right now.
> XX/OO

Brent called Michael; he wouldn't give up without a fight. I saw it now. I just didn't have the strength to fight all the challenges that were coming at me in full force. The fact was he didn't trust me to tell me what he knew. But I had to put the thought of Brent and what might be on the backburner. My dad's recovery was my focus. I saw my Aunt Josie coming down the corridor with her rosary beads. It actually put a smile on my face. She was very dramatic. Sure, my dad was in ICU, but my aunt didn't even know what prayer to say for each bead. It's comical really.

"Alisa, how is he?" she asked, clutching the rosary with a concerned look on her face.

"Aunt Josie, he lost a lot of blood. They will know better in the morning." Speaking to my aunt was an art; you needed to play it simple. Any emotion caused her to always think the worst. My mother was the same way.

"I'll stay with him. You get something to eat. You're so skinny. I bet you only had one of the awful Greek yogurt breakfasts."

A smile formed, the first one since all this happened. It's a typical Sicilian behavior. When we get nervous, they tell you to eat. This time, she was absolutely right. I hadn't eaten since this morning. I took her up on her offer to stay with my dad.

"Aunt Josie, would you like a coffee or something to eat? I am going to the cafeteria."

"No, sweetie. You go now, before they run out of salad." She winked at me knowing her comment would release some of the stress that was eating me up inside.

I was downstairs getting a cappuccino from the machine. I knew it's that powder crap, but I was desperate. When I reached the cashier with my piece of pound cake and coffee, I looked around not knowing what I was looking for. There's a table in the corner I went to. Picking at the pound cake, I felt the sense of loneliness and sadness with the loss of my friend. A tear fell once again for the umpteenth time today. I shook off the feeling and gathered my garbage to throw out. As I walked back to the ICU, I heard the mumbling from the outside of my father's room. The guard must have left his post.

As I turned the knob, I heard my aunt yelling, "You bastard, you had to be selfish. You had to get everyone in trouble. Rosalie would spit at you right now. Alisa was never to find out about our connections. Do you remember the promise you made to her on her deathbed, on your wedding day?"

My eyes went wide. A rush of anger overcame any sadness I had felt just minutes ago.

"You knew! Aunt Josie, everyone knew besides me. I feel like such an idiot. How can you all keep this from me? Why would you keep this from me?" I went to her for answers, the answers to the questions that now have redefined my life.

"It was for the best, my Alisa. It was for the best. Now, our family is out after today. Marco is dead. Uncle Carmine and Anthony will be in jail. Your father…" She looked to the ceiling and did the sign of the cross as she kissed her rosary beads still clutched in her hands. She gave a last look at my father, grabbed his hand, and kissed him. "We are free now, Alisa. You do not need to know any more than today. No more debt to pay to the family!" She turned toward the door and walked out.

She grabbed the door jam and swiveled her head to face me. "I'll call you tomorrow. Alisa, be well." The look on her face showed the relief and fear of the unknown.

Her rosary beads lay on my father's chest, and I was left in a state of confusion. If I thought Brent's withholding was a betrayal, what should I consider my family's secret ties to the mafia? How could I have been so clueless? I sat down by my father's bedside, shaken to my core by my aunt's confession. My head was pounding. I rested my head next to my father's bandaged hand to rest my eyes.

Just as I was about to nod off, I felt Michael's energy enter the room. I ran into his arms to get one of the bear hugs that helped me when I was upset. The only person I wanted to be with right now. The only person I could trust.

"I'm here, Alisa, let it out. It's been a hell of a day, huh?"

Just hearing his voice and the comment he made, the waterworks flew. He started to rock me back and forth as if I was a child.

Michael's shirt was now drenched with tears. He kissed the top of my head and lifted my chin to look at me.

"Are we good? I mean I didn't bring an extra shirt, and this one is wet."

I whacked his chest as a giggle was released from my mouth. "I'm good. Thank you for being here."

"Where else would I be?" he said as he shrugged his shoulders and hugged me again. Our conversation was interrupted when the doctor came in to examine my dad.

"Ms. Rossi, I presume."

"Yes, that's correct. Vincent is my father."

He nodded his head before he started his diagnosis. "He will be in the intensive care unit until we see improvement. The next forty-eight hours will be critical. It's too early to tell if he will make it. He lost a lot of blood, and the surgeons had many wounds to tend to. We are afraid we may not have gotten to them all. Your father is very lucky man. Normally with that amount of blood loss, people wouldn't even survive the ambulance ride to the hospital. If he keeps fighting the way he has been, we should see some good signs within that two-day window."

It was so much information to take in, but there's hope for recovery, and right now that was enough.

"Thank you, Doctor," were the only words I could let leave my mouth without another breakdown.

"You're welcome. There is hope, Alisa. As I said, your father is a fighter." He put his hand on mine. "Do you have any questions?"

"No, Doctor, thank you for everything."

As the doctor left the room, I saw the officer return to his post.

Michael embraced me, chin on my head. "We'll get through this. Why are there guards at the door?"

"Why? Why am I in this shit show? There're police outside waiting for answers from my father. My heart is broken, Sharon is dead, my dad is in critical condition, and apparently my father was part of a mafia family. Michael, my world has been turned upside down and inside out." I looked out the window shaking my head. I verbally said it this time without a tear in my eye. I needed to find my strength and climb these mountains my life was bringing me. I wanted to reach the top. Only then will the universe provide me with clarity of why this all is happening to me and what the future holds.

Destiny is the journey. Fate will tell me where I stand.

Would you like to know what happens next? Will Alisa grow from this experience? Will she find a new love, or will her journey bring her back to Brent?

The next chapter of her life starts in *Fate*.

Fate

C. E. Giannico

Book II of the Destino Trilogia

CHAPTER 1

Alisa

In the last two weeks, my life had become a roller coaster. I had been put through every emotion a human being could go through. The sadness, betrayal, passion, grief, and a sense of happiness had been my mini tornadoes of hope. I looked over the Long Island Sound watching where the sun and water met. The colors of the sky—yellows, pinks, and purples—brought some peace for a moment. The memories of the last few weeks began to melt into a kaleidoscope of images, intermingled with various events from my life as if they were somehow connected by a common thread. Will I ever be able to make sense of it all? I moved over to the chaise lounge and sat with my wine. I closed my eyes and tried to relax. The cool breeze hit my face, but nothing will ease the feeling I had about today.

Today was the day I said my final goodbyes to the closet person I had in my life. I looked at all the people with their heads down walking to the site where Sharon will be buried. It was the hardest thing I ever had to do. We were inseparable ever since the day we met in junior high. She was so much more than a friend, she was my sister. We went through everything together. A shadow of a smile was on my face when I remembered all our firsts we've shared. Everything including our period, music concerts, first kiss with our first boyfriend, and virginity. Luckily, I lost mine in time to talk about it. She was my rock, through the tough times when I needed it, and the first person I would talk about my successes. She was always there to talk things through, tell me her thoughts or opinions to see things from a different perspective. She would encourage me to shoot for the stars and capture my dreams. Now I will go through the rest of my life without her wiseass remarks that totally made sense. The memories would always be part of me especially when she told me to never to give up on my dreams.

It was hard to see Louie, Sharon's boyfriend, at the cemetery. He was hard to recognize at first; he grew a beard and dyed his hair. It was if he wore a disguise for some reason. You could tell this was hard on him as it was for me. His eyes were darkened and teary. He approached me cautiously. It was quite odd. He came in from behind me and held my hand. He came around to face me, then kissed my cheek and leaned into me.

"Just know I did love Sharon the way she should have been loved."

He reached into his pocket and showed me an engagement ring. My eyes lit up at the same time a tear fell from them. He was going to propose to her. He looked into my eyes with such remorse. He was hiding something, I felt it, but I had no clue of what it could be. As he went to hold my hand, a folded piece of paper touched the middle of my palm.

"Please read the letter tomorrow. You will always be part of my life, Alisa, the part that made me find true love with Sharon."

"Where are you going?"

"I will be away for a while. You won't be able to contact me. Just know I feel your sorrow too and will be thinking about Sharon every day. Goodbye, Alisa."

He turned to the coffin; a tear fell from his face. He made the sign of the cross, kissed the box, and placed the ring in her grave. With one last glance at me and with a nod, he left with his head up kissing the sky. I felt the emptiness again knowing I wouldn't even have him to talk to. I hoped that one day our paths would cross again. If not, he would always be part of my life knowing how much he meant to Sharon.

Once everyone left the services, Sharon's mother and I had our own time alone to discuss our future without Sharon. She wanted me to visit her as often as I could. She made me understand that I, too, was a daughter to her. She made it quite clear she did not want to lose another daughter. After some crying and reminiscing, she reached behind the couch and gave me a familiar box. The box was filled with Sharon's personal treasures. I didn't want to open it with her there. This was something I needed to do alone, knowing I would break down. I needed to be strong for her. I was thankful she never brought up my father's doings in all this. I was not ready to go down that road with her. I really didn't know the entire story myself.

It had been weeks since Sharon's funeral, and I missed her dearly. I found myself calling her phone just to listen to her voice-mail recording. I was a mess. The box that Sharon's mom gave me has been on my coffee table staring at me. I didn't want to open it. I wasn't ready to say the final goodbye. So instead of dealing with my feelings, I worked. I went in at 6:00 a.m. ordering, prepping, and scheduling. Michael, that wonderful friend of mine, told me to put on my big girl pants and get my closure. He was right. I needed to do this. The days have been crazy, only because I needed to be busy. Now, I needed to take the time and get a hold of myself, continue to live my life and to achieve my dreams. Sharon would have wanted it that way.

Right out of the shower in my lounge pants and tank top, I grabbed a large glass of pinot noir, sat on my couch, and stared at the box. I was amazed when I finally lifted the lid. The trinkets and pictures she saved over the years, memories only I knew what it meant to her. Digging through the box, I found a picture frame with an engravement of "best friends." On one side was a picture of Sharon and me graduating high school, and on the other of us graduating college. My eyes welled with tears, remembering both days so vividly.

After our college graduation, we were partying so much we wound up in Atlantic City. Till this day, I still don't know how we got there. The fun we had sitting at the roulette table. Black 22, it was for two by two, two peas in a pod, and together we would conquer the world. We hit it three times. We were up $5,500.00, and by the end of the night, we had a toga outfit on including the fig leaf crown and gold bracelets. The security couldn't help but laugh at us as they escorted us to our room that was comped because of the entertainment we provided the casino for free. The hotel concierge said that we were more entertaining than their regular talent and deserved the best room they had. The security guards brought us to the penthouse suite and stayed with us for a bit. They left to continue their shift, but thirty minutes later they came back with more of the staff. We didn't sleep until early hours of the morning and drank until the last bottle of Jose Cuervo was gone. I was not sure how we managed, but we left by 11:00 a.m., check-out time.

The smell of alcohol coming from our pores and the endless voicemails from our parents trying to find us made for a wicked five-hour drive home. I learned not to eat greasy food after the night we had. Sharon needed to pull over. By the time we went over the Verrazano Bridge, my stomach was craving a release of the ham and cheese omelet I had at the breakfast buffet. A true friend holds your hair back when you vomit. I shook my head and laughed to myself until I came across a piece of paper. My tears released like a waterfall when I picked up our "Contract to our Friendship."

It meant everything to us back then. We thought for days to make up ten rules or commitments that we would base our friendship on. Sharon checked off all the items we completed. My fingers ran along number 9 and 10, knowing it would never happen now that she was gone. These were the two that we were really waiting for. This was where we knew we had to share our bond with the men we loved for the rest of our lives. I think Sharon left this earth finding hers, and for me, I thought I did. The ninth on the list stated that we would be each other's maid of honor, and the tenth commitment was for us to be the godmother of our firstborn child.

There was envelope with my name on it. I opened it. It was a legal document. She willed me her photographs and the rights to her publications. Attached was another envelope; in it was a letter. The letter said if I was reading it that she was gone. She wrote how she knew I needed the letter to move on. She made me cry and laugh at the same time. She was right; this is exactly what I needed. Wiping the tears off my face with the back of my hand, I raised my glass in the air. "To you, my friend," and took a sip.

On the coffee table was the newest addition of *Society*. This was the paper Sharon's photographs were published in. I ran through it finding the page where they talked about Sharon. They did a wonderful tribute to her and her work in the paper. The writer was a dear friend of hers. I met him twice; Scott was his name. Very polished man, intellectually handsome was the best way to describe him. At one time Scott and Sharon dated. After four months, Sharon broke up with him. She told me "Some guys are just meant to be your friend." Scott wrote as if he still loved her. He highlighted her best pieces and explained how her passion for photography was more important than the words in an article. He continued by stating her reason: people needed pictures to give clarity to the meaning of the words. How photography was her first love. The words that he used to describe Sharon's truest talent. She timed herself to take the perfect shot. She knew when the lighting and the subject were in perfect position. He mentioned her eye for detail, making sure the audience saw the emotion or the reason for the photograph. My eyes moved to the one of me at the beach she took. I displayed it on my mantel. She told me that my eyes were pure gold in the picture, and the angle of my face brought out my best features. The picture next to it was a landscape picture of Port Jefferson Harbor. It was taken at dusk. The pinks and purples along the coastline brought out the best of my favorite place. I had photographs of hers in my restaurants too. Some of them were taken when she was on location in Florence and Monte Carlo. There was one picture that was in my East Hampton restaurant; it's of a Tuscan vineyard. The picture was gorgeous. The vivid colors blared out against the high grasses and vine trellis with dangling grapes. In the background, you saw the villa true to the Tuscan region, with the clay roof, iron gates, cobblestone walkway.

I continued to read the article, which included other writers chiming in to talk about her work and her passion for humanity. At the end, they added Sharon's motto, "Every moment in life is worth the click of a camera."

The article made me realize what to do with her photographs—a charity event for the Brady Law. This charity will help prevent the wrong people to carry guns. It required one background check on the individual before you can purchase a firearm. The proceeds from the sale of her photographs would go directly to it. This event would showcase her talent, and it would help me get through the guilt that I had for not being there for her. I should have fought harder for Brent to tell me what he knew. I should have been more attuned to my father's business dealings. If I wasn't so oblivious, I could have stopped her from going to the bowling alley, and she would be alive today.

My thoughts reverted to the men in my life. All but one betrayed me. My dad recovered from the broken bones and swelling from the beating he received. He was out of the hospital, but he didn't come home. The feds placed him on Ryker's Island awaiting his sentencing for the felony he had committed. He was separated from the other members of the organized crime family for obvious reasons. My uncle and cousin were also quarantined from the other members for similar reasons. It was a reenactment from a scene from the movie *Godfather* or *Goodfellas*.

"You don't betray the family."

Who knew I was the daughter of a mobster? I shook my head in disgust to the three men I loved who betrayed me. I guess the crime family or blood family didn't matter because they betrayed us both. Apparently, my father was the one who stole Kim Killian's necklace. He used me and my restaurant to pull off the most notorious jewel heist on Long Island. I couldn't even trust the man who raised me.

I replayed that night over and over, to find any clues that would have led me to believe it was him. My father masterminded the plan himself. I shook my head in disgust. My whole life he kept being part of the mafia from me. I mean I was twenty-seven years old. I never saw anything that would make me believe it to be true. My mother even did a great job of changing the subject or making up an excuse for certain things I may have questioned. I was not sure how to feel about them hiding that from me. I guess they wanted me to have a normal upbringing and not one wondering if my father was coming home or if he would be swimming with the fishes. Even worse, coming home with blood on his shirt. I didn't even want to think about what other horrible things he has done.

That fateful day started out as another perfect day with Brent, little did I know it would end in disaster, deceit, and death. Marco, who was now dead, was supposed to get a piece of the profits from the sale of the necklace but never received a dime. My dad was a lieutenant in the Marino crime family. My uncle was next to be the head of the family. Cousin Anthony was a soldier, working himself up the ranks to earn the respect of the members of the family. My Aunt Josephine, she knew everything that had happened and the plan they had to be at the top.

She called me several times. I still hadn't responded to her voicemails. The drama was in her voice. "Alisa, we are family. We need to get through this together. Call me." I was disgusted with her too. She called me again the night of the burial. She wanted me to know that my father loved me and tried to get out of the mafia but couldn't. I no longer had any interest to talk to Aunt Josie either. I left her a note in her mailbox. I made her understand she also had many opportunities to let me in on the family secret that was hidden from me. If she didn't have respect for me, I no longer had respect for her.

With anger and embarrassment of my naive self, it took a couple of days to pass before I went to see my father. It was not for a pleasant visit. It was hard at first to look into his eyes. I could see his need to explain everything to me. He did some talking, but I stopped him. I could tell the truth from the lies. I told him how disappointed and ashamed I was of him. "My whole life is a lie, Papa. Everything you did for me to protect me was really to protect you from being the evil man you are. You used me and my restaurant to benefit you with scheme you planned. You risked my life, my livelihood and my reputation for your own personal gain. How was that protecting me?"

I couldn't hold anything back from saying what I needed to say. I informed him the next time I saw him would be the day of his funeral. The look on his face was one I never saw before. His stoic stance was interrupted by him clearing his throat and the tears welling up in his eyes. He thought his apology for Sharon and for betraying me would be accepted. I made sure he knew it wasn't. Oh, and hearing him repeat the cliché several times, "I did it for you," at that point I slammed my hands on the counter and walked out. "*Le bugie, le bugie devono fermare*," I yelled at him while slamming my fist on the table. The lies needed to stop. Nothing could repair this relationship. Before he could even say goodbye, I got up from the table and walked out of the visiting room without even turning back for a second look.

I sat in the parking lot of the penitentiary. I realized I was all alone now. That's not exactly true. I did have my restaurants and Michael. Michael has been a great sounding board for me. The last couple of weeks were bearable because of his support. He allowed me to scream, cry, yell, and he even introduced me to yoga to help calm my anger. Anger that has brought me to my backyard looking out into water with the moon shining and the ripples of water shimmering. It's time to rid of the anger and go on with my life. The life that is now shed from lies and deceit. The life I now have renewed hope for, with goals and dreams to reach. A new beginning awaits, and I am ready to take the leap into the unknown.

Printed in the USA
CPSIA information can be obtained
at www.ICGtesting.com
LVHW021316070824
787583LV00002B/201

9 781684 985067